High Praise for
NO STOPPING US NOW
by Lucy Jane Bledsoe

A TIMELESS AND triumphant story of courage in the face of opposition, as well as a glimpse into the early days of Title IX's implementation. Knowledgeable about, and appreciative of, the trailblazers who fought for fairness and equal opportunities for women in sports, *No Stopping Us Now* is an excellent historical novel.

> FOREWORD REVIEWS (starred review)

THE CAUSE IS just, the action absorbing, the sexist flack still all too familiar.

> KIRKUS REVIEWS

LUCY BLEDSOE CONJURES up everyday sexism on the cusp of Title IX with powerful immediacy. From Shirley Chisholm and Gloria Steinem, to macrame and hip-huggers, we are solidly in 1974. Yet there's something absolutely contemporary in the way Bledsoe captures the perils, the highs, and the awkward, nonverbal jostling of high school social life. *No Stopping Us Now* takes a historic moment for women's sports and replays it in all its sweaty, visceral glory.

> ALISON BECHDEL, author, *Fun Home* and *The Secret to Superhuman Strength*

IN THE FABULOUS *No Stopping Us Now*, Lucy Jane Bledsoe tells two stories of transition—of a high school girl discovering her voice and her strength and of a society grappling with the evolving expectations of women. We cheer for Louisa as she speaks truth to power, has her eyes opened to feminist intersectionality, and shines on the basketball court. On the fiftieth anniversary of Title IX, this is an important and necessary book for young people, a poignant tribute to the women who demanded equality in athletics, and an inspiring call for a new generation to fight its own battles for justice.

> ANDREW MARANISS, author of *Inaugural Ballers: The True Story of the First U.S. Women's Olympic Basketball Team*

THE CHARACTERS ARE beautifully drawn, the story expertly plotted and moving and as a former D-I basketball player, it is close to my heart.

> MARY VOLMER, author of *Reliance, Illinois*

SO MANY YOUNG women athletes today grow up without understanding the importance of Title IX and how hard previous generations struggled for the opportunity to participate in the sports they loved. In writing *No Stopping Us Now*, Bledsoe not only informs and entertains, she directly connects young readers to an integral part of women's sports history that should never be forgotten.

> LYNDSEY D'ARCANGELO, sports writer; co-author of *Hail Mary: The Rise and Fall of the National Women's Football League*

NO STOPPING US now is full of such heart, love and courage. A stunning and brave journey from start to finish, I loved Louisa and her bold crew of superstar athletes who rose up together to be seen, valued and heard. This is a book to be treasured, taught and shared. I want my children and students to know what it means to fight for what you believe in. To take up space, to raise your voice and most of all, to get on the court and play.

> ELLEN HAGAN, author, *Don't Call Me a Hurricane*

IT'S TEMPTING TO say that *No Stopping Us Now* transports us back to the intense battles teen girls faced in the early years of Title IX, except that similar battles rage on today. This timeless story is a must-read for adolescents trying to find themselves and their powerful voices both personally and politically.

> SHERRY BOSCHERT, author, *37 Words: Title IX and Fifty Years of Fighting Sex Discrimination*

FEARLESSLY INVOKES A recent past we must become reacquainted with, the better to understand how far women have come and what's at stake for our rights and opportunities.

> BONNIE J. MORRIS, women's history professor; author of *What's the Score? Twenty-Five Years of Teaching Women's Sports History*

No Stopping Us Now

No Stopping Us Now

a novel

Lucy Jane Bledsoe

THREE ROOMS PRESS
New York, NY

Y
Fic
BLE

No Stopping Us Now
A NOVEL BY Lucy Jane Bledsoe

© 2022 by Lucy Jane Bledsoe

ISBN 978-1-953103-20-8 (trade paperback)
ISBN 978-1-953103-21-5 (Epub)
Library of Congress Control Number: 2021947713

TRP-096

Pub Date: April 26, 2022

Young Adult Fiction: Ages 14 and up
BISAC Coding:
YAF059020 Young Adult Fiction / Sports & Recreation / Basketball
YAF022000 Young Adult Fiction / Girls & Women
YAF031000 Young Adult Fiction / LGBTQ+
YAF024170 Young Adult Fiction / Historical / United States / 20th Century

COVER DESIGN:
Victoria Black: www.thevictoriablack.com

BOOK DESIGN:
KG Design International: www.katgeorges.com

DISTRIBUTED IN THE U.S. AND INTERNATIONALLY BY:
Publishers Group West: www.pgw.com

Three Rooms Press
New York, NY
www.threeroomspress.com
info@threeroomspress.com

For my sisterhood,
especially Margaret and Laura

"First it was voting, then it was professional wrestling, and now women think they can play basketball! The men who ratified the 20th amendment didn't know what they were getting into."

THE STATESMAN, WILSON HIGH SCHOOL NEWSPAPER, PORTLAND, OREGON, DECEMBER 20, 1974

"The gymnasium was swarming with girl-watchers Friday afternoon. And did the girls ever put on a show."

THE OREGONIAN, MARCH 8, 1975

Based on a true story.

No Stopping Us Now

PART ONE

1

WHEN MY ALARM GOES OFF AT five-thirty a.m., I wake up hugging my basketball. I let my fingers feel the nubbly surface, the indented lines, the comforting roundness. I imagine all of that spinning off my fingers and heading for the hoop. The nearly silent swish of the ball falling through the net.

Basketball is the correction to all things askew. It's like traveling to this secret universe in the deepest part of myself, where thinking just stops, and my muscles and bones and blood take over. It's the one place where I can forget everything else.

I need that badly this morning.

I roll out of bed, pull on sweats, and stuff my school clothes and transistor radio into my backpack. Before going out the front door, I take a good long look at myself in the hall mirror. Tall with a tangle of short blond curly hair and serious gray eyes, I wish I looked more striking. I don't know what my style is. Carly once said I should aim for bohemian, which I didn't really appreciate, since the implication was that wild child was the best I could hope for. She said that wasn't what she meant. But this morning I definitely feel shaggy. If I can just stay focused on the team, our game tomorrow, then maybe I can survive the day.

I leave the house well before dawn, walk up the street, and then into the woods: my shortcut to school. I've walked this route hundreds of times, could probably do it with my eyes closed, but this morning everything is making me uneasy: the creek gurgling beside the trail; something scampering in the nearby brush; even the nonstop rain. I was an idiot at the party on Saturday night, and can't bear the thought of seeing Steve in school today, but what I'm feeling goes deeper than worrying about that. A profound uncertainty, something between dread and hope, is lodged in my chest.

It's 1974 and the American president is a crook. I'm stuck in soggy Portland, Oregon for the unforeseeable future. Seventeen years old, in the middle of my junior year, I'm hardly a kid anymore and yet I have plenty of high school left to go. My three older siblings have all moved out already, and their being gone gives me a sense of velocity, like everything is moving forward too fast. It's like I'm hurdling toward a cliff and maybe that's a good thing, a launch and flight, or maybe it's a bad thing, an impending crash into the bottom of a canyon.

I toss my basketball from hand to hand, keeping my fingers spread, imagining the dark Douglas fir trunks to be opponents. Trying to calm myself. When I reach the highway, I can see, through the thick cloudy rain, smudges of light up ahead, and I run the rest of the way to the high school. Sometimes the night janitor forgets to unlock the entrance before he leaves at five a.m. and I have to bang on the window until the day janitor happens by. One morning last week the other girls and I had to sit outside in the cold drizzle, backs against the door, until eight o'clock, and we missed our entire practice.

The door opens this morning. I jog down the hall and step into the dark gym. As I clunk on the light switches, brightness splashes across the varnished wood floor, the bleachers lining the sides of the gym, and the big green and white Woodrow Wilson Trojans banners hanging on the walls behind both baskets.

I toss my backpack on the bottom bleacher and dig out my transistor radio. Tuned to KISN, I wheel the volume dial to high and set it on the bleacher. Perfect: The DJ is playing Janis Joplin doing "Piece of My Heart." That song matches my ache this morning. I wish I could have been part of the Summer of Love a few years ago. A big free-spirited gathering of hippies wearing jeans embroidered with rainbows and peace signs, listening to real music, insisting on love, all kinds of love, over hate. It tore me up when Janis Joplin died of an overdose. I loved her rebellious, hoarse, wild-eyed voice. My sister left the *Cheap Thrills* album behind when she went off to college and even though it's six years old, I still listen to it all the time.

I channel the lyrics as I start shooting, and everything starts to feel better. I love the bonk of the leather ball on the court. The mingling smells of wood and sweat and competition. The loosening of my muscles as I warm up. My brothers taught me how to drive for layups, shoot jump shots from five, ten, and fifteen feet out, roll off a pick, snag rebounds by using my body to block out defenders. Luckily, they taught me the boys' version of the game. Until three years ago, the rules for girls basketball were completely different. Girls teams had to put six, rather than five, players on the court. Even worse, the team was divided into three forwards and three guards, and the forwards could only play on the offensive end of the court and the guards could only play on the defensive end, which meant everyone could only play half-court. Some girls never got to shoot and some never got to play defense. I guess they thought girls were too delicate to run full court.

The rules for girls basketball were recently changed to be much more similar to those for boys, but none of this matters because the Portland Public Schools do not have a basketball program for girls. The only place we can play basketball is in city rec leagues.

Still, I'm glad my brothers taught me the boys' game. I love running full court. I love playing offense *and* defense. I love basketball, period.

Val and Diane come into the gym together. They do everything together. Val is tall and gaunt, has sallow white skin, which is usually broken out in bad acne, and wears her hair in a dishwater-colored mullet. She doesn't talk much, and when she does, it's often to say something negative, but I like her. She has this smoldering anger that I respect, though I have no idea what she's angry about. She can do everything on the court: shoot, guard, rebound. She's our best forward. Her sidekick Diane is also tall, but clumsy. She has a hunching way of moving, as if she's trying to make herself smaller. She wears big blue plastic-framed glasses and a floppy ponytail. Her pale skin gets bright red when she's playing basketball. She's a great rebounder, and I'm glad she's on the team.

Next Helen floats sleepily into the gym. Willowy and toothpick-thin, she has enviably high cheekbones, huge brown eyes, and wears her hair in a giant afro. Remarkably, Helen never seems to sweat. Even after a two-hour practice, her skin looks as soft and dry as nutmeg. We call her Spider because although she's not a forceful player—she glides rather than runs and only rebounds if no one is around her—her hands are sticky. She catches anything coming her way. Also, like a spider, she's all skinny arms and legs.

Helen and I have a couple of classes together. She's the only one of these girls I knew until a few months ago when I put up a sign in the gym announcing the start of a basketball team. Exactly five girls, including me, showed up at the first meeting. I got us into a city rec league and talked the principal, Dr. Merble, into letting us use the gym in the early mornings.

The fifth girl, Barb, our point guard, arrives at six-forty-five, shouting, "Worry about nothing! I have arrived!"

Val rolls her eyes. Diane then rolls her eyes too.

Helen smiles at Barb's bravado.

"Turn it up!" Barb shouts, pointing at my transistor radio. "This is my favorite song."

Stevie Wonder is singing "You Are the Sunshine of My Life," and I flush as Barb shouts the song with him, looking at me.

"You're late," I say to cover my surprising delight. Barb's always late, but without her, we don't stand a chance at winning any games. She hits from the outside with incredible accuracy. She can also drive through a crowded key and still finish at the hoop. Short and chunky, with dark brown skin, she wears her hair straightened and pulled back in a stubby ponytail. She has this super mobile mouth, like it's always in motion, laughing and talking and just making faces. She's very free with eye contact, too, which sometimes makes me nervous.

"How're we getting to the game tomorrow night?" Diane asks as she puts up an air ball. "My mom is working a night shift all week, so she can't take us."

"Can you get the car?" Helen asks.

I know she's talking to me since I'm the only one with a driver's license and access to a car. "I already asked," I say, putting up a long shot from the corner. It swishes through the net. "My parents need the car tomorrow night."

"What's the point?" Val asks.

"To what?" Helen asks Val, but with a smile. "Get a grip. We always find a way."

"I'm not taking the bus again." Val throws her basketball against the backboard, hard, purposely missing, so she can leap to rebound it.

"I got in so much trouble that time," Diane says. "I got home at like midnight."

"It's a drag," Barb says, dribbling the ball between her legs. Her ball-handling skills are crazy good. "Practicing in the middle of the night, no coaches, no uniforms, nothing."

I set my basketball on the floor and sit on it. I don't want to have this whole conversation again. It doesn't help our game. But my teammates are right: nothing about having a basketball team, if you can even call us that, is working. I get back on my feet and try to sound encouraging as I call out, "Let's run our play."

Val coughs a sarcastic laugh. "The play. Our one and only play."

"It never works," Diane says.

"That's because you always fall for my fakes," Barb says. "Which are meant for the other team." She takes her hair out of the band, gathers it into a tighter ponytail, and snaps the band back in place. I can't help grooving on how easy and loose she is in her body, even if she's a hotdogger. After every practice she rubs lots of lotion into her arms and legs, and once when she caught me staring, she said, "What's up, white girl? Black people use a lot of lotion, okay?"

"I use lotion," I'd said stupidly.

Barb had laughed. "Just ribbing you." And she'd swatted me on the butt with her towel.

"Okay," I say now. "Then let's start with the fast break drill. Come on. Look alive. Let's go."

As we fall into the drill, running the weave pattern, passing, and dropping layups, Elton John sings "Crocodile Rock," and soon my favorite part of being an athlete takes over. It's an endorphins high, but it's not *only* an endorphins high. There's this other part, where my arms and legs and feet and hands know exactly what to do, and all my worries—party behavior, college applications, crushes, jealousies, and Grandpa's health—melt away. I'm just me, pure me, moving in sync with my teammates.

A little after eight o'clock, as we're scrimmaging half-court, playing three on two, making the team of two work extra hard against the team of three, sweating profusely (except for Helen), concentrating hard, a group of boys clang in the gym door. They shout comments about our playing and our bodies, but we're above all that, soaring in the zone, and we just ignore them. They start horsing around on the other end of the gym, getting more and more rowdy, trying to get our attention, and still we stay in our game until we finish and hit the showers.

2

THAT AWESOME ENDORPHINS HIGH EVAPORATES QUICKLY. Steve is in my first period class. Do I just say I'm sorry? Do I pretend nothing happened on Saturday night? Maybe he doesn't even remember. I wish I didn't. Those gin and tonics, with all that lime juice squeezed in, tasted too much like delicious and innocent limeade. Carly says I'm an inexperienced drinker. I'm not sure I want any more experience. Here are the facts: I plunked myself in Steve's lap, told him I loved him, and then hurled all those gin and tonics.

Okay, I flew off his lap and made it to the hallway before the barfing part. Carly assures me that Steve saw nothing.

Still. The first part, that stuff I said to him, is unbearable enough. I wish I could just stay on the basketball court, sprinting hard and shooting baskets until Saturday night fades from my memory. If that's even possible.

I'm doing my best fast-walk hustle to get to class on time. My hair is wet but at least I managed to remember all my school clothes. Last Friday I forgot every single piece of underwear and had to wear my sweaty basketball bra all day, along with nothing under my pants. Until my eighth grade year, girls weren't allowed to wear pants to school, only dresses and skirts. Imagine how disastrous forgetting my underwear would have been if *that* rule hadn't changed.

The hall is pretty much empty by now because I'm so late. I hung out in the shower too long, listening to Barb brag about beating her best friend, a girl from her church, in a pushup competition. Right there in the shower room, Barb held out both palms and said, "Gimme five," I guess to celebrate her pushup prowess. Then, in the locker room, while we were still in just our underwear, she grabbed me by the arm, pulled me close, and whispered, "Why does Val always dress in the toilet stall?" I'd noticed that too. She never undresses in front of us. Val's extreme modesty makes me feel protective about her. That, along with her gruff way of talking, must be shielding some kind of hurt.

Now in the school hall, I break into a run to beat the bell.

"Hey, hey, hey now."

The voice comes from behind me. I stop and turn. It's Mr. Stanton, the football coach. He doesn't say anything more for a few seconds, just lumbers toward me. Mr. Stanton has red-rimmed, narrow eyes and a fleshy, also red, face. He has a beach ball stomach, a crew cut, and is kind of old for a teacher, like between my dad and grandpa's ages.

"If you got an earlier start, you wouldn't need to be running in the halls."

"Sorry."

Mr. Stanton nods at the basketball under my arm. "Furthermore, the classroom is no place for sports equipment."

"Oh." I want to say, you just pointed out I'm late, so yeah, I don't have time to put the basketball away in my locker right now. But you don't talk back to teachers, especially not ones who are also coaches. They're usually extra strict.

"And you need a basketball at school why?" he asks.

"We have practice. Early."

"Who's we?"

"Some girls are playing in a city rec league. Dr. Merble said we could use the gym before school."

"Is that so." He punches the words into a statement, not a question.

I want to tell him that no one else is using the gym from six-thirty to eight-thirty in the morning, and so why shouldn't we? Instead, I feel my face collapse into a wince of apology, as if to say I'm sorry I play basketball, that I use the gym. Luckily, the tardy bell rings, saving me from having to respond. I look purposefully past Mr. Stanton, down the empty hall, and start to step around him.

"How're your brothers doing?"

"Fine."

"You tell them both hello for me. Fine quarterbacks. A couple of the best the Woodrow Wilson Trojans have ever had."

"Thanks. I will."

Then I do apologize. "Sorry. But I better get to class."

Finally, Mr. Stanton walks on and I hustle down to Room 206, open the door as inconspicuously as possible, and slip in. Mrs. Hernandez's back is turned as she chalks an algebra problem on the board. I drop silently into my desk and slide my backpack under the chair, but my basketball is still on the desktop when she turns around. She makes this indulgent face, like she's so happy she caught me, and says, "Since when is Louisa tardy?"

Some of the kids laugh.

"Sorry." I put the ball on the floor and hold it between my feet so it won't roll.

"Excused. This time."

Helen got to class well before me and is sitting in the front row, as usual. She told me she's going to be a civil rights lawyer and needs to get a 4.0 grade point average. She said that sitting in the front row sends a subliminal message to teachers, and without even knowing they're doing it, they'll round your grade up at report card time. This morning she turns and gives me a judgmental look, as if my tardiness somehow reflects on her. I'm so glad she wasn't at the party on Saturday night. Or any of my teammates.

My best friend, Carly, *was* there, however.

She's sitting behind me, to the right, and she clears her throat. I turn to see what she wants and she bugs her eyes at me. With her long, straight black hair and dark eyes to match, she always manages to look sexy. Today she's wearing a slinky blouse, in a blue and green paisley, with long pointed collars. In some ways, I feel like we're opposites. At least unlikely best friends. I feel dumpy in my gold turtleneck with the yellow sweater vest. I can't remember if I brushed my hair in the locker room. I shrug at her.

Steve sits in the desk right behind Carly, and I know just saying hi would be the least weird thing to do, but I can't even look at him. When Mrs. Hernandez returns to the chalk board, he hisses, "Carmichael!" I rotate all the way around in my chair but keep my gaze on his desktop rather than his face. He taps his watch. When I finally look up, he wags his eyebrows, still tapping his watch, making fun of me for being late. He has this mock cocky way of acting like he's more laid back than he really is. He's both smart and a jock, and it's hard to straddle those two identities at our high school. When he smiles, a wave of relief washes through me. He's obviously not dwelling on whatever happened on that couch on Saturday night. For all I know, he'd had a few personality-altering beverages of his own.

Mrs. Hernandez asks for a volunteer to work the problem on the chalkboard. No one raises a hand. She adjusts her glasses and smirks at the class, wearing that sarcastic face she's really good at, the one that says, *Really? No one can do this problem?*

"Did you just volunteer, Louisa?" Her favorite ploy. If she catches you passing notes or talking in class, she pretends you raised your hand.

Lucky for me, just in time, Mort shoves out of his chair and starts for the front of the classroom. He didn't even raise his hand or get called on by Mrs. Hernandez. As he passes my desk, he gives me one of his long predatory looks. You get the feeling he has X-ray vision, like he can see what you're thinking. He's the assistant editor of the *Statesman*, the school newspaper, and never goes anywhere without his big Nikon harnessed onto his chest. He always keeps one hand on its lens, ready to snap anything interesting. For him the camera is like a body part, a third eye with special powers. You never know when he'll lift that long lens and shoot a picture of you, like when you're scratching your butt or sneezing really hard.

But right now he's saving me, so I smile at him, just a little bit. He starts chalking his way through the math problem, and as he writes the final digit to the answer, his fingers slip on the tiny piece of chalk and a fingernail scrapes across the green slate. A hard shiver ratchets through me. Carly groans.

Mort turns and looks right at me as he says, "That was definitely unnecessary."

Why is he speaking directly to me?

Before taking his seat again, Mort takes one of those small black calculator things out of his back pocket. He taps at the tiny keys and then looks up at Mrs. Hernandez. "I am correct," he says, and she rolls her eyes. Earlier in the year, she'd try to tell him he couldn't use the instrument in class, but he'd taken his case—for a calculator!—to the school board and won.

Just then the classroom door swings open.

It's Diane, who works first period in the admin offices. Without Val at her side, she looks afraid of her own footsteps. "Excuse me, Mrs. Hernandez, but Mrs. Hodge wants to see Louisa in her office."

"Me?" I squeak. For being late to class? For carrying my basketball in the hallway? Mr. Stanton told on me to the vice principal?

"Right on," Carly says. "Louisa's finally in trouble."

"I doubt it," Steve says. "She's probably getting an award."

"Most Likely to Please Teachers," Carly says.

"Best Rule Follower," Steve jokes.

"Wholesomeness Incarnate."

"Carnal Wholesomeness."

"Funny," I whisper to my two friends. "You're both hilarious."

Even as I'm nervous about this trip to the vice principal's office, I do note that Steve is teasing me about my supposed innocence and wholesomeness, which is further proof that he missed, or at least took for a joke, what I said Saturday night in his lap.

Taking my basketball with me, I duck out into the quiet hallway lined with gray metal lockers, and look in both directions for Diane, hoping she might have some information on why I'm being summoned, but she's disappeared. Tightly embracing the ball, I make my way to the vice principal's office. I wish I knew what she wanted. Could she know about the party? But you can't get in trouble at school for something you did on the weekend.

Then it occurs to me that this might be about Grandpa. He has dementia and sometimes wanders off. That thought kicks me in the stomach. Those couple of times we had to search the neighborhood for him were so scary. But Mom wouldn't pull me out of school for that. Unless it were even more serious. Maybe this time he isn't just down the street petting someone's cat. He could have gotten hit by a car. I run the rest of the way to the admin offices.

The secretary waves me through to Mrs. Hodge's lair. I step up to the front of her desk and she makes me wait while she finishes writing something on a big yellow legal pad. People make fun of Mrs. Hodge, with her stiff hairdo, rhinestone-studded cat-eye glasses, and bright red lipstick, but I like her. She's acerbic and always gets right to the point.

"Don't bother sitting," she finally says, not looking up from her legal pad. "This will be brief. Gloria Steinem is coming to speak at the Civic Auditorium in a couple of weeks. On Saturday afternoon, February twenty-third. She wants a youth representative on stage with her." Mrs. Hodge pushes a piece of paper across the desk at me. "The particulars are here."

It takes me a few seconds to take in that I'm not in trouble, that Grandpa is not lost or hurt. What she *has* said is kind of crazy, though.

"Me?" I ask.

"Speak to your parents. Let me know tomorrow."

"Gloria Steinem? *The* Gloria Steinem?"

Mrs. Hodge finally looks up at me, the pen gripped in her right hand. I stand facing her, the basketball balanced on one hip and the fingertips of my other hand on my chest in a gesture of incredulity.

"No," she says in a deadpan voice. "An Avon saleslady who shares the same name."

Nodding, I start backing out of her office.

Mrs. Hodge actually smiles. "That *was* you, wasn't it, who wrote a letter to the administration at the beginning of the year insisting that girls who lettered be admitted to the Letterman's Club?"

Last spring I got my letter in tennis, one of the few sports available for girls at my high school. There's a club of lettered athletes that meets once a month, but girls can't be members. This fall I went to a meeting anyway, the only girl sitting there, and the boys and teacher advisor all discussed whether the rule could be changed. One of their biggest problems, or so they said, was that they didn't want to change the name. "What," Doug Carter had said, "we're going to call it the Letter*people*'s Club? No way."

"I never got an answer to the letter I wrote to the administration," I say to Mrs. Hodge.

"Well. Consider this invitation your answer." She flaps the sheet of paper at me. "Take this. It has all the details."

I snatch up the sheet, and leave her office, wishing I didn't have to go back to algebra class. Stalling, I stop at my locker and put my basketball away.

Gloria Steinem? I know who she is. Everyone knows who she is. She's the most famous feminist in the world. She's all over the newspapers, magazines, and TV, with her curtains of straight blond hair and tinted aviator glasses. She looks like a beautiful model, only defiant.

The idea of meeting her in person, of being on stage and having a public conversation with her, all that is just plain terrifying. But also kind of thrilling.

3

AT THE END OF THE DAY, I stop in the doorway to the gym to watch the boys basketball practice. They have a head coach, Mr. Ward, plus two assistant coaches, and they get to practice from three-thirty to five-thirty every afternoon, conveniently right after school. Steve sees me standing there and he breaks away from their shoot-around to say hi.

"What'd the Hodge want?" he asks.

He smells good. I love basketball sweat. It's completely different from stinky clothes sweat or nervous class presentation sweat. Basketball sweat comes from a place of pure effort. I don't think I'd even tell Carly that I want to lick the sweat from that indent at the base of his neck, between his collarbones. She would understand, in a way, but she'd insist on a very specific interpretation of that desire, an interpretation that might not be completely accurate.

I tell Steve, "She wants me to be in some program with Gloria Steinem at the Civic Auditorium."

"Really?" He looks briefly intrigued, and then smiles the beginning of a joke, but before he can voice it, a loud clapping interrupts our conversation. We both turn to see Coach Ward, a twitchy man who wears thick-lensed, rectangular wire-framed glasses, and who nearly vibrates with intensity, slapping his hands together and glaring in our direction.

Coach Ward shouts, "Get your ass back on the court, Barrows."

"Sorry," I whisper.

Steve runs back onto the gym floor and joins the elaborate shooting drill the team is now running. I stand there for a while, wistfully watching the fully supported, highly disciplined practice, all muscle and precision and focus.

I startle when Carly pokes me in the back.

"Whatcha looking at?" she asks with a sassy knowingness.

I shrug, pretend I don't know what she's talking about. But I do. She's talking about Steve.

"Lust," Carly whispers in my ear.

I elbow her. She always uses the most extreme words.

"Maybe," I say.

I do feel lust. A big confusing lust. In all the parts of my body, including my brain.

"Then do something about it," Carly says before she turns and leaves. I watch her go, admiring her self-possession, her crazy confidence, her sensuous hold on life, all displayed in the way she kicks down the hall in her high platform shoes. I look down at my cloddy earth shoes. Carly says they suit me, but I'm not sure that's a compliment. We both want to be writers, but Carly has so much more figured out than I do. She's already planning on moving to Paris where she says the writing scene is tons more dynamic than it is in this country. I love her big appetite—for everything.

Carly knows me better than anyone, so yeah, she's right, I'm looking at Steve, his tall lanky ease on the basketball court, his cute crooked smile, the fact that he risked Coach Ward's wrath to come talk to me.

But I'm also looking at the basketball practice in its full glory. They have a whole rack of basketballs, a pile of fresh towels to wipe off their sweat, a plate of orange slices for energy, and a big chalk board for the coaches to draw and explain at least a dozen different plays. I want that, I want all of that.

4

TUESDAY NIGHT'S GAME IS A DISASTER. Diane gets her older sister to give us a ride, but she chain-smokes the whole way to the gym and by the time we get there I can hardly breathe. Then during tip-off, one of the girls on the other—all white—team says, in this extra friendly voice, as if she's just curious, "So is this a bussing thing?" She smiles and adds, "I mean do you all go to the same high school?"

Barb ignores her, waiting for the ref to toss the ball. The spot below Helen's right eye twitches.

The girls on the other team make comments throughout the first half. They speak quietly, under their breath, to Barb or Helen. After halftime, Barb starts playing rough to get back, throwing an elbow here and sticking out a foot there. When Diane tells her to cool it, Barb says, "Shut up." To her own teammate.

The refs are no help. They pretend to not hear any of the insults. I keep glancing at Virginia, hoping that she'll somehow intervene. She's the closest thing to an adult in our group, but she just sits on the highest bench in the bleachers with her legs crossed, smoking.

When one of the girls shoves my back so hard I fly onto the floor, my knees cracking on the court surface, the ref somehow decides to call the foul on *me*. The second time the girl does it, she holds out a hand to help me up. I take it, giving her the benefit of the doubt. Maybe the decking had been a mistake. But when I'm on my feet, she doesn't let go of my hand. Instead she yanks her arm to the side so forcefully that I fall down again. She laughs and says, "Clumsy bitch." The ref blows his whistle, and I think, at last, thank you, a technical foul. But no, he calls traveling on Barb. Who, in the next play, gets in perfect position for a rebound, and in so doing shoves her butt into the player behind her, which you are allowed to do if you're in position, but the ref calls a foul on her anyway.

"That's not fair!" I cry.

"That's not fair!" two girls on the other team mock in unison. They slap hands and crack up.

I step up to the ref and begin a flustered protest, but Helen grabs my arm. She shakes her head at me. With her other hand, she's holding back Barb.

"But—" I try.

"No," Helen says. "Just no."

"Who you?" one of the girls says to Helen. She holds up her hands about a foot away from either side of her head. "Angela Davis? I thought they locked you up."

I freeze in place, wishing I had the nerve to say something. Say something right. Say something that calls out the girl's racism. I guess I'm just standing there with my mouth hanging open, because as Barb runs past me, she says, "They're not worth your breath, girl. Leave it."

We lose the game by twenty-three points.

There are no locker rooms or showers at the rec center, and so as we step out into the wet night, cold air seizes my tired muscles. Virginia lights what must be her hundredth cigarette as we walk to her car in the parking lot. We're all silent, which I hate, the absence of our usual joking, or at least playful bickering. This is supposed to be fun.

Into that silence, Virginia lets loose a string of curses. We all look at each other. What is her problem?

Then I see. The passenger side front tire of her red Chevrolet Impala is flat.

I look around for a gas station. Beyond a weedy empty lot, there's a Piggly Wiggly and a shoe repair place, a church and a record store, but no gas station.

"Pay phone," Virginia says pointing with the burning end of her cigarette at the booth on the far side of the parking lot. "Anyone have a dime?"

Helen fishes one out of her gym bag and gives it to Virginia.

"Who are you going to call?" Diane asks in an incredulous voice, and the sisters exchange a look that I can't read.

"Your dad?" I ask, trying to move this along.

Diane crosses her arms and turns away, facing the empty lot. Virginia drops her cigarette butt on the pavement, grinds it with the heel of her sneaker, and gets a fresh one out of the pack in her pocket. There's a nearly audible crackling between the two sisters. It's pretty clear I've asked a bad question.

"I could try calling mine," I say. "Maybe they're back home by now."

"Shit," Barb says. "We don't need anyone's dad. Don't you have a spare?"

Everyone stares at her.

"Open the trunk."

Virginia does.

"Yep. Right here. Cool. We can do this."

Barb hands me a flashlight from the trunk, as well as a lug wrench and a jack. I'm glad to be the designated helper. She hefts out the spare tire and sets it on the ground. Next she takes the jack from me, fits it under the car's carriage, and pumps the handle, lifting that corner of the car until the flat tire is elevated off the ground.

Wow. How does she know how to do that?

Barb looks over her shoulder at me with her cocky smile, as if she could see my awe. "Dig it," she says. "I'm multi-talented, okay?"

"Okay," I say like a dork.

I stay close, wanting to help but having no idea what needs to be done. Helen stands a few yards away with her arms crossed, looking around the dark and now empty parking lot, as if she expects danger. Virginia paces and, of course, smokes. Diane and Val huddle, talking quietly out of the sides of their mouths. I'm not sure, but Diane might be crying a little.

Barb asks me to hold the flashlight as she uses the long-handled wrench to unscrew the lug nuts. She's squatting, her leg muscles tensed. Her arm muscles contract and loosen as she works the tire free.

"Company," Virginia says.

"Lovely," Helen comments and steps closer to me, Barb, and the car.

All six of the girls on the other team walk toward us. When we left the gym, they'd stayed inside to shoot victory baskets, crowing about their win. I look around now for their car and there isn't one. When they arrive at ours, they stand in a circle around me and my teammates. Barb keeps working on the tire.

"Nice game," one of our opponents says.

"Thank you," I answer, and Val shoots me a look that can only mean shut up.

"What school you gals go to?"

"Wilson," I say, still tuning out Val's silent advice.

"Figures."

"We're busy," Virginia says with a scowl. "So scram."

"What's that girl doing with a weapon?" asks the one who twice knocked me down.

Again I look for their ride. All the other cars in the parking lot have driven off. Just then the flood lights on the outside of the rec center blink off.

"It's a lug wrench," I say. "We have a flat."

As if that's not obvious.

Barb has finished unscrewing the lug nuts, and she sets down the wrench so she can lift the flat tire off the axle. The skinny girl steps forward and snatches the long tool off the ground. She whips it around in the air over her head, howling with laughter.

Barb stands up slowly and squares her shoulders. Helen folds her arms across her chest and looks at the ground. Val and Diane step away from each other, as if standing too close puts them in danger. I don't know what to do. Virginia is three years older than us. She should take charge. But she just sucks in smoke, huffs it back out again, all the while staring blankly into the dark night.

"Give me a cigarette," the girl with the lug wrench says, and Virginia pulls out the pack. "Yeah, actually, just give me the pack. The whole pack."

When Virginia shakes her head no, the girl lunges. Virginia drops the pack on the pavement like it's a burning coal. The girls double over laughing as their leader picks up the pack and crushes it in her fist, saying, "I don't smoke." Then she hauls back her arm and tosses the lug wrench off into the weeds. She throws the crushed pack of cigarettes in the same direction.

A white Mustang rolls into the parking lot. The driver looks like someone else's older sister. The girls pile in the car, calling out polite comments, like, "Nice to meet you!" and "Good game!" and "Looking forward to next time!"

The driver accelerates hard and the Mustang screeches out of the parking lot, a stink of exhaust fumes puffing back at us.

"Every one of them is a dyke," Virginia says. "They were so butch."

"Yeah," I say and then wish so badly I hadn't.

Diane looks at Val who scowls and walks to the other side of the car, as if she needs an entire automobile between the two of them.

Barb lifts the spare and fits it onto the axle. "Go get the wrench," she says angrily.

By the time I get back, she's already placed all the lug nuts on the bolts. As she starts to tighten the first one, I say, "Let me do that."

She looks at me for a long time, as if making some kind of decision, and then hands me the tool. I crank each bolt clockwise, glad to be doing something physical and helpful.

When I finish, Barb huffs quietly before taking the lug wrench from me.

"Wimp," she says and gets each of the nuts to turn another full rotation. She pops to her feet, holds up her arm, and flexes her muscle.

"Strong," I say, wishing I had more of every kind of strength.

Barb bats my shoulder and says, "Daily pushups."

We throw our gym bags in the trunk and start climbing in the car. Diane gets in the front seat with her sister, as Barb, Helen, and I slide into the backseat. Val starts to get in the front, next to Diane, but then changes her mind and scoots out again.

"Take the front," she says to Helen.

"Don't you want to sit next to Diane?" I blurt, trying to make up for my previous "yeah."

"Hell, no," Val says with a strange ferocity.

"Why would we want to sit next to each other?" Diane adds, less convincingly.

Her sister's word *dyke* echoes in the cold dark air. I scoot toward the center of the backseat so Val can get in next to me. Helen climbs in front.

When we're finally on our way, hurdling down the highway, me squeezed in the backseat between Val and Barb, I point out that if we had a school team, with real adults and a bus, then none of this would have happened.

"None of what?" Barb asks, as if the bad referees, game loss, obnoxious girls, and flat tire hadn't happened.

Virginia coughs derisively and says, "Life isn't fair. Get used to it."

"I don't believe that!" I say. Everyone ignores my outburst. We're all cold and hungry and have homework to do. Still, I can't resist persisting. "Life *can* be fair. Sometimes." My voice cracks, and now all my teammates laugh, as if I'd said a joke.

But then Helen starts talking about Shirley Chisholm, who ran for president two years ago, both the first woman and the first Black candidate for that office. Virginia interrupts to say, "That's never going to happen," though it's not clear what exactly she thinks will never happen. Helen ignores the comment, talks right over it, saying that Chisholm inspired her to get a law degree. I stay quiet, wanting to hear more, but Val and Barb start trading boasts about their prowess on the court, one-upping each other in a funny competition of who can state her skills with the most hyperbole, made all the funnier because Barb shouts hers and Val mumbles hers.

By the time we reach the high school, we're all laughing like usual, but I feel so frustrated. It *isn't* fair. And no one else seems to care.

5

I START WALKING HOME IN THE dark, completely capsized by the game. Those awful girls with their racism and the flat tire and Virginia's comment, using that word, and the way I said, "yeah."

I need to see Carly. I can tell her anything. And she always has answers.

At the turnoff to the path through the woods, I stay on the highway and walk the mile to her house. Carly's parents won't appreciate me showing up at ten o'clock on a school night, so I sneak through the bushes on the side of the yard. Craning my neck, I look up at the one window in Carly's upstairs bedroom. There's a pile of rocks around the bottom of the cast iron drain pipe that runs up the side of the house and alongside her window. I scoop a handful and toss a small one at the soft, muted square of light.

"Carly!" I shout-whisper.

My next rock, a bigger and sharper one, misses the window— luckily, because I throw it too hard and might have broken the glass. It thunks against the wooden siding.

What's she doing? Why doesn't she hear me? I cock back my arm, about to throw another, when I hear a voice. "Hello? Who's out there? Hello?"

Busted.

I have no choice but to walk around to the front of the house, into the brightness of the porch light, where I find Mrs. Mazza standing in her bathrobe, arms folded on her chest.

"I'm sorry, Mrs. Mazza. I didn't want to wake anyone up."

"So you're throwing rocks at the house and shouting at Carly's window?"

"I'm sorry." What else can I say?

"Are you all right?"

"I'm fine." I'm not. I feel all torn up. "I just need to talk to Carly for a minute. It's about an important homework issue."

Mrs. Mazza looks dubious. She clearly does not buy my story. But she holds open the front door, nodding toward the stairway that leads up to Carly's room. I glance at the statue of the Blessed Virgin Mary, in her white veil and blue robe, standing in the entryway. Then I vault up, two steps at a time, calling over my shoulder, "Thank you, Mrs. Mazza. I'll only stay a second. I'm so stuck on this one algebra problem."

I grab the doorknob but the door doesn't open. Carly never locks her door. I peek back down the stairs in time to see Mrs. Mazza disappear into the kitchen. I knock as quietly as possible, not wanting to raise any more red flags than I have already.

"Mom?" Carly's voice comes out in a strange quiet rasp from the other side of the bedroom door. She sounds panicked.

"It's me," I whisper. "Louisa."

The door cracks open. "Does Mom or Dad know you're here?"

"Your mom let me in."

"Oh, boy. Okay."

Carly pulls me into her room, quickly shutting and locking the door behind me. I stand there confused, wondering what all the secrecy is about, until I see Doug Carter sitting up in her bed. The football player, maybe the most muscular boy at school, is naked, at least the part I can see. His red lips look swollen and bruised.

"Oh. I didn't realize—"

"It's okay," Carly says. "You look really uptight."

"I should just go. I'm sorry."

Doug crosses his arms, rubs his meaty triceps, grins. "What's up?"

"No," I say. "No. Sorry. I'll just go."

"Do you realize how often you say 'sorry?'" Carly asks me, tipping her head to the side.

"Sorry."

Carly sighs.

"Yeah," I say weakly. "I see what you mean."

"Didn't you have a game tonight? You're usually so jazzed after games."

"I should go."

"Not on my account," Doug says. "I'm leaving anyway."

Carly puts a finger against her lips, cautioning him to keep his deep voice down.

I stand there staring at his pale chest until I realize he's waiting for me to leave, even though he said not on his account, or at least turn my back, so he can get out of the bed. His boxers, jeans, and a T-shirt are wadded in a pile on the floor. I reach for the doorknob.

"You can't leave yet," Carly says, pulling me back by the shoulder. "You'll make my parents suspicious."

How did he even get in her room?

I keep my back turned. Carly's bedroom floor is covered by a powder blue shag carpet, which softens the sound of Doug's big feet landing on the floor. A moment later, I hear the whispers of fabric sliding on skin, him pulling on his boxers and jeans.

To my horror, tears well up in my eyes.

"You're *not* okay," Carly says.

"It's just . . . just everything. I gotta do that thing with Gloria Steinem next week. And Grandpa is getting so much worse. And I didn't sleep last night. And the refs at the game were so unfair. And the girls on the other team were awful. It all just kind of makes me feel . . . I guess kind of lonely."

I didn't mean to say that last sentence. But it's exactly what I feel. Helen has her eyes on a law degree, if not the presidency. Val and Diane have a kind of love/hate thing going on, but they do have each other. Barb has her best friend from church.

I thought I had Carly.

But apparently she has Doug.

"Sorry," I say. Then I say it again, for having said it. "Sorry."

"You want to stay the night?"

"No, that's okay. It's too late to call my parents. I just—"

"Carly!" Mrs. Mazza's voice sails up the stairs and all three of us freeze as we listen to her footsteps follow. "It's time for Louisa to go home."

Carly gestures frantically at Doug. He's got his shirt, jacket, and pants on now, but is still threading his belt into the loops of his jeans. His sneakers lie on their sides on the far side of the room, as if they'd been tossed.

"Hurry," Carly whispers.

Doug grabs the sneakers, leaving his tube socks—bright white and obvious against the baby blue shag rug—on the floor by the bed, and pushes the window open. He lobs out his shoes. Then grins at us both as he swings out one leg.

"Okay, Mom," Carly calls out. "We're just—"

She widens her eyes at me and frantically circles her hand in front of her mouth, meaning for me to articulate what we're doing.

"—finishing a math problem," I hiss.

"—finishing a math problem!" she screeches, her voice exposing total panic.

Now it's my turn to widen my eyes at *her*.

We both watch the rest of Doug—his other leg, hips and torso, and finally his head—slide out the window. It's like a twenty foot drop. He'll break both legs.

The door knob rattles as Mrs. Mazza tries to get in.

My mouth hangs open, expecting the worst, that Carly is going to get into huge trouble. But she flashes her wildest, nuttiest smile, the one that says you can get away with anything if only you dare.

"Carly? Why is this door locked?"

Doug has completely disappeared into the black hole of the open window. I can hear him huffing, and wonder if he's hanging by his fingertips on the window trim.

Carly again circles her hand in front of her mouth, gesturing for me to speak, to say something that will help with the distraction. I nod, trying to think of something. Finally I manage, "I'm leaving now, Mrs. Mazza. I think I have the math problem under control. Like, I see where I was going wrong. Like, I could have just called but it was too late to call, and anyway, I needed to show Carly the problem on paper because I wouldn't have been able to describe the numbers over the phone. Anyway, she was so helpful and—"

Carly flattens her hand and slices the air in front of her throat, meaning enough already. I shut up.

She wags her thumb at the window and I run over to shut it, but I can't help pausing, for just one tiny moment, to look out. Doug is clinging to the cast iron drain pipe, his hands and knees gripping the thick tube, as he inches himself down toward the grass. I shut the window.

Carly opens the bedroom door. "Hi, Mom."

My gaze pounces on the white tube socks on the pale blue rug next to the bed. They're obviously a huge size, much bigger than

Carly's feet, and besides, she would never wear tube socks. She just wouldn't. I make a snap decision, realizing as I do that it might backfire.

"Sorry, Carly! My dirty socks from the game came out of the backpack when I pulled out my math book!"

She gives me a look of disbelief as I grab the socks and shove them into my backpack. Of course I never took out my math book and so it is nowhere in sight.

I add, "Which is already in my backpack, because I'm ready to go."

"Why was the door locked?" Mrs. Mazza demands, her thoughts thankfully riveted on that other suspicious factoid.

"I guess the button got pushed accidentally," Carly says.

"That's happened before," I say. "I mean, here in this room. That doorknob particularly. The lock button is super sensitive. My finger barely taps it, and click, it locks. Sorry."

Carly widens her eyes at me in an attempt to get me to, again, shut up.

"Carly's trying to get me to say 'sorry' less," I explain to Mrs. Mazza. "I say it constantly. Anyway, thanks for the math help."

"We'll do fine on the test," Carly says.

I smile weakly. "Good night, Mrs. Mazza. I can let myself out."

"Oh," Carly says. "That would be rude. Mom and I will see you to the front door. Mom, come on down—" She tries to push her mom out of her bedroom, but Mrs. Mazza breaks away and walks to the window.

"You should shut your curtains at night, honey."

"I know. I just got so caught up in my homework."

That's too much, and Carly knows it the minute the words come out of her mouth. She looks at me beseechingly, like I'll be able to say something to save her.

Mrs. Mazza gazes out the window for too long. Then she lifts it open. "Is that someone in the backyard?"

"What?" Carly squeals. "Geez, should we call the police?"

Mrs. Mazza takes another long silent gander out the window. Then she shuts it tight and pulls the curtains closed. "Probably just a dog," she says.

"Yep," I chime in. "There was one out there. Like when I was throwing rocks. Which I shouldn't have been doing. Sorry. I was just really worried about this math problem. And our test tomorrow."

"No one looks after their dogs anymore," Carly says.

"I know!" I agree too emphatically. "It's late. People should have their dogs inside." I nod at Mrs. Mazza, as if to say, now it's your turn to talk.

She sighs, as if she gets that something is going on that she doesn't understand, but she only says, "Time for you to go home, Louisa."

"Yep. Here I go."

As Mrs. Mazza leaves the bedroom and starts down the stairs, I begin to follow, but can't help turning back. I smack into Carly who is right behind me. I make a "you have got to be kidding me" face and whisper, "Doug Carter?"

She shrugs. "He's kind of nonverbal. But I like his bod."

"Nonverbal is an understatement."

"He wasn't here for conversation."

I can't help it. I feel shocked. In a reverential kind of way, but still shocked. Carly laughs at the look on my face.

She says, "Like you're so virginal."

"No. I mean. It's just—" My first, and so far only, boyfriend Jason and I did pretty much everything except go all the way, but that's not even the point. Carly is so unapologetic. She revels in her libido.

"I didn't really love Jason," I say, trying to explain.

"What's love got to do with it?" Carly asks, hands on her hips.

I wish I knew the answer to that question, but I don't, so I walk back to her bedroom window. I speak loudly, for Mrs. Mazza's sake, but also to make Carly laugh, saying, "I'm just going to make sure that dog is gone before I go back out there. It might bite."

I shove the window open again and, gripping the sill with two hands, slide half my body out into the night. Doug is gone. I can hear Carly snorting as she tries to suppress her laughter. I pull back into the room and shut the window.

"Really?" I say. "Doug Carter?"

Carly smiles and shrugs, looking happily sated.

6

"Let's just scrimmage," I say at practice the next morning. Why bother with drills and plays? No one takes us seriously, anyway, and the games are jokes. No, worse than jokes, they're humiliating and definitely not fun.

"We can't scrimmage for two whole hours with only five players," Val argues. Even as she objects, her long fingers spread around the basketball, as if she can't wait to get started.

"Sure we can," I say, trying to hype myself up. "We'll switch up the combinations, but this will challenge us. Running full court with so few players will get us in shape. It'll be really good for our game."

As if the quality of our game even matters.

"I might just go to the vending machine and get a Tab," Diane says. Sometimes I think she cares more about diet pop than anything else. She's lost a lot of weight this winter. At first everyone was complimenting her, using words like "svelte," but to me it looks like she's trying to erase herself. This morning her cheeks look hollow.

Val drives to the basket and drops in a layup. Diane watches her and apparently decides to stay.

"Let's play," Helen says quietly.

Barb announces, "I can take you all on, four against one. Let's do it." She tosses me a ball, beaming her daredevil smile.

Instantly I feel better. We may not have a coach or uniforms or even a league, but my team is here. I set my transistor on a bleacher bench and turn the volume on high. Gladys Knight and the Pips are halfway through "Midnight Train to Georgia," a song that always fills me with longing for my nonexistent true love. We scrimmage full court for a solid two hours, and we've never had more fun. The uneven matchups bring out our goofiness. We're loose. We run fast, shoot from thirty feet out just for kicks, make full court passes, hoot at the air balls, use our fanciest dribbling skills.

Afterward, in the locker room, I tell Barb about the Gloria Steinem event coming up in a week from Saturday. "I don't know why I said I'd do it."

"Cool!" Barb's enthusiasm surprises me. "My mom loves her."

"Really?"

"Mom says it's about time someone spoke truth to power."

I drop down onto the bench to take in this phrase. I want to ask what it means, but it's kind of clear, if you think about it. What's *my* truth?

"What are you going to say?" Barb asks.

Good question. "I guess I'll just listen."

Barb squints at me. Then she holds out her bottle of lotion. "Want some?"

I take the bottle and squeeze a little out, rub it into my legs. It feels unbearably intimate using her lotion. Roberta Flack's voice drifts from my transistor with "Killin' Me Softly." A knot lodges in my throat. Everything makes me feel like crying these days, and half the time I don't even know if it's happy or sad crying.

Maybe I'm not the only one. Halfway through practice the next day, Diane bursts into tears and runs to the locker room.

"What happened?" Barb asks.

We all look at Val, who only gives us her signature shrug.

"Go see if she's okay," Helen tells her.

"She's okay."

"She didn't look okay," Barb says. "*Go.* Go see."

"Her dad," Val says, not moving toward the locker room.

"Could you maybe use a full sentence? Just this once?" Helen asks.

"He left a few weeks ago."

That explains the moment, in the rec center parking lot, when I asked if Virginia was going to call their dad. She and Diane both went mute and looked so instantly adrift.

"Is that why she's losing all that weight so fast?" Barb asks.

Val reverts to shrugging.

"Just go get her," I say.

Val walks heavily toward the locker room. It's obvious that closeness of any kind, even with her supposed best friend (or whatever they are), is difficult for Val. She opens the door and shouts into the damp room, "Diane! The team wants to know where you went."

"Sweet," Helen says.

"A gentle touch always works," Barb adds.

We all snort a little. It's funny, but it's not.

To everyone's surprise, Diane emerges from the locker room. Her cheeks are extra red under the blue plastic rims of her glasses, and her mouth is twisted in an effort of control, but she clunks out to the middle of the court and says, "Okay."

"You, me, and Helen," I say to her. "Against Barb and Val."

We run even harder than the day before, as if hurt can be sweat out. As if deep in the core of basketball is the secret to life.

7

ON THE MORNING OF THE GLORIA Steinem event, I get up before dawn and take off on a run to calm my nerves. I set a fast pace all the way downtown and then jog along the Willamette River waterfront, watching the rays of the rising sun strike Portland's twelve bridges. Above me, on top of one of the city's buildings, sits the giant White Stag Sportswear sign, glowing in the early light.

When I get back home, I find Grandpa sitting at the kitchen table, with the lights out, eating a bowl of ice cream. His dementia messes with his biological clock and he often gets up well before morning. Faintly from my bedroom upstairs, I hear my alarm clock going off. I hardly slept last night, and then I took off for the run, forgetting I'd set it. I'd meant to take some notes for today's event.

Grandpa nods at his huge bowl of ice cream and says, "Good stuff."

"You know you're not supposed to have ice cream for breakfast, Grandpa." It's almost impossible to remember that he doesn't know what he's doing half the time. Despite his advanced age, he still *looks* pretty good, athletic even. Back in the day he was a semi-famous football coach. I've always been jealous of the

39

interest he used to take in my brothers' sports teams. Now he pretty much just clings to a couple key memories. And repeats them endlessly.

I flip on the kitchen light, pat Grandpa on the shoulder, and run up the stairs, taking them two at a time, to shut off my alarm. Returning to the kitchen, I sit at the table with Grandpa. I know he doesn't understand most of what I say, but I still want to ask him for advice. I try to formulate my question in a way he *might* understand, but he beats me to the punch.

"Did I ever tell you about the 1945 championship game, Cougars versus the Wildcats?"

Only about a million times.

"See, both teams were feline, so right there—"

Often I just let him tell the story. Again. And again and again. But I'm prickly this morning, despite the run, and so I interrupt. "I love that story. What are you doing up so early?"

He stares at me blankly.

"I bet my alarm clock woke you. Sorry about that."

"Apologies are unnecessary," he says with a patient smile, "after forty years of marriage."

"Grandpa! I'm not Grandma." I catch myself and sigh. People with dementia get on jags. Confused jags. It does no good to correct them. I know that. But it's so hard to not try steering Grandpa back to his healthy mind.

He's looking sad now, so I say, "Lean over here. Give me your head." I rub the bald top of his head. He looks at me blankly, and I can tell that, in this moment, he doesn't remember our ritual. I wink at him, hoping that will spark his mind back. He grins suddenly and widely. It's worked. He winks back at me.

"Ha. Thanks. Now I know it'll be a good day. Here—" I open the refrigerator and take out the can of Hershey's chocolate syrup, pour some on Grandpa's ice cream, and kiss his cheek. "Don't tell Mom, okay?"

"Well, after forty years of marriage—"

"Hey, I have a game next week. I wish you could come."

"Cougars versus the Wildcats."

"No! *My* team. *My* game." I watch Grandpa spoon bite after bite of chocolaty ice cream into his mouth, counseling myself to just let it go. But I can't. I say, "No cougars. No wildcats."

I've spoken so loudly and harshly, that Grandpa looks startled.

I don't stop. I say, "Not even the Wilson High School Trojans, who it would be if we had a real team at school. Which we don't."

"Would you like some ice cream?" Grandpa pushes his bowl toward me.

Finally, my frustration unsnarls. How stupid to try to get a person with dementia to understand issues of fairness. I take the spoon out of his hand and scoop out a big bite. "Delicious," I say, and then remember his favorite expression and use it. "Good stuff."

My alarm clock probably woke up my parents, too. I hear the bathroom sink faucet running and Dad's rumbling voice. Maybe I should take the ice cream away from Grandpa. I don't want him getting in trouble. But Mom can't get mad at someone whose mind isn't all there, can she?

"What's going on?" she says, coming into the kitchen tying her bathrobe shut and squinting at the light. "Why are you two up so early? Dad! Ice cream and chocolate syrup at seven in the morning?"

Grandpa grins at his breakfast and digs in again.

She turns and looks at me, as if I'm to blame.

"What should I say?" I ask Mom.

"Tell him he should eat something healthy. He listens to you."

"I mean this afternoon. With Gloria Steinem."

"Oh . . ." She rubs her brow and then bangs the frying pan on top of the stove. She opens the fridge, takes out two eggs, and cracks them into a bowl. I guess she's going to make Grandpa a couple of scrambled eggs to counter the ice cream. When she turns to finally speak there's a stubborn look on her face, almost angry. "Tell them that there's nothing wrong with being a housewife. It's a perfectly good choice. People shouldn't denigrate housewives."

I think about that for a moment and know it's true. My mom takes care of our family of seven, plus Grandpa, and it's a lot of work, even now after three kids have moved out.

I grab my basketball off the kitchen counter and slam the backdoor on my way out to the hoop in our driveway. I run about a hundred layups, practice my left-handed dribble for ten timed minutes, and then shoot a bunch of jump shots. My favorite and most accurate shot is from the corner, so I stay out there on the driveway until I hit five of those in a row.

8

Mom pulls up in front of the Civic Auditorium, and I get out of the car. The sun is out today, and in Portland that means all the people come out, too. Oregonians take advantage of every ray of sunshine possible, even in February when it's still cool. The Forecourt Fountain, directly across the street from the auditorium, is packed with people. Designed to look like the waterfalls in the Columbia River Gorge, the fountain is made of big slabs of cement, with water cascading down the vertical ones and sunbathers, mostly hippies, lounging on the horizontal ones, their bare feet dangling in the pools.

I spot Carly and Doug sitting on one of the highest platforms, his big arms holding her close. Carly's mouth is wide open and I know she's laughing, even though I can't hear her over the splashing fountain water. She said she would come to the event today, but somehow I doubt they'll move from their sunny love perch.

Grandpa is riding in the front seat with Mom, and will be coming with her to the event, after she parks the car. Dad is staying home with my little sister. Mom reaches across Grandpa and rolls down the window. I rub the top of his bald head, and then tap my cheekbone, just below my eye, to remind him of his part in our ritual. Delighted with himself for remembering, he gives me a big wink.

"Perfect," I tell him. "Now everything will be all right."

"What?" Mom asks.

"Nothing."

Grandpa's expression dulls back to his usual confused dementia. He echoes, "Nothing."

"See you soon," I say, turning toward the big glass doors of the auditorium.

"In 1945," Grandpa calls to my back, "when I was coaching the Cougars, we made it all the way to the—"

"You're a winner, Grandpa," I call back to him. "You're my good luck."

Once inside the lobby of the auditorium, I get light-headed with nervousness. This is where the symphony performs. John F. Kennedy once spoke from this stage. Led Zeppelin played one of its early concerts here. The place seats about four thousand people.

Me, on stage. Four thousand people in the audience.

After a few false starts, I find the door leading to backstage, which is full of ropes and heavy equipment. The two giant curtains between the stage and the audience are closed. Intensely focused people rush around carrying furniture, microphone stands, and clipboards. I just try to breathe.

A woman in a red suit bustles up. No hello or how are you doing, just, "Your name?"

"Louisa Carmichael."

"Good. You're here."

Did they think I wouldn't show up?

"So have you given thought to what you want to say?" the woman asks.

"Say?"

"Yes," she snaps. "To the audience."

"Uh. Well."

"I take that as a no. Figure it out. About four thousand people are taking their seats right now." As if I'm not aware of that number. "They don't want to hear, 'Uh, well.' They want a coherent, meaningful point of view from the youth representative."

I must be staring at her blankly, because she adds, "That's you. You're the youth representative."

"Sorry." I'm practically hyperventilating.

"Wait here," she says.

I stand perfectly still until she grabs my arm a few minutes later. "Take your seat."

I glance behind myself, into the dark recesses of backstage, looking for a chair.

"*On stage*," she hisses, giving me a little shove. "The chair closest to us."

I step onto the stage and take the first of four seats. Two older women, following me, take the middle two. In front of me is a sea of faces and a swell of murmuring voices. To distract myself from my stage fright, I look for Mom and Grandpa, starting in the very back rows, scanning from left to right. I only get through about five rows before the lights go down. Then, coming from the other side, Gloria Steinem steps onto the stage.

She looks exactly like her pictures in all the magazines and newspapers. She's tall and thin, with that long blond straight hair hanging on either side of her face. She peers out at the audience through her tinted, wire-rimmed aviator glasses, and then bows slightly. Turning to the three of us on stage, she speaks softly, saying, "Welcome." Her smile is kind, almost sad.

I don't hear the introductions of the other two women and myself. I don't hear anyone announce the topic of this forum. I don't hear a thing. I keep trying to find Mom and Grandpa in the audience, but now the stage lights shine directly into my eyes and the audience is just a dark mass.

"Good stuff!" a male voice in the audience says too loudly. I almost laugh. Poor Mom is going to have to try to keep Grandpa quiet. But he's worked his usual magic. Hearing his voice helps me rein in my nerves and start paying attention.

"That's just it," the curly-headed woman on my left is saying, "we're not asking to be *given* anything."

"Anything that's not our due already," agrees the woman to the left of her.

"Exactly."

"Nor is anything going to be won without a fight."

"It took *years* of hard work for women to win the right to vote in this country. The vote! What can be more of a basic human right than that?"

"And that only happened fifty-four years ago. In the lifetime of many women in this audience."

"Oh, and how those suffragettes—Elizabeth Cady Stanton, Harriet Tubman, and Susan B. Anthony—were vilified."

"Yes. In 1917, when a group of women demonstrated outside the White House for the right to vote, they were arrested and thrown in prison. The male guards at the Northern Virginia prison fastened Lucy Burns by her hands to the bars above her cell and forced her to stand all night. Dorothy Day had her arm twisted behind her back and they threw her, over and over, against an iron bench, viciously roughing her up. None of the women were allowed lawyers."

I'm impressed by all the historical details these women know. I'm also a little bit shocked. When I think of the suffragettes, I think of women in long white skirts and funny hats marching down the street in parades. I didn't know that they'd been beaten and imprisoned. I'm also surprised by Gloria Steinem. Newspaper reporters and television commentators make her seem abrasive, unreasonable, demanding. Instead, she's cool and witty, with a dry sense of humor. She listens carefully to what the other women are saying.

After a long quiet pause on stage, Gloria Steinem says in her soft voice, "Any woman who chooses to behave like a full human being should be warned that the armies of the status quo will treat her as something of a dirty joke. She will need her sisterhood."

During the thunderous applause after that comment, I wonder if I have a sisterhood. Is Carly my sisterhood? My mom? My two actual sisters? My teammates?

"Here's the problem, though," says the curly-headed woman. "The history books don't tell us about the decades of incredibly hard work and persistence—including the imprisonment and beatings—of women who won us the vote. Not to mention those in the forefront of the Abolitionist Movement, like Sojourner Truth and Lucy Stone, who worked so hard to end slavery. Because young girls aren't taught our history, we have to reinvent how to make change every single generation."

"Just two years ago, in 1972," says the woman sitting next to Gloria Steinem, "Congresswoman Shirley Chisholm became the first female and the first Black candidate of a major party to run for president of the United States. Will she make it into the history books?"

Helen should be here! I wish I'd thought to invite my teammates.

"To quote Virginia Woolf," Gloria Steinem says, "'Anonymous was a woman.'"

The curly-headed woman nods vigorously and leans forward. "Exactly. And without these examples of women's leadership in social movements, there are no visible road maps for the young women trying to make change today."

The conversation pauses and all three of the others on stage lean forward in their chairs and look at me, the "young woman" on stage. I open my mouth, because I know I'm supposed to speak, but nothing comes out.

The woman sitting next to Gloria Steinem gives me a sympathetic smile and saves me. Speaking clearly into the microphone, she says, "What isn't said enough is that the culturally entrenched gender roles are just as inhuman for men as they are for women. Imagine men who could be free enough to share their feelings. Or who could be released from the weighty responsibility of being the sole breadwinner."

"A feminist," Gloria Steinem says, "is anyone who recognizes the equality and full humanity of women *and* men."

I sit back and listen to the storm of applause. For a hot second, I think I might get away without having to say a word. Until I notice Gloria Steinem is once again leaning forward in her chair and looking at me. She says, "I'd like to hear from the next generation. Tell us what you think about the conversation we've been having, here today and also nationally, about women's roles in public life."

I wish I had a basketball in my hands.

"I think," I say, my voice tight and high. "I think it should be okay to want to be a housewife. Women who stay home and take care of children and do the housework shouldn't be denigrated."

A scattering of tepid applause follows my remarks. Gloria Steinem watches me with a cool and neutral face, as if she's waiting for me to say something more. When I don't, she turns away.

"I'd like to take some questions from the audience," she says. "Yes, you, the young woman in purple. Please step over to the microphone."

The girl, about my age, scoots out of her row, grabs hold of the microphone stand, and speaks with confidence. "Title IX was passed two years ago. And yet at our high schools here in Portland, girls have so many fewer sports options than boys. Basically, we can play golf or tennis. For team sports, there's the swim and track teams, but no basketball, no softball, no soccer, no volleyball. The boys have all the sports we have, plus football, basketball, baseball, soccer, and wrestling. What can we do about this?"

Gloria Steinem nods at me. I guess she's giving me another chance. I try to will her attention away, but she says, "Can you address that one?"

I'm still embarrassed about my housewife comment. My mind is blank.

A long awkward silence ticks by.

A tall man in the front row stands up. The woman next to him is tugging on his arm, trying to get him to sit back down. There they are! Right where I can see them, with some of the stage light spilling into the first couple audience rows. Grandpa is bigger and stronger than Mom, and he pulls his arm away. People turn to stare as he begins rubbing the shiny skin on the top of his head.

I smile and wink at him.

Grandpa winks back.

All at once, the words come tumbling out of me in a flood of genuine feeling.

"I know what you mean," I say to the girl in purple. "I organized a girls basketball team at my school, but we have to play in the city's rec league. And because the boys have the gym after school, we have to practice at six-thirty in the morning. We have to scrounge rides to games while the boys go on a bus paid for by the school. We don't even have a coach."

"That's illegal, you know," Gloria Steinem says.

"Playing . . . basketball?" The audience laughs at my question.

Gloria Steinem shakes her head. "Title IX is a federal law, passed two years ago. The law states, and I quote, 'No person in the United States shall, on the basis of sex, be excluded from participation in, be denied the benefits of, or be subjected to discrimination under any education program or activity receiving federal financial assistance.'"

I nod, trying to not look like a complete idiot, pretending I already knew this. But even as I'm trying to look informed, I'm thinking about what she just said. *No person . . . on the basis of sex . . . excluded from participation.*

I lean into the microphone and the words shoot, unpremeditated, out of my mouth. "I'm tired of being benched."

A whooping cheer goes up in the audience. A few people even stand to applaud. When they finally quiet down, Gloria Steinem lowers her microphone and looks right into my eyes.

"The truth will set you free," she says in a quiet but firm voice, "but first it will piss you off."

9

On Sunday morning, while Mom makes pancakes, I search the *Oregonian* for coverage of the event. When I find the article, I fold the paper in half to make reading easier, and settle in, excited to see what details the reporter includes.

I read the first paragraph once, and then a second time. I check the headline, thinking for a moment that I have the wrong article. I don't. The reporter is definitely talking about Gloria Steinem yesterday at the Civic Auditorium. But the conversation he describes is completely different from the one I remember. How can that be? Words were said, *specific* words. I heard them. I read all the way through to the bottom of the article, confusion knotting my thoughts. I start at the top and read it all again and then set the paper down, just as Mom slides two pancakes onto my plate.

"He just made stuff up." I'm so shocked my voice barely comes out.

"What?" Dad asks, lowering the sports section.

"It's their job to report the facts. This reporter put words in Gloria Steinem's mouth. She didn't say any of this."

Dad looks at me for a second, then goes back to reading the sports page. Mom puts a plate of butter and the bottle of maple syrup on the table. My eleven-year-old sister Sarah looks at me curiously.

Since Mom and Dad continue to ignore me, I say to Sarah, "All Gloria Steinem said was that women should get paid for their work. Paid the same as men. That men should be free, too. Here the reporter writes—Mom, Dad, are you listening?— and I quote, 'In attendance were the usual lesbians, lunatics, and bra burners.'"

Mom pours more coffee for Dad and tells Sarah to finish her pancakes.

"No one burned any bras," I practically shout. "There were a bunch of regular people there. Middle-aged ladies. College kids."

"I need you to watch Grandpa after school tomorrow," Mom says. "I have a meeting that will run late. I'll barely have time to get dinner on the table."

I set down the folded section of newspaper. No one is listening to me. "But Steve and I are going to the library after school tomorrow to work on our English papers."

That's only partially true. Or it's true with complications. Steve has basketball practice from three-thirty to five-thirty. I'm supposed to be home in the evenings by six. When he asked me to meet him at the library after his practice so we could do our English papers, I didn't tell him that I pretty much would only have a half-hour window. More like fifteen minutes if you count travel time. I just said yes and figured I could work out the complications later. I'm just so relieved that he seems entirely oblivious to what happened at the party a couple of weeks ago. I can almost forget it myself.

"Our *King Lear* papers are due at the end of the week," I say now, hoping that pending homework and time spent in the library will excuse me from a ridiculously early curfew. Maybe just this one time.

"Good," Mom says in her distracted voice. "So you have plenty of time to finish the paper later this week." She flips more pancakes with one hand and puts the orange juice jug away with the other. She kicks a cabinet door shut with her foot.

"But Mom—?"

When she finally stops, spatula in hand, and looks at me, I realize trying to get out of looking after Grandpa tomorrow afternoon is futile. So instead, I use my moment of her attention to go back to the newspaper article. "Mom, you were there. Did you read this yet? It's as if they were at a completely different event. Gloria Steinem was calm. Reasonable. She didn't say anything outrageous."

This article makes her sound like a total fruitcake. An angry one. Steinem was right: they vilify women who speak out.

Mom seems to be actually thinking about what I just said and is about to answer when Grandpa pushes himself up from the table and goes to the refrigerator. He opens the freezer and takes out the carton of vanilla ice cream. Mom intercepts him, takes away the ice cream, and guides him back to the table. "Are you still hungry, Dad? I could fry you a couple of eggs."

"After forty years of marriage, you'd think—"

This time his voice trails off as he forgets what he was going to say.

"They're lying," I say hotly, my voice getting loud. "Doesn't anyone care about fairness? It's . . . it's . . . it's simple math. Equal is equal. Everyone should get the same. And—" I shake the newspaper. "—tell the truth."

No one answers me. We all sit and listen to the eggs sizzling in the frying pan until Dad gets up and pats my shoulder before leaving the kitchen. Mom slides two lacy-edged eggs into the pool of maple syrup on Grandpa's plate and he breaks the yolks, smiling. For an old man, he has a big appetite.

I wad up the newspaper and throw it across the kitchen.

"Hey, hey, that's enough now," Mom says, and she too leaves the kitchen.

Grandpa finishes his eggs in about thirty seconds. I get up and scoop him a big bowl of ice cream and he winks at me.

Sarah says, "I'm telling." Then she changes her mind and says, "No, I won't."

"Good stuff," Grandpa says. "Now you may not know this, but I'm head coach for the Washington Cougars."

I stand at the kitchen window looking out at the driveway and basketball rim above the garage door. With my back to Grandpa, I say, dully, "No way. That's awesome."

"Yep. We won the 1945 championship game. We were playing the Wildcats. See, both teams were feline, so right there—"

He falters again, forgets what he's saying, and I take the opportunity to run upstairs to my room. I flop down on my bed and open my copy of Shakespeare's *King Lear*. The paper is due on Friday. Maybe if I get some done today, Steve and I can just goof around in the library tomorrow, assuming I find a way to show up. We always have a blast when we're in the English Resource Center on our free period. All that forced quiet, those dead serious walls of books, triggers uncontrollable bouts of laughing, which only get worse when the on-duty teacher shushes us. This library plan, meeting outside of school, feels like a step up, a relationship promotion. We'll be untethered, freer. We can laugh even harder. And maybe actually talk seriously.

10

As I walk to school in the dark, navigating the path through the woods, I make a strategy for getting to my date this afternoon. Okay, maybe date is too strong a word, but it feels like one, as in a get-together outside of school, planned in advance. Sarah will be at her macramé class, so I don't have to worry about her. I would never blow off taking care of Grandpa, but I can go home right after school and stay with him until shortly before Mom gets home. Then I'll take off for the library. I'll be a no show for dinner. Big deal.

I really want to meet Steve this afternoon. Finding Doug Carter in Carly's bedroom a couple of weeks ago made me feel not just lonely, but ignorant, too. It's like there are whole codes of intimacy I don't understand. I know what actually happens between boys and girls, men and women. I know what sex is. I've done it. Most of it, anyway. But I have this ache in my center that won't go away. I feel like I've missed the best part of sex, some kind of secret door I have yet to pass through to get to that happy—*blissful*—place Carly describes.

Maybe it could be like that with Steve. He's perfect: smart, funny, a basketball player. I don't care if I get in trouble tonight. I mean, seriously, I'm not sneaking off to a smoky motel room to have sex with a stranger. We're talking about going to the library with a guy who's practically the boy next door.

Algebra class is excruciating. Steve says nothing about our plans. He's wearing those brown cords and his tan crew sweater, the same clothes he had on at the party, and the memory of that night paralyzes me. I can hardly look at him. When the bell finally rings, he stops briefly by my desk.

"Miss Carmichael," Steve says, making fun of the way our English teacher Mr. Murray calls all the students by their last names, fronted by either Miss or Mr. "See you in English."

Okay. English is last period of the day, so I figure he's mentioning that class as an indirect confirmation of our after-school plans. We'll see each other in Mr. Murray's class, and then he'll go to basketball practice and I'll run home, watch Grandpa for a while, and then take off for the library.

The day limps along and finally last period arrives. Mr. Murray, my favorite teacher, is short and thin, with eczema flaring across his face. He always wears an old-fashioned gray suit with thin lapels. He often stands with his hands in front of his chest, fingertips pointed up and pressed together like a steeple. In his class, we sit in a horseshoe so we can see everyone. Besides calling us Miss Carmichael, Miss Mazza, and Mr. Barrows, he encourages discussion and different points of view about the novels and poems we're reading, and he actually respects our ideas.

"Ah!" Mr. Murray says after Judith Langstrom makes a typically brazen comment about Walt Whitman. "Would anyone like to comment on what Miss Langstrom has opined?"

No one wants to comment on what Judith Langstrom has opined. She said that Walt Whitman clearly wants to have sex with nature. She compared him with D.H. Lawrence and cited a scene in the novel, *Women in Love,* where a female character pretty much makes love with a tree trunk.

Steve has an admiring smirk on his face. He's nodding his approval of Judith pushing the discussion outside the usual bounds.

"Leda and the swan," I blurt, citing a story from Greek mythology, and a poem by W.B. Yeats, where the god Zeus turns himself into a big white bird to seduce Leda.

"That's not eroticism," Judith argues. "That's rape."

Now the room goes silent and I feel stupid. Maybe she's right. I need to reread the Yeats poem.

Thankfully, Mr. Murray asks another question, about the cadences in Whitman's *Leaves of Grass,* and the discussion swerves off in that direction.

Steve crosses his arms, smiles, and quietly says, in a voice only the students sitting nearby can hear, "I wasn't done with the sex part of the conversation."

He makes eye contact with me as he says this, and I wonder if he's referring to our future. Our immediate future. I'm not done with the sex part of the conversation either.

When the last bell of the day finally rings, Steve takes his time packing up his books. I'm not sure what to do. Should I wait for him? Or should I just leave and show up at the library a little after five-thirty?

Mort steps up to me, as if I'd been waiting for *him,* and says, "I find Whitman a bit flaccid."

What does that even mean?

"I love his poetry," I say, because it's true and also because Mort's criticism annoys me. "It's cosmic. Trippy."

Mort looks startled, like he didn't expect me to contradict him.

But then he smiles and says, "I was just trying to make a joke about the erotics of poetry. I guess it wasn't funny."

I fake a laugh and say, "Oh. Yeah."

Steve is leaving the classroom, talking to Judith. I quickly follow him, and Mort follows me. I call out to Steve, "Five-thirty at the library?"

I'm trying to sound casual, but my hands and feet feel icy with embarrassment. That I had to prompt him. The way I said the words with a question mark.

Mort does a little salute, fingers at his brow, and takes off. Judith pauses a second, a worldly expression on her face, before also sauntering away.

"Ah, man, I gotta take a rain check," Steve says. "I forgot about my sister's cello performance. She really wants me there. I'm gonna already miss the first half because of practice."

"Oh, yeah! You definitely should be there!" I'm practically shouting to cover up my disappointment.

"Rain check?" he says.

"Rain check," I agree.

He doesn't leave, though, he just stands there looking at me. I swear there's a softness in his chest. I can see it right through the wool sweater. He nods slowly, like he's thinking. "We do have to do our *Lear* papers," he says.

"Yeah, and they're due on Friday."

"Is there any sex in *King Lear*?" he asks.

"There's lots of sex in all of Shakespeare," I hear myself saying, although I have no idea if it's true. We both laugh.

"What are you doing tonight?" he asks.

I want to say, *looking for the sex in* King Lear, but that might be taking the joke a little too far. The best I can do is, "Reading *King Lear*, I guess." Even though I've already read it.

"I could come by tonight after my sister's concert."

"Sure," I say, still reaching for casual, as if it's all the same to me whether he comes or not.

"Seven o'clock?"

"Sure." Apparently it's the only word I know.

When Steve arrives, a half hour late, Mom asks how his parents are doing and then says, "You can use the den," which is code for, *remember, no boys in your bedroom.*

"Let's shoot a few first," Steve says. "Exercise helps me think better."

I'm still wearing the dove gray bellbottoms and lemon yellow turtleneck I wore to school, not exactly basketball clothes, but I say, "Okay."

Mom scowls a little bit.

"Join us for a quick game, Mrs. Carmichael?" Steve asks.

That dissolves her scowl. Mom loves boys. Their jokes are funnier than girls' jokes. Their ideas are smarter.

"I'll be right out," she teases.

I grab the basketball and Steve and I go out the backdoor. It's cool, but not wet. I switch on the driveway light.

"One on one," Steve says. He pops up a short jumper, misses, and I rebound.

I take the ball to the top of the key, and he guards me by placing a hand on my right hip, his other hand high in the air. I dribble right and then left, spin, trying to get around him, wondering if he's going to let me.

He doesn't. We play hard and we keep score. After just a few minutes, he's way ahead, but I'm trying my hardest, sweating through my yellow turtleneck.

I fake left and drive right, losing him for an easy layup.

"Damn, you're good," Steve says. "Try that again."

I fake left and lunge one leg right. He drops back to guard the key. But I don't drive. I shoot a fifteen-footer, sinking it.

"Maybe I should talk to Coach Ward about getting you a spot on the boys team," Steve says.

"Barb and Val are a lot better than me."

His lead is not exactly in danger, but he doesn't let up. He shoots all of his next shots from the perimeter, dropping each one.

The kitchen window is a buttery square of light, with Mom in the center of it, looking out, watching us as she does the dishes. I keep wondering when she'll finish. Eventually she does go away, but comes back several times to peer out at our game.

Finally, though, I forget about her and what homework is due tomorrow and how Grandpa is doing. That switch inside me flips on, and I enter the intoxicating basketball place, as if my limbs are flowing with a happy drug. We're all hands, no body part is off-limits, slamming chest to chest to block shots, butt to stomach to get in position for rebounds, playing at full tilt, trying to win every single possession.

I even forget that it's Steve. That I'm supposed to have a crush on him. That he's perfect for me. I'm all about hoops. Pure hoops.

"Excuse me, kids," Mom calls out the back door. "If my memory serves, you were going to work on your *King Lear* papers?"

Steve and I both bend at the waist, bracing our hands on our knees, and gulp air. Despite my mom breaking our basketball spell, the competitiveness is still coursing through me and I make a point of straightening up first, as if I'm not *that* out of breath.

"Intermission," he says, and I interpret that to mean we have unfinished business.

"*King Lear?*" I ask.

We retreat to the den, all sweaty, our faces flushed bright red.

For the next hour, we crack jokes about King Lear. Steve makes lewd remarks about his daughters, we talk to each other in our own version of Shakespearean English, and we don't do a single thing that actually advances our papers. The door to the den is shut, but nothing is going to happen. We're both sticky and stinky from the basketball.

Mom bursts in at nine o'clock and says it's time for Steve to go home. He gets up right away, saying good night to Mom. To me, he says, "And I bid adieu to the fair lady." Mom thinks this is hilarious. As he's going out the door, he shouts in the direction of the living room, "See you later, Mr. Carmichael!"

I run upstairs and hop in the shower. After changing into my pajamas, I sit at my desk and begin work on my *King Lear* paper for real.

"Honey," Mom says, coming into my room without knocking. I can tell that she's bothered by something and it must have to do with Steve, but I can't imagine what it would be. Especially when rather than ditching Grandpa and playing hooky for dinner, I had him over to the house for a wholesome game of basketball and a bit of studying. Of course Mom doesn't know about my aborted plans, or that we didn't actually study.

"I'm surprised you're still so keen on basketball," Mom says, sitting on the edge of my bed.

"What?"

"Most girls outgrow their . . . sports phase." She doesn't use the word *tomboy* but it hangs there between us anyway.

I want to say, *I love basketball,* but in this moment, it feels like that would be akin to saying, *I love farting in public.*

She says, "I was watching you and Steve play."

"We had fun."

"You won't want to hear what I'm about to say, but it's a fact. Boys don't like to be beat by girls."

"I didn't beat Steve. We kept score. He beat me by thirty-two points."

"Why keep score at all?"

"Because we were playing basketball?"

Mom sighs. "I remember once when your Grandpa was struggling to carry a heavy suitcase to the car for me. I tried to take it from him, thinking I'd be helping him. My mother pulled me back. She told me it's always better to let the man do it, even if you can do it better."

I'm confused. I can't do basketball better than Steve.

Okay, no, I'm not confused. I know exactly what she means. I shouldn't have been playing so hard. Competitiveness is unlady-like. Steve won't think of me as a girl, as a potential girl*friend*, if I sweat and grunt and try with all my might on the court. I'm supposed to defer.

"I disagree, Mom."

She shakes her head, like I'm too young and inexperienced to understand.

"Why would I want to be with a boy who can't take being beat by a girl? Seriously, Mom."

"I don't want you limiting your choices, is all."

Mom is never completely wrong. I do know what she means. Some guys can't stand for you to know more or to perform better than they do. But Steve isn't like that.

I make the mistake of saying, "This isn't the 1940s, Mom, like when you were dating. This is the 1970s. We get to be freer. Were you even listening at the Gloria Steinem event on Saturday?"

Mom gives me a look of unfiltered fury and leaves my bedroom.

11

WE ACTUALLY WIN OUR GAME ON Tuesday, which puts us in a really good mood for practice on Wednesday morning. I blast my transistor and we scrimmage through a lot of great music, including Carole King singing "I Feel the Earth Move," and I think I do feel the earth move under my feet. All of us are hot this morning. We're connected. We're unstoppable. When Stevie Wonder comes on with "You Are the Sunshine of My Life," Barb points at me and says, "Our song," and then sinks a ten-footer right over my hands.

I'm thinking that maybe it's time to return to our drills, get serious again, because the truth is, we have some serious skill on our team. Even if we are only five. Even if we have lost a couple of early games. I think we're at the beginning of a winning streak.

For now, we keep playing full court, running hard, changing up the two on three teams. Even Diane and Val seem happy.

A little after eight o'clock, two brothers, a sophomore and a senior, Jerry and Sam, guys I know only by name, start playing at one end of the court. They're in street clothes, shirt tails flying and shoelaces untied, as if they left home partially dressed. This isn't the first time boys have crashed our court. We usually just shrink our game back down to half court.

Not today. We're on fire.

"I'll tell them to leave," I say.

"Don't bother," Val says. "It's eight-fifteen."

"I'm done anyway," Diane says.

"No, you're not," Barb tells her.

"Come on," Helen says. "Let's finish strong. We can play the last fifteen minutes half court."

"But—" I start.

"Let it go," Helen says.

As we regroup on one end of court and go back to our game, three more boys join Jerry and Sam. They get loud, rough-housing, throwing their basketball at the backboard as hard as they can to make it ricochet into our game. We toss them their ball and keep playing, trying to tune them out.

When one of the boys makes a long pass out to Jerry who is standing at the center court line, rather than driving toward their own basket, he turns and dribbles toward ours. He drives right through our scrimmage and makes a layup.

"Boom!" he says. "Two points."

"Excuse me," I say. "We're having a practice here."

He doesn't even look at me. He catches the ball falling through the hoop and tosses it down court. His brother Sam snags the pass, and dribbles our way again. All five boys galumph into our game, laughing and passing the ball. One puts a shot up, misses, and they tear down to the other basket again.

Our beautiful mojo, the exhilaration we were feeling, caves. No one knows what to do. The boys' boorishness is a floodlight glaring onto the tender synergy we'd just found. As if we'd somehow shown too much of ourselves to each other this morning and it had to break. It couldn't last.

Val, Helen, Diane, Barb, and I clear off to the sideline. The boys will run us down if we don't. We stand there gaping, still breathing hard from our scrimmage, as they continue their game, now playing full court, running back and forth between the two baskets. I want to reclaim the court, but I don't know how.

Val makes a couple of snarky comments, but surrenders, slouching off toward the locker room. Diane and Helen follow.

That gets me. Seeing my teammates quit. Just give in.

I look at Barb and she shakes her head, says, "Dunno, girl. Boys will be boys."

I hate that line. It's so bogus. I fly onto the court and intercept a pass. Tucking the basketball against my hip, I inform them, "We've signed up for the gym, the *whole* gym, from six-thirty to eight-thirty."

One of the boys grabs another basketball sitting on the side of the court and they continue playing, as if I haven't even spoken.

Val, Diane, and Helen wait at the entrance to the locker room to see what will happen. Barb stays on the side of the court, dribbling the ball, acting cool.

"You're going to have to clear off," I say, raising my voice. "We're scrimmaging."

Finally Jerry stops the play and turns to me. He has straggly brown hair and food crud on the sides of his mouth. Circles of sweat darken the armpits of his striped shirt. He coughs out a laugh and says, "You can't do a real scrimmage with only five players."

"Sure we can. It's good that way. We play two on three. It makes us work harder."

"You want it harder?" he says, eyes lit with what he thinks is a hilarious remark.

"She wants it harder," his brother Sam joins in, his voice cracking on the last word.

"It's good that way," Jerry says.

The boys all laugh. Sam gets so overwhelmed by the hilarity that he bends over and slaps the floor.

"We're just trying to have a practice," I say.

"Tell you what. We can help. There're five of you and five of us. You against us. Full court."

The boys hoot their approval of the challenge.

"No," I say, "We're—"

"What's the matter? Think we might win?"

"Come on," Sam says. "Boys against girls. Let's do it."

"Let's do it harder!" shouts Jerry.

"You can have first possession," Sam says in a phony-generous voice, and he hurls the ball at me. I don't react fast enough, and it hits me in the shoulder, bounces away.

Defeated by the boys' uproarious laughter, my teammates watching from the locker room door give up and head for the showers. Barb still stands nearby, on the sideline, and I half expect her to take up their challenge. Truth is, we could probably beat them. They aren't on the school team. They're just sloppy kids killing time. But that's not the point. The point is that the gym belongs to us from six-thirty to eight-thirty. Already all we get are crumbs, basketball crumbs, and I'll be damned if I'm giving up even those.

I glance at Barb and can tell that she gets it. She nods at me, an unusual seriousness on her face, but she doesn't say anything. What is there to say? She drops onto the bottom bleacher, next to my transistor, and waits for me to finish my protest.

I just stand there, in the middle of the court, while the boys resume their play, surging around me as if I were invisible. As one of them almost knocks me over, a flash catches my eye. It's a camera flash.

Mort stands in the gym doorway, photographing my humiliation. I want to give him the finger. Instead I duck as the boys storm back down the court, nearly trampling me. Throughout it all, Mort holds his camera against his face and snaps a series of pictures.

12

WE HAVE A QUIZ TODAY IN algebra. If I shower, dress, then run home and back to school, it'll take me at least forty-five minutes. Which means I'll be late, very late, for class. And the quiz. It's a bad idea, assuming I want the rest of my life to go well, as in get good grades, get into college, not piss people off.

But.

That was exactly what Gloria Steinem said. Being pissed off is the first step in getting free. And I'm pissed as hell.

I run the whole way home—up the highway and down the path through the woods—and burst in the back door. Thankfully, Mom is out and she has Grandpa with her. Dad, of course, is at work, and Sarah is at school. I vault up the stairs to the laundry hamper, hoping that Mom hasn't had time to do a wash since Saturday afternoon. I dig through the dirty clothes, throwing them on the bathroom floor as I go, looking for the plaid pants I wore to the Civic Auditorium. They're not here. Mom *has* done the laundry.

I sit on the cold bathroom floor tiles and let the anger pulse through me. I'm pissed off, but I don't feel very free, that's for sure.

Why rush back to school now? I'm pretty much guaranteed a no-show F on the algebra quiz. I walk slowly back downstairs and am about to head out the back door when my eye catches the laundry basket, sitting on top of the dryer, full of clean and unfolded clothes. I paw through the shirts and underwear until I find my freshly laundered plaid pants. I reach into the back right pocket, but it's empty. I try the back left pocket and feel the wad of paper. I take it out and hold it in my palm.

As I made my way through the crowd in the auditorium lobby, after the conversation with Gloria Steinem, two women wearing pale purple T-shirts with the words *Lavender Menace* stenciled on the front had stopped me.

"Hey, sister," one said. "You were right on. Thanks for speaking out."

"Oh. You're welcome."

The other one handed me a pamphlet. "Have you read *The Woman-Identified Woman?*"

"Oh," I said again. "No, thank you. I'm looking for my mom."

"Cool. Thanks again." They both held up fists. The first one said, "Sisterhood is powerful."

"Yeah," I said, glancing at their pamphlet in my hand.

Turning away quickly, I almost ran into another audience member who wanted to talk to me. This one was my mom's age, dowdy in comfortable loose clothes and a soft voice, much less intimidating than the *Lavender Menace*—whatever that meant—girls. The older woman pressed a piece of paper into my hand. She said, "Louisa, do you want to help us get a girls basketball league in the Portland public high schools?" By then I was feeling so overwhelmed, I'm not sure I even answered. She said, "My name is Mrs. Armstrong. Call me."

When I got home, I stuffed the pamphlet under my mattress and forgot all about Mrs. Armstrong's phone number wadded up in my back pocket.

Until now.

Slowly, carefully, and without much hope, I try to unwad the paper. It's about the size of a lima bean, white with visible bits of washed-out blue ink. They're smeared, but not entirely indecipherable. If I can peel the layers of paper away without tearing it in too many places, I might be able to piece together her phone number.

I set the laundered clump of paper on top of the dryer and use my fingernails to tease apart the layers. Five minutes later, I have several tiny flat pieces which I Scotch tape together to reveal, maybe, a phone number. One digit could be either an eight or a three, but the rest of the numbers are reasonably clear.

I run up to my parents' bedroom, snatch the phone's handset, and dial so furiously—trying the three—that my finger slips out of the holes a couple of times. A lady answers in a high voice and drags out the second syllable of her greeting. "Hellooooo?"

"Mrs. Armstrong?"

"I'm sorry, dear. You must have a wrong number."

"Thank you." I hang up and try the number with an eight instead of the three. This time a man answers and says he doesn't know a Mrs. Armstrong.

I sit on my parents' bed, staring at the blurry blue ink on the tissuey paper, feeling completely defeated. The boys ran us off our basketball court and it doesn't matter because we don't even have a real team. Mom is probably right: I should let go of basketball and move on with my life. Which means right now I should get up and get to class. But I don't move, I just sit there studying the laundered, unfurled, and taped piece of paper as if it's a key to something.

One of the digits of the phone number is a straight line with a little cap on its top. I thought it was a one. What if it's a seven?

I dial, slowly this time, holding my breath.

"Hello?"

"Is this Mrs. Armstrong?"

"Yes, it is. Who's calling?"

"This is Louisa Carmichael. The girl from the Gloria Steinem event on Saturday? I do want to help get a real basketball program for girls in the Portland public schools."

PART TWO

13

"Excuse me." I raise my voice to be heard over the chatter of kids in the hall between classes. "Excuse me!"

The stoner girl stops and looks at me with hooded eyes. Maybe she's high, I don't know. But I'm trying to be fair and include a wide variety of students in my survey, not just talk to the ones who I think will agree with me. Mrs. Armstrong and I developed the questions together and I'll report the findings to the school board meeting next week.

"What?" the stoner girl says flatly.

"I'm doing a survey. Do you have a second to answer a couple of questions?"

"Maybe," she says.

"I know class starts in a minute, so I'll be quick."

"Like I care when class starts."

"Oh. Okay. Well, thank you. I just wanted to know if you think school sports are important."

"Not really."

"But—"

"I'm gonna change my vote to a definite no."

"Okay." I mark her answer down on the chart on my clipboard. "Second question: Do you think girls should have the same opportunities as boys?"

The stoner girl shrugs and I think she's going to walk away. But she crosses her arms and says, "Yeah, I guess. What's your point?"

"Thank you for your time!"

I'm excited to have an affirmative answer and I mark her response before flagging down another student, a guy on the swim team. His hair has that shiny green tinge that blond people get from spending so much time in chlorinated water.

"Excuse me! Do you think school sports are important?"

"Absolutely."

"Do you think girls should have the same opportunities as boys?"

"In sports?"

"Yes." My heart sinks. I know I'm not supposed to advocate for the answers I want. A researcher should be neutral. I'm just gathering data. Still, it's really hard to not want a certain outcome.

The guy blows air out of his mouth, like he's thinking really hard about this. He cocks his head from side to side. Then, "I guess so. Why not?"

"Cool! Thank you for your time!"

Judith Langstrom is coming down the hall toward me. She looks like a poet in her flea market clothes—a purple peasant top with white embroidery and worn Levis. Big earrings catch in her messy long shag, which she repeatedly shakes back, as if throwing off all things boring. Judith's wide mouth makes her look brainy, like she has so many important things to say that she needs a bigger mouth than most people. Spray-painted in silver across the side of her leather book bag are the words "Hell no, we won't go" over a peace sign.

"Hey, Judith."

"Hey."

"I'm doing a survey about girls and sports."

Judith squints, looking both beautiful and intellectual. She reminds me of an ocean wave, deep splashy fluidity. I think I have a crush on her brain.

"Um, do you think school sports are important?"

"You're kidding, right?"

"No. I'm actually not."

Judith laughs, tosses her hair.

"I mean," and here I go, arguing for my side of the question, which I'm not supposed to do. "Do sports hurt anything?"

"Yeah, I guess I would argue that they do. All that ramming each other. And the pointless competitiveness. Sports are kind of violent, actually. What exactly do sports do for mankind? Seriously."

"You said 'mankind.'"

First she shrugs, like my observation is inconsequential, but then she smiles, acknowledging my point, and says, "Okay, so what do sports do for *people*?"

I want to find the words, for myself, but also to convince Judith. "It's about fairness. Girls don't even get a chance to—"

"Ram each other?" Judith laughs again.

"Compete."

She does that beautiful/intellectual squint again, and pauses, thinking. I feel ridiculously pleased that Judith Langstrom is seriously considering my question.

She nods as she says, "I dug that runner chick who crashed the Boston marathon a few years ago."

"Yes!" It was on the news, and even though I was only ten years old, I remember it well. A woman named Kathrine Switzer signed up to run the Boston marathon using just her initials so they wouldn't know she was female. When the race director heard a girl was running the race, he located her in the pack and physically attacked her, trying to pull her off the course. He screamed, "Get the hell out of my race and give me those numbers." He tried to rip her race number off her shirt. A television crew caught the entire interaction on film. Kathrine's coach and boyfriend fought off the race director, and she finished the race, proving that women can run twenty-six miles. Even so, it was only two years ago that women were officially allowed to enter the marathon.

"I thought she was right on," Judith says, and I nod vigorously in agreement.

I tell her about Mrs. Armstrong and the group of older women I've been working with for the past month. We've already testified twice to the Oregon State Legislature in Salem. A bunch of the women lawmakers signed a letter in support of our request for the Oregon public schools to be in compliance with the new Title IX law.

Judith looks interested, maybe even impressed, but then she says, "Cool. But right now I think we all need to focus on ending the Vietnam War."

Can't people do more than one thing?

"But," I say, "if there *are* school sports, do you think girls should have the same opportunities as boys?"

"I'll give you that. Sure."

Judith rushes off as if she personally is going to end the Vietnam War this very moment. The bell rings, so I shove the clipboard into my backpack, and head for class.

"I heard you're doing a survey."

The cheerleader, dressed for the boys game this afternoon, wears a short green pleated skirt. A big green W for Wilson High School is sewn on the front of her white sweater. She's wearing lots of blusher and blond ringlets bounce on her shoulders.

"Yeah," I say in a rote voice, forcing myself to ask the question. "Do you think school sports are important?"

"I sure do!"

"Do you think girls should have the same opportunities as boys?"

My face clinches into a grimace as I brace for her answer.

"I sure do!"

Then, right here in hall, the cheerleader girl does a short ditty, waving imaginary pom-poms. "Look to the left! Look to the right! Trojan girls will fight, fight, fight!"

She flutters a girl-wave, all fingers, and joins the rush of students trying to get to class on time. With a swell of optimism, I laugh out loud.

As I get my clipboard back out of my backpack to record her answers, I see Coach Ward heading my way. He's wearing brown polyester pants and a tan, white, and brown plaid sports coat. Though he's not wearing a tie, he tugs at the collar of his shirt as if it's choking him. I guess he's nervous about this afternoon's game.

Why not include him?

"Coach!"

He looks at me as he passes, the thick lenses on his wire-framed glasses magnifying his eyes, but he doesn't stop. I know he heard me but he's probably super focused on the win today. I shouldn't bother him. But getting support from the boys basketball coach would be so helpful. If anyone thinks sports are an important part of education, it would be the school coaches.

I run after him.

"Coach Ward? Do you have a sec?"

But he doesn't turn around.

14

"CHICA!" BARB SWATS HER TOWEL AT me as I come out of the shower, buck naked, after practice. "How come you haven't researched me yet?"

"Researched you?"

"Yeah. I hear you're asking everyone's opinion. You want mine?"

"Sure. Let me get my clothes on first. Then I'll get my clipboard."

"I like a girl with a clipboard," Barb says. She squeezes a big mound of lotion into her palm and rubs it into her calves, working up to her thighs.

"How's your pushup contest going?" I ask, even though she already told me she won.

"What?"

"With your friend from church."

"Oh. That. I won." Her face closes up, just briefly, but I see it.

"Is she your best friend?"

"Her best friend is Jesus." A hint of bitterness, so uncommon for Barb, flavors the comment.

"What do you mean?"

"What do you think I mean?"

"So she can't be friends with you too?"

Barb looks at me like she's wondering why I'm asking so many questions, and I do feel embarrassed about being so interested in her church friend.

"It does sort of mean that. For her."

"What's her name?"

Barb ignores that question, which should be my cue to stop already with the interrogation, but I say, "Okay, I'm gonna call her Church Girl X."

Barb looks at me blankly for a moment and I think she's going to tell me to butt out. But then she laughs out loud.

"Me," she says, beginning to lotion her pushup-winning arms, "I say Jesus is all about love and there's never anything wrong with love."

I step into my plaid pants, the ones I wore for Gloria Steinem. They're hip-huggers with flared legs, and I hope Barb notices my new wide leather belt tooled with flowers. I wish I had on a newer bra, one that isn't so gray and ratty. I also wish I had something equally profound to say about love. She's right: There's never anything wrong with love. It's such a simple and perfect statement.

"In fact," Barb says with her playful grin, "I like all the L words."

"The L words?" I blush hard and hope it just looks like post-practice face.

"Yeah. L as in Lounge. Loaf. Languish. Leisure. Lollygag. Loiter. Languorous. Loll. Layabout." She ticks the words off on her fingers.

I crack up and say, "Laugh."

"Laugh's a good one."

We're grinning at each other, and I'm trying to think of another L word to make Barb laugh.

She says, "Love. And Louisa."

I turn my back quickly and yank my blouse out of the locker, tearing the neckline on the hook. I finish dressing and shove my sweaty basketball shorts and T-shirt into my backpack. By the time I turn around again, Barb is at the mirror doing her hair. She asked to be a part of my survey, but I'm too flustered to give her the questions now. So I just head out the locker room door.

"I know the questions," she calls after me. "My answers are yes and yes."

She laughs again, this time, I think, at the look on my face.

"Yes," she clarifies, "I think sports are important, and yes, I think girls should have the same opportunities as boys."

"Thanks," I say. "I'll record your answers later today."

"Do that," she says.

It's not really a crush. I feel this way about all the girls on the team. Well, everyone except for Diane. I'm sorry, but her cringing is just unattractive. The crush feeling is about basketball. The way it claims your whole body. This might sound crazy, but basketball is downright erotic.

Maybe I should present that idea to Judith. Maybe it'd win her over to my side on the value of sports. I try to imagine Judith on the basketball court, but I know she'd never want to play a sport. Still, she knew the story about the marathon runner Kathrine Switzer. I bet she'd have something to say about last year's Billie Jean King and Bobby Riggs tennis match.

Later that day when Barb passes me in the hall, she says, "Chica, did you write down my answers?"

"Of course. I said I would, didn't I?"

"That's my girl."

The following evening I pull into the high school parking lot to drive us to our game, arriving as Barb is shutting the door to her ride. The two adults in the front seat, a man and a woman, are white. Barb catches me gaping like an idiot.

As they drive off, she walks up to me and says, "My parents."

"Oh!"

"My mom had an affair with a Black guy, I'm the product of that union, and my dad hasn't figured it out yet."

I deserve that. I look at my feet and nod. "Sorry. I didn't mean to stare."

"Believe me, you aren't the first."

"You're adopted?"

"Bingo." She deploys that reckless smile that unravels me. Then she gives my shoulder an affectionate shove.

In our game that night, she and I have a particularly effective on-court alliance. I score the most I have all season, nearly every goal with an assist from Barb. She sinks fifteen points herself. We win by a healthy margin.

In the rec center parking lot after the game, she says, "Pushup tournament! Let's go!"

She's looking at *me*.

"Now? Here?"

Barb drops to the cold pavement, her body planked, and waits for me.

Helen, Val, and Diane clap and cheer, so I don't have a choice. I get down onto my hands and toes, parallel to Barb, and when Val says, "Go!" we start as the other girls count.

I'm done at fifty, but Barb keeps going for another twenty. She's not satisfied with just winning, she wants to blow me out of the water. When she's done, she leaps to her feet and throws an arm around my neck. "Thanks, chica. I needed that."

"You can just forget about Church Girl X," I say.

She waits for our teammates to pile in the car and then she looks me right in the eye and says, "Yeah, I can."

15

STEVE AND I ARE SITTING SIDE by side, our thighs and arms touching, on the short stone wall that circles the top of Council Crest, the park covering the highest hill in Portland. In the distance, Mount Hood is pink with twilight.

We're supposed to be studying. At the library. But as soon as we got there, Steve said he wanted to come here instead. I think we might be on a date. It's Saturday evening, after all, and Council Crest is where couples go. The place has a reputation.

As the sky turns a soft lavender, and the city lights twinkle on, I prime myself for what's going to happen next. I think about Mom and Grandpa's suitcase, how I'm supposed to make myself smaller around boys, at least according to Mom, but I feel huge right now, the moment awkward and potent.

I hear myself say, "Dad's going to kill me."

"For what?"

"For not being home in time for dinner."

Why did I break the spell by talking about Dad and dinner? Am I trying to put a time pressure on what's about to happen? Nudge it forward with a deadline?

"Even on Saturday?" he asks.

"Yeah."

"You eat dinner the same time every night?"

I nod.

"But we're studying for our English test," Steve says. "Doesn't that trump everything?"

"You'd think."

"Mellow out already. You got a freaking A on your *King Lear* paper."

"A minus."

"Oh, wow, did you forget to put a period at the end of a sentence?"

"In my family," I try to explain, "straight As and library time aren't rewarded, they're expected. No extra privileges for doing well in school. Besides, I've been spending so much time working with Mrs. Armstrong on the Title IX thing, I'm probably going to flunk the English test we're supposedly studying for right now."

"It's probably mathematically impossible for you to bring your grade point average down at this point. I mean, you're applying early decision to Williams, right?"

"My spring grades will still count."

Steve pulls away and then bumps me with his whole body, as if to remind me that we're at Council Crest at sunset, not at the library. He wears his most flirtatious smile as he says, "You're such a good girl. What does that get you? Anything?"

I stare at the mountain, its shape darkening with shadow, trying to sort out how I feel. What I'm supposed to *do* right now.

I know what Carly would do. She'd flirt hard. She'd probably make the first move, put her hands over his ears and draw his head forward, press her mouth against his.

Steve slides off the stone wall and stands facing me. I look up at him and try to hold eye contact.

"We should go," he says. "Get you home. So you can study."

"We can stay here," I say, trying to salvage the date.

"I don't want your dad on my case," he says.

I can't think of a single thing to say that might fix this, make him sit down again, take us to the next level. I'm pretty sure these are not the right words, but they're the ones that come out of my mouth. "Are you coming on Thursday evening?"

"Coming where?"

"To the school board meeting." Mrs. Armstrong said I should get as many students as possible to show up and support us, and I'd told Steve about it earlier in the week.

"Do I have a choice?" he says. "Now that you've been recruited, I guess I have to stop being a male chauvinist pig."

I punch him lightly in the chest. "You've never been a male chauvinist pig."

He reaches behind me and snaps my bra strap. "So you haven't burned your bra yet."

"Like anyone actually does that."

Steve takes my hands and pulls me to my feet. Our faces are inches apart and I stop breathing. The tension is too much, though, and I look away, over his shoulder at the city lights.

He drops my hands. When I look back at him, he has that mocking expression, the way he pretends to be a jerk, even though he isn't. He cocks his head to the side and squints one eye. "Sooooo," he says in a jesting voice, "How many boys have you kissed? Come on, you can tell me. Fifteen? Twenty?"

I'm totally confused by the shift in tone. By the overt reference to kissing. As if it's something that would never happen *between* us, just something we could discuss as friends. It's as if I've totally misread the previous few minutes. He's in his forced ironic mode now, like all of life is a joke, one that we're in on together, but just as pals.

"I've lost count," I say, trying to also be funny. But silently, I figure it out. There was Calvin freshman year, followed by Angus,

George, and then Jason. Four. I've kissed four boys. That's a lot, isn't it? For a seventeen-year-old?

Or maybe it's not supposed to be a lot. Maybe he wants to hear zero.

I sound like my mom, wondering what *he* wants.

"Let's go." Steve turns and heads down the grassy slope toward the parking lot. I stay for another few seconds. As the sky darkens all around me, I'm swamped with that familiar feeling of floating alone.

16

CARLY SITS NEXT TO ME IN the front row of the audience. Mrs. Armstrong, and the other three older feminists I've been working with, sit in the row directly behind us. The members of the school board are at the table in the front of the drab, windowless room, talking quietly among themselves. The meeting is about to begin.

Mom got a babysitter to stay with Grandpa and Sarah so that she and Dad could be here, and they're sitting smack in the middle of the audience, not up close but also not in the very back. They're a little nervous about me making waves and at the same time don't appreciate people limiting what I can do.

Earlier this week, I got up my nerve to ask Judith to come and she responded enthusiastically. I like that she's a person who is willing to change her mind about things. She made sure I knew that she still finds sports "dull, maybe even offensive," but said that "justice matters, no matter what the arena." I see her now near the back, sitting with a couple of her smart, war-protesting friends. Helen is the only member of my basketball team who's come. She's sitting in the front row of course, on the far side of the room from me, her giant afro making its own lovely statement. She's using the minutes before the meeting begins to get in some studying. Once I thought I was complimenting her when I said she'd probably get into Harvard. She made a face and said, "Nope. I'm going to Howard."

I'm craning around in my seat, checking to see who else is here, when Steve walks in. He stays in the very back of the room where he leans against the wall with his arms crossed. When our eyes meet, he doesn't even do that ironic mocking thing. Instead he nods slowly and smiles, genuine and sweet. Mort is here too, sitting in the last seat of the row behind Carly and me, next to Mrs. Armstrong's group. Naturally his camera is strapped to his chest and he holds a pencil poised over a yellow legal pad, ready to catch the first word of news.

"What time do you suppose we'll be home tonight?" I over-hear one of the older women asking. "Bill is staying with the kids, but he's no good at putting them to bed."

"Listen to yourself," says Mrs. Armstrong.

"For God's sake, don't be so sanctimonious. You put your kids to bed every night, just like I do."

"I certainly don't apologize to my husband for not being home in time to do it."

"Who said anything about apologizing?"

Carly bats my knee, rolling her eyes back toward the women, and we both crack up. Once I start laughing, I can't stop, even though it is so inappropriate for me, who is about to speak to the school board, to be laughing uncontrollably in the front row. Partly it's my nerves. And partly it's like being in the library. The more you're not supposed to laugh, the more you want to laugh.

The school board chairman slams his gavel on the table top, and for a second I think he's shushing *me*. I'm mortified. But then I realize he's only starting the meeting.

"We'll begin with the budget," he says. "Roger, would you please report on finances?"

Roger drones on about the costs of building maintenance and possible enhancements to the school lunch program. I look around again, and Mort catches my eye. His mouth sort of kicks up at the corners in what I suppose is a smile. Then he gives me the thumbs up. I guess he's saying good luck. Which is nice of him. I try to smile, but my mouth isn't working normally. Now I'm full-on, can-hardly-breathe nervous and wish Carly and I could go back to cracking up about the older women sitting behind us arguing about their husbands.

I whisper, "Where's Doug?"

"He doesn't believe in this," she whispers back.

"This?"

"Girls sports? Equal rights? How do I know what he believes in?"

"He's your boyfriend. I guess you'd know what he believes in."

"Not anymore."

This is news. Why hasn't she already told me this?

"*What*?"

"He said our relationship was 'cheap.'"

A too-loud guffaw escapes my mouth. Mrs. Armstrong taps me on the shoulder. I know she means for me and Carly to quit whispering. But I have to hear the end of this. I lean in and ask quietly, "Meaning?"

"Meaning me. *I'm* cheap."

"You're not doing anything he's not doing."

"He's seeing Marylou now."

"No way. Marylou Fitzpatrick?"

"He's been getting really active in Young Life and I guess he's decided sex is dirty. Or girls who like sex are."

"That is so hypocritical."

"I'm guessing that Marylou is as pure as the driven snow."

A potent silence fills the room. The entire school board is looking at me expectantly as another wave of mortification floods me.

"Ready, Louisa?" the school board chairman asks.

I nod.

"Next up is Louisa Carmichael who has a few words she would like to say."

I stand and begin to make my way up to the table where the school board is seated, but the chairman says, "From right there is fine. Go ahead."

He didn't say, *make it quick*, but I feel like he did.

It's awkward speaking from my seat. Should I face the school board or the audience? I look behind me and as I do, a camera flash brightens the room. Mort has taken my picture. I freeze, as if the camera flash catches me in a trap.

After several long moments of my petrified silence, Mrs. Armstrong whispers, "The survey."

I hold my prepared statement in two hands. All I have to do is read it. I keep my back to the audience and address the school board, trying to speak loudly enough for everyone in the room to hear.

"Thank you for this opportunity to speak. I'd like to start by reporting on a survey I've taken in my high school, Woodrow Wilson. Of the 350 students I questioned, 76% believe sports are an important part of education and 68% believe that girls should have the same opportunities in sports as boys. These numbers are backed by Title IX, the law that says any institutions receiving federal funds must present equal opportunities for boys and girls, men and women.

"But this is not the case in my high school. I would like to read the petition I've written: We, the Wilson High School female city rec league basketball team, state our desire to have a school-sponsored varsity program in which to participate. It is only fair that school funds be provided for girls basketball as well as for boys basketball; and once girls basketball is school-sponsored, it is only fair that use of the gymnasium at convenient hours be made available to us."

Mom and Dad applaud nervously as Carly, Mrs. Armstrong, and her friends applaud enthusiastically. Helen sits with her legs and arms crossed, and she's not clapping but she's nodding solemnly at me, as if she's in a courtroom. From the back wall of the room, Steve puts two fingers in his mouth and whistles. I grin at him, relieved by his support. Mort flashes more photographs.

When I turn back to the school board, I'm surprised to see them leaning to the center of their table, quietly conferring. The chairman takes off his jacket and rolls up his shirt sleeves. He says, "We'll take comments from the floor. Yes, you, there in front."

I wasn't finished, but I sit back down. What choice do I have?

To my astonishment, dozens of people take turns speaking up. Students, parents, and coaches all make comments.

"In my high school," one girl with shiny swimmer's hair says, "when the school pool was shut down for repairs, the boys swim team got to practice at the Multnomah Club but the girls swim team didn't."

"We have a track team, but the coach only coaches the boys," says a stocky girl with short hair. "The girls have to coach themselves. The school has eight javelins, but the girls are only allowed to use one of them, the oldest one."

"There's no girls soccer team, but we're not allowed to play on the boys team."

"I've offered to coach a girls softball team, but was told there is no money for girls softball."

"My brothers all have earned varsity letters, but when I earned mine for golf, they didn't give me a letter, just a certificate."

"We organized a soccer team and a P.E. teacher agreed to coach us, but she isn't paid one cent. She's doing it for free. All the male coaches get paid."

"I coach girls tennis and get paid half of what the male coach gets."

"We have to buy our own uniforms . . ."

". . . buy our own equipment."

". . . practice outside in the rain."

The school board chairman smacks down his gavel again and announces, "All right. We need to move on to other agenda items. Thank you for your comments." He makes a big show of scowling at his wristwatch.

I raise my hand and he directs the scowl at me. Another member of the school board leans across the table, holds a hand up to the chairman, and speaks to him in a hushed tone. I can't hear the exact words, but I can see he's telling the chairman to let me speak. Then all the members of the school board stand up and move to the side of the room where they gather in a huddle for a mini-meeting, speaking among themselves. When they sit back down, the chairman leans back in his chair, hoods his eyes, and nods at me. He doesn't say my name or call on me, so I'm not sure what the nod means, but Mrs. Armstrong prods me from behind. She hisses one word, "Speak."

As I stand up I realize I'm no longer afraid. All the voices in the room the last few minutes rose like a tide, lifting me. Also, at least some members of the school board have agreed that I have a right to a voice about my own education. I feel confident and clear making my final statement.

"I organized a city league team and our principal, Dr. Merble, said we could use the gym in the early mornings for our practices." I glance over at Helen and she nods at me. I take a breath and go on. "But a group of boys often disrupt our practice and when I asked Dr. Merble to enforce our reservation of the gym, he said we'd have to share. In other words, a group of boys horsing around before school are given more rights than a group of girls trying to play serious basketball.

"We are here today to ask that the Portland Public School Board take steps to enforce the new federal law, Title IX, in our city's schools. I am particularly interested in gaining the chance to play basketball. Sports are not just games. Competition inspires striving for excellence. Being on a team is an important educational experience: players learn to work cooperatively with others and to share common goals. On a team, success is only possible when everyone contributes her best. I want the opportunity to play on an interscholastic basketball team."

As I sit back down, the room erupts in boisterous applause.

17

On Friday, I'm eating lunch in the cafeteria with Steve and Carly when Helen sets down her tray. She's never sat with us in the cafeteria, so I'm a little surprised but happy to see her. I pull out a chair for her, but she doesn't sit.

"You were awesome last night," Helen says. "You should consider law school."

"She's going to be a writer," Carly says. "We both are."

"Cool."

Mort arrives holding a brimming tray, as in two hamburgers, two orders of fries, and a large dish of vanilla soft serve swimming in strawberry sauce. I'd be embarrassed to be seen with that much food. He asks, "Can I sit here?"

We all look at him. No one *asks* to sit somewhere. Especially if they want to be included. They just sit, act like they own the chair. Yet he stands there waiting for permission.

I shrug.

Helen shifts from one foot to the other as if she's anxious to leave.

Steve says, "Dude. Whatever."

Carly holds up her hands, making them into a frame, and looks through them at Mort. She cocks her head to the side and keeps looking. Finally, she says, "Cute." Dropping her hands, she pats the empty metal seat of the chair next to her. "Over here."

Steve and I meet eyes and he draws down the sides of his mouth in a, *wow, look at that* expression. I haven't yet thanked him for showing up last night but I can later this afternoon in the English Resource Center where we always go for our free period.

"Anyway," Helen says, as if we were in the middle of a conversation. "I can't come to the game Tuesday night."

"What do you mean?" I ask.

"I have other plans," she says, averting her eyes.

"What other plans?"

"That's actually not your business."

"But we can't play without you. We'd only have four players."

"I know. I talked Marcia into taking my place."

Marcia? Marcia Abelman? Can she even play basketball? Talking someone into something that requires specific skills is not a promising scenario.

"No. We need you, Spider." I'm hoping the affectionate nickname will win her over.

"Can't. Anyway, Marcia is actually a better player than I am. I had P.E. with her in ninth grade."

This is slightly intriguing. We could use more players. And good ones. But I don't want to lose Helen.

"You'll be back next week?"

"Maybe."

"Maybe? Helen! This is so not okay! You're like the most serious player on the team. You already know you're going to Howard. And to law school. But you can't stick with a commitment to a basketball team?"

"I actually don't need you to lecture me about commitment," Helen says, picking up her tray that holds an untouched salad and apple.

Steve and Carly aren't listening to me and Helen. They've paired off to heatedly discuss the merits of last week's episode of *All in the Family*. But Mort is all ears, following every word of Helen's and my argument, as if he's a gossip columnist for the *Statesman* rather than a news reporter and photographer.

"Is this about studying?" I ask, trying to ignore Mort.

Helen shakes her head and looks away. I see the truth in the expression on her face, the open hope and anticipation in her big brown eyes. As she starts to walk away, holding her head high, her long neck stretched out like an ostrich, I also see the vulnerability there. She's afraid of something.

I get up and chase after her.

"This is about a boy, isn't it?"

"I already said it's none of your business."

"You told me that your parents won't let you date until college, so you're using the cover of our game to go out with someone."

She slams her tray down on another table in the cafeteria, causing the kids sitting there to flinch. A crouton pops out of her salad and onto the table. One of boys sitting nearby says, "Girl fight!"

"How many times do I need to tell you it's none of your business?" she demands.

I know I should shut up. But I just spoke to the school board about the importance of teams. Helen was there. More than that, with her political smarts, she should understand better than anyone what's at stake. I've been feeling such a rush about the way our team is cohering, coming together as one force. To abandon that now, for a date with a boy, that's wrong.

"It's just that we need everyone. You're our rock."

"I'm tired of being anyone's rock," Helen says. "And yeah, I do have a date. He's hot and smart and he likes me too. I'm not giving that up. Sorry, Louisa. I'm just not."

Helen leaves her tray on the random table of students and walks out of the cafeteria. I go slowly back to my table where Steve, Carly, and Mort are now talking about the Watergate break-in, debating how much President Nixon knew and when he knew it. I slump into my chair and take a bite of my grilled cheese sandwich.

"I wish you hadn't chased her off," Mort says.

"Okay," is the only response I can think of.

"She's the smartest kid in Larson's American history class. I'd like to hear what *she* thinks about impeachment."

I shrug. "Ask her in class then."

"Okay. Good idea. I will."

"What's up?" Carly asks me, reading how upset I am.

I'm not going to betray my teammate, so I don't tell them about Helen's secret date. Anyway, I don't think they'd understand how I feel, as if the rug has been pulled out from under me. Maybe Steve would. He's an athlete. But the stakes are not so high for a team of boys: they have everything they need, including twelve players.

"You two were arguing," Mort prompts and waits for an explanation.

"I gotta study," I say and leave the table quickly.

"Wait, I'll come with you," Mort calls after me. "The library?"

"No. Sorry. I have to study alone right now."

"Mort," Carly calls to him. "Stay here with us. We haven't finished off Nixon yet."

The three laugh and start shouting opinions all at once.

18

I'm still mad at Helen, so on Tuesday I'm pretty curt in Mrs. Hernandez's first period class when I march up to where she's sitting in her first row seat and say, "So Marcia. She's going to be in the parking lot this evening? In time to ride with us to the game?"

"She'll be there," Helen says. She bites her bottom lip, looking uneasy.

"If she's not there, you realize we forfeit the game."

"Shit, Louisa. What is your problem? It's a *basketball* game. But she'll be there."

I guess I do have a problem. The team has made so much progress, but our unity feels fragile. Diane is even thinner, and okay, she's never been my favorite person, but I'm worried about her. She and Val seem to be keeping a distance from each other, as if there's a negative force, like the repelling ends of magnets, at work between them. Barb shows up regularly, and her game is great, but I can't always read her and it throws me off balance. Now Helen is abandoning the team for a new boyfriend.

In the afternoon, just as Mr. Murray begins our discussion of Steinbeck's *East of Eden,* two cheerleaders prance into the room giggling. Mr. Murray takes a few steps back and temples his fingers, purses his lips, and lets the cheerleaders do their ritual. On game days, they give the athletes pep presents, messages written on construction paper cut-outs with candy attached. So it might be *Crunch Lincoln!* with a Nestle Crunch bar glued to a boot-shaped piece of paper. Or *Whip Washington!* with a piece of black licorice attached. This time it's a piece of bubble gum with *Pop Roosevelt's Bubble!* scrawled on pink paper, cut in the shape of a bubble. A cheerleader pins one of these on the front of Steve's shirt. He looks a little sheepish, but also pleased. The girls canter out.

I wouldn't have thought Mr. Murray knew anything about my basketball team, or my testimonies to the State Legislature and the school board, but he pauses now, fingertips still pressed together, eyes dancing in amusement, as he looks right at me and holds my gaze for a long time. It makes me feel like an adult. Like he and I can share a joke, the silliness of this cheerleader ritual. I remind myself that at least one of the cheerleaders did support my survey and that my older sister was a cheerleader. Still, it's gratifying to have a teacher understand the irony and unfairness.

"Miss Carmichael," he says, "which character in *East of Eden* did you find most affecting?"

After class, I walk slowly to my locker. The boys have their last game of the season, here in our home gym. I'm going to go cheer them on. Then I'll run home for a quick bite, get the car, and come back to get my team to drive us to our game. Watching the boys game will help get me in the competitive spirit. As I slam my locker shut, I see Mort weaving in and out of the pack of kids in the hall. He's carrying a stack of school newspapers. When he reaches me, he lifts the stack and swats me on the head with them.

"What are you *doing?*" I yell, shoving him away with my hand.

"Oh. Uh. That was a bit abrupt. You okay?"

I step around him and head for the gym.

Mort calls to my back, "The paper just got back from the printer. I wanted to make sure you saw it right away. You're this week's lead story."

I stop, turn, and face him. "What?"

He holds up the *Statesman.* "The meeting on Thursday? That was you, wasn't it? Making trouble at the school board meeting?"

When I don't answer, he takes a couple of steps toward me, cautiously, like I'm a dog that bites. "Fresh off the press." He holds the stack of papers under his nose and takes a big sniff. "Don't you love the smell of fresh printing press ink?"

I have no idea how fresh printing press ink smells.

"The paper comes out on Tuesdays. Surely you know that." Like he's hurt I don't follow the schedule of his school activities.

Mort hands me a copy of the *Statesman.* On the front page, top of the fold, are two pictures of me: one he took at the early morning practice last month when the boys game swarmed around me; and the other he took at the school board meeting as I delivered my statement.

"I'm pretty proud of that first one," Mort says. "I mean, it's not a great shot of you. In fact, you look a little psycho. But journalistically speaking, it's gold. Look carefully: that's evidence, right? Better than a thousand words, to use a cliché."

I stare at him, still completely mute.

He speaks slowly now, like I'm totally dense. "The photograph in question corroborates your testimony to the school board. Look, I even got the clock in the shot, showing that indeed this was the time when you had the gym reserved. Ha!"

"Why would I need corroboration? I just stated facts."

"Don't be naïve."

"It's all pretty straightforward," I say.

"Nothing about politics is straightforward. For example, the First Amendment defends my right as a journalist to say anything I damn well please—well, short of crying fire in a crowded theater. Nevertheless, The Powers That Be will do everything they can to censor journalists if they're telling a story that's incriminating to the said Powers. But that's what I love about journalism: the facts come out, eventually. And as you say, we're on the side of truth here, which is why you should be happy this picture is being published because it supports your statement."

I *don't* feel happy. I feel confused. I told the truth. Isn't that enough?

"No one," Mort carries on, "is going to hand you your rights on a silver platter, or even on a paper plate. You may have a fight on your hands. This is the first time in my career as a journalist, which admittedly is only two years long, in which the *Statesman* advisor insisted I get Dr. Merble to sign off on a story before going to press."

"Dr. Merble read this story?"

"My understanding is that Coach Ward also had a crack at it."

I stare uncomprehendingly at the words, long paragraphs of print, in columns under the two pictures of me, as if the story is written in Russian.

"What's more," Mort says, "they edited it, which, were I to take them to court, would be illegal. Don't worry, though. They made me take out some of the more incriminating parts of the story. But I still got a lot in. Read it. I'm pretty sure you'll be happy with how I finessed the reporting in spite of the unlawful censorship. The best part is that they had no idea this picture—" He snaps his fingers at the first photograph—"tells your whole story: they were too stupid to realize that it is more proof than any of my words. Proof, that is, that you're right and they're wrong."

My eyes travel from the newspaper print, to Mort's hands, the fingers inked and his nails bitten to the quick, and up to his face, which I study for a long time, as if I've never seen him before. He's exactly my height with brown eyes and limp brown hair, combed to the side, hanging just below his ears. He always wears off-brand jeans that are too big, a white T-shirt, and a green army jacket, also too big. He smells like laundry soap, as if every night he washes the one outfit he wears everyday. Mort does everything so fervently: his walk has an extra jaunt and his voice cracks with conviction. I remember Carly calling him cute yesterday. His eyes do have a compelling fierceness.

"What's missing," Mort says, "is the interview. We can do that right now. It'll run in next week's paper."

His eyes search my face, as if he's just asked me out on a date rather than requested an interview.

"That's okay," I say. "I should read the article first."

"Smart. How about tomorrow after school?"

"Maybe." He's so intense. And this article on the front page of the *Statesman*, I didn't ask for that. It feels like a lightning rod in my hand.

I hustle back to my locker, pretending I forgot something, and make a big show of digging through my stuff, but really I'm just waiting for the hall to empty so I can be alone. When all the kids have cleared out, I slide to the floor and read the article. Unlike the reporting in the *Oregonian* the day after the Gloria Steinem event, Mort's story is all true, despite Dr. Merble's and Coach Ward's "editing." He writes about the Title IX law passed two years ago, explains what it means, and integrates the events here at Wilson High School, the ones I outlined at the meeting, into his explanations. He also reports on what the other students, teachers, and coaches said at the school board meeting.

I wonder which parts Dr. Merble and Coach Ward changed or took out. Why do they care? They obviously have strong feelings or they wouldn't have insisted on vetting Mort's article. But I don't see what's so controversial. At the meeting I only stated facts and asked for fairness. For compliance with a federal law about education. How can anyone be against kids wanting more school activities?

I skip Steve's game. I need my best friend. Between basketball practice and games, meetings with Mrs. Armstrong and her friends, testifying to the legislature down in Salem, writing my speech for the school board, and a big load of homework, I've barely talked to Carly lately. Until she told me at the school board meeting on Thursday night, I didn't even know she and Doug Carter had broken up. Actually, I hadn't known they were together until I found him in her bed. I tried to call her over the weekend, but she said she was too busy to talk. Which isn't like her. She always wants to talk. She's been absent from school both yesterday and today.

Rain pummels the parking lot pavement, the drops hitting so hard they splash back up again. I run up the highway, skip the turnoff through the woods, and go directly to Carly's house. It's four in the afternoon, a perfectly acceptable time to show up, so I knock on the front door.

"Oh, hello, Louisa," Mrs. Mazza says, opening the door. Her face is drawn, extra pale, and little worm lines of worry score her forehead. "It's not a great time."

"Okay, can I just say hi? Then I'll leave."

"Not today."

"Is Carly okay?"

"Just some bug," Mrs. Mazza says. "She'll be grand soon."

Behind me the rain sloshes down. In front of me Mrs. Mazza blocks entrance to the house. I need to see Carly. I need to hear her bold declarations about our lives, our futures, the books she'll write and the sex she'll have when she moves to Paris. I open my mouth to insist on coming in, but Mrs. Mazza just shuts the door in my face, as if I'm a Fuller Brush salesman she doesn't want on her porch.

19

"I THINK WE SHOULD TAKE OUR game to the Olympics," Barb crows.

We're finishing up practice on Wednesday morning, and even though we won our game last night, even though Marcia Abelman has joined the team, and even though Helen has shown up for practice today, the gym has a bad vibe. I wish I could identify what's causing it.

"Right," Val says in her driest voice, "because we're so good they're going to put us on the American men's team."

"Shiiiiit," Barb shoots back. "I'll play for the Russians. The Chinese. Whoever."

As if nationality, rather than gender, is the issue.

We all shuffle grumpily to the bleachers.

"Okay, forget you all," Barb says. "I'm gonna be the first girl to play for the Harlem Globetrotters. Watch."

She sprints back onto the court and executes a reverse layup.

Val rolls her eyes. Helen collapses on the bench. Diane leaves for the locker room. Marcia just looks confused. Barb spreads out her arms, palms facing up, as if to say, *hey, what's wrong with these girls?* As she returns to the bench, I stand up and hold out both palms. She slaps them, and then doesn't let go after the contact, holding on for a second, squeezing my fingers.

"I saw the *Statesman* article," she says. "Truth to power."

"Truth, anyway," I say.

Marvin Gaye is singing "Let's Get it On," and Barb sings along with him as she heads for the locker room, followed by everyone else. I turn off my transistor and stuff it in my pack, then walk over to the electric panel and throw the big light switches. Twice Dr. Merble has asked me to not waste electricity when we use the gym, and I can't help wondering why I'm trying so hard to save the school district money when they won't spend a fair amount on my education.

Once the lights are out, I turn and look into the big cavernous space. It's a little depressing, even eerie, when it's empty and silent and dark. We only have one more game, and I'm almost glad. Why even bother?

The gym door whooshes open. Coach Ward strides in like he owns the place, clearly unbothered by the murky silence. He looks around quickly, as if he's late for something, and spies me by the electric panel. In a few long strides, he's at my side and clutches my elbow. I'm so stunned I squawk. He pulls me deeper into the space under the bleachers and pushes me against the wall.

"A word," he says.

I wish I'd left the gym lights on.

Even so, his face is so close to mine that I can see it perfectly. His blurry eyes behind those thick-lensed glasses. The thin line of his lips. The greased strands of hair slicked back on the sides of his head. He's still holding my elbow too hard. It hurts.

For a long few moments he just stares, saying nothing, his jaw clenching and unclenching, his nostrils quivering.

Coach Ward has no reason to be in the gym at eight-thirty in the morning. He knows, from Mort's article if he didn't already, that I'm here early every morning. Did he purposely come to find me?

"I'd advise you to zip it," he says, anger razoring his words.

I think I say, "What?" but maybe no sound comes out at all.

"You'll be sorry, if you don't," he says.

It's dark. We're alone. And he's hurting my arm.

Yet if my fear is a cloud, the truth is a rock, a whole mountain, under that cloud. I'm a kid. The job of teachers is to support kids. I've only asked for a federal law to be enforced. He can't erode that mountain with his bullying.

So I say, "I just want to play basketball."

The little muscles around his mouth twitch, and he's still pinning me against the wall. "I won't let a little girl and her lies destroy my program."

Lies. That word gets me. "I haven't told any lies."

"This is your one warning."

I can't look at him any longer, so I look over his shoulder, at the court painted with lines that define the game of basketball, at the blank scoreboard, at the empty bleachers. Coach Ward couldn't be more clear: This gym is *his* territory. Basketball is *his* game. I do not belong.

"Do we have an understanding?" He lets go of me and takes a step back. He straightens his rust-colored leisure suit jacket and sinks a hand in the pants pocket, as if striving for a look of relaxed nonchalance.

I turn my face away from the foul smell of his coffee breath.

Coach Ward leaves abruptly, kicking the gym door open on his way out. I slump onto the floor wondering what has just happened. The tardy bell rings and I am, once again, late to Mrs. Hernandez's class. Instead of racing there now, I just stay here in the gym, on the floor under the bleachers along with the gum wrappers and dust balls. My hands and feet are icy and I feel hollow inside.

I don't know what to do.

Forty minutes later, when the end of the first period bell rings, it's like an alarm clock shocking me to my feet. I have two choices for my immediate future. Walk home and get Mom to write a note saying I'm sick, in which case I'd have to fake a convincing illness, or go talk to Mrs. Hernandez. The fact of the matter is, I don't want to miss the rest of my classes today, especially not Mr. Murray's English. So I rush over to room 206 to get there before the next class piles in.

"Louisa!" Mrs. Hernandez says. "Why weren't you in class today?"

Despite her smirks, Mrs. Hernandez is a nice person. For a second, I consider telling her what just happened. But she probably wouldn't believe me. What teacher would push a kid against a wall and threaten her? Anyone would think I made it up.

Instead, I say, "Something bad just happened. I'm sorry I missed class."

"Are you okay?"

"Yes," I lie.

"Can I help in any way?"

"If it's okay, maybe if you could just excuse my absence. This one last time. It won't happen again. I promise."

Mrs. Hernandez looks at me for a long time. She nods slowly. "Okay," she says. "Maybe stop in and see Mrs. Evans on your free period?"

I must look really bad. Mrs. Evans is the school counselor. "Okay."

Of course I don't do that. For lots of reasons. One being that I'd rather talk to Steve on my free period. I get to the English Resource Center first this afternoon, right on time, and collapse into a chair at our usual table. Coach Ward is his coach. Maybe Steve can help me make sense of what happened this morning.

Steve is often late so it's not that weird when he still hasn't shown up by two o'clock. But it's a *little* weird. We're not allowed to be in the halls—loitering, one of Barb's L words—during class periods. Which means I can't exactly get up and go see if he, for some reason, decided to go to the Social Studies Resource Center or the library instead today.

But why would he? We always, every day, meet here.

Carly too, but she's absent again today.

Later, going into Mr. Murray's English class, I say hi to Steve, but I don't want to ask why he didn't show up in the English Resource Center. It's not like we have an official agreement. It would sound clingy. Or presumptuous. But I can't say I'm not a little hurt. And maybe worried.

At the end of class, I'm purposely taking forever to pack up, hoping to talk with him. But he walks right by my desk without stopping. Mort does stop and talks for a long time about the compliments he's getting on his article. I wish he'd never written it. Finally, I just get up, even though he's in the middle of a sentence, and fly out of the classroom. I run to Steve's locker, but he's not there. I walk to the gym and look in. The lights are blazing, but the place is empty. The boys season is over. Steve is probably already on his way home.

For the second day in a row, I walk to Carly's house, and this time, Mrs. Mazza doesn't even open the door. I know they're home because the car is in the driveway. Did she look out a window, see me on the porch, and decide to ignore the doorbell? I miss Carly. I miss her a lot.

20

I'm surprised when that evening I get a call from Helen. She's never called me before and so I'm not sure how to act on the phone. Besides, I'm still mad at her.

I take the call on the extension in my parents' bedroom.

"Hey," she says. "How's it going?"

It's going awful, but I say, "Fine."

Even though Helen bailed on our game yesterday, she'd come to the school board meeting last week. I'm pretty sure she would understand. So I amend my answer and say, "Actually, not that fine. Coach Ward told me to shut up about Title IX and getting a girls basketball team."

"*What?*"

I nod, realize she can't see me, and say, "Yeah."

"When? And how?"

I don't want to tell her about the way he grabbed and held me, his coffee breath in my face. "This morning. In the gym."

"I saw him coming in as we were leaving."

"Yeah."

She's quiet for a long pause and then, "You won't shut up, though, right?"

I love the clarity in her voice. I guess I've been thinking all day of shutting up. But I would never admit to Helen, with her brains and big hair and deadly serious way of moving through the world, that maybe I would shut up. "I guess not."

"You *guess* not?"

Helen wasn't the one there in the dark gym with that man's knuckled grip on her arm. I literally have a bruise coming up.

"Mort's article was so right on," Helen says. "The way he laid out the issue for everyone to see so plainly. You've just gotten started."

I pull a thread on my parents' bedspread and slowly start unraveling a patch until I realize what I'm doing and leave it alone. It hadn't occurred to me that I'd only gotten started. I'd collected the facts and evidence. I'd presented it to the school board. I was done, wasn't I? Wasn't it their job to make the correction? To fix the problem?

But she's right: you don't win games by making one or two shots.

"Anyway," Helen says, "I called to apologize for missing the game."

"Oh."

"You have a right to be mad at me."

"I do?"

"Sure."

Just like that my resentment sloughs away. "So how'd your date go?"

"Forget that."

"Seriously. I'd like to know. You said he was both hot and smart. Tell me, Spider." I use her nickname in the hopes it'll soften her up.

I'm so surprised to hear what sounds like a tiny sob.

"Helen? Spider? What's wrong?"

"Stupid," she says. "I'm so stupid."

"No, you're not."

"My parents saw right through the whole scheme. They went to the rec center last night, looked in on the game, and saw I wasn't there."

"How would they know you were . . . lying?"

"One, my mom is clairvoyant. Which caused her to, two, read my journal."

"That's totally wrong. She has no right to read your journal."

"Agreed. But she did. And since she caught me in a lie, she argues it was justified."

"Wait. Oh my God, I saw them!"

"You did?"

It's not like we ever have more than a handful of spectators at our rec center games. I saw a couple come in part way through the first quarter. The woman was elegantly skinny, and come to think of it, built just like Helen. She wore gold lamé slacks, a leopard print top, and her hair swept on top of her head. The man was darker-skinned than his wife and had a chubbier build. He wore his hair just like Helen's, only not as big. His round, wire-framed glasses made him look bookish. They were definitely her parents.

"Yes. I thought it was weird that these two middle-aged people came in late and then left after five minutes."

"I'm sure they just popped their heads in to confirm their suspicions. When I got home they grilled me about the game. Did we win. How many points I scored. Thank God I could tell immediately that they knew. If I'd started a string of lies about the game, I'd have been sent off to boarding school this morning."

I laugh. I can't help it. It's funny, the picture of Helen being sent off to boarding school. I imagine her in the places described in *Jane Eyre* or *David Copperfield*. Maybe it's not so funny after all.

"It's not funny, Louisa."

"No. It's not. I'm sorry. It's not fair. Your mom shouldn't read your journal. You should be able to date a boy you like. They should trust you. You're super mature."

"I don't expect you to understand."

I'm taken aback by the comment. The tone of her voice throws up a roadblock.

"My parents can be strict too," I say.

"I'm not talking about strictness. Look, do you know why they won't let me date until college?" Now she sounds nearly angry.

I shake my head. "Because they want you to focus on your studies?"

"That, yes. But also they're afraid I'll date a white boy."

"Wilson's not all white."

Helen sighs.

It was a stupid, defensive thing to say, so I concede. "Sorry. I see your point. I mean, Wilson is mostly white."

I want to ask, *does it even matter?* But I'm pretty sure that's part of what she doesn't expect me to understand.

"It's so messed up," Helen says. "I mean, Gerald is Black. He's the student body president of Jefferson High School. You'd think that'd be good enough."

"You would think."

"But it's not just the white thing. Dad says high school boys are all idiots. He says he wants me to wait until boys catch up with my maturity. My dad is a Howard graduate. He says he'll be damned if I date anyone but a Howard man."

"That's crazy."

"It *is* crazy, and yet it turns out he's right," she says, her voice full of tears, and then repeats, "I'm stupid."

"You are so not stupid."

"Gerald goes to my cousin's church."

"So he's a church-going student body president. How could your parents object?"

"My cousin told me—she told me two weeks ago and I didn't believe her—that he has a girlfriend already."

"How would your cousin know?"

"That's what I said when she told me. I figured she was just, you know, jealous or something."

"Yeah. She probably is."

"On Tuesday night I asked him pointblank," Helen says.

"If he had a girlfriend?"

"Yeah."

"What'd he say?"

"Never mind." I can tell she doesn't trust me with the answer. "Let's just say that he more or less confirmed it. And that the date went badly overall."

"I'm really sorry."

"Yeah, well. I called to say I'm sorry I missed the game. Especially after what you're doing with Title IX and all. You're right: trading a date with a boy for showing up for my team is just wrong."

"I'm glad you didn't get in trouble with your parents."

"Did I say I didn't get in trouble? I said they aren't sending me to boarding school."

"Are you grounded?"

"Being grounded is my usual state of affairs. I'm *always* grounded. Except for school-related events. I did get a little leniency because of Mom reading my journal, which Dad agrees was wrong, though they both say that my lying overturns her wrongdoing."

"Sounds complicated."

"I probably would have put up a bigger fight if it hadn't turned out that Gerald is a major drag. Anyway, Dad says for penance I have to do a study course over the summer. He'll decide the topic."

That doesn't sound too bad to me. Helen would probably study all summer long anyway. Still, I hear the sadness in her voice. Summer is for swimming at the river and lounging in fresh cut grass with your best friend. Not for staying inside at a desk studying. I think of Helen saying she's tired of being a rock. Sitting in the front row of every class. Having to be perfect all the time. Now the screws will be tightened down on her life even more. I wonder if Helen feels lonely, too.

21

ON THURSDAY, I MAKE SURE TO get to first period well ahead of both bells. Mrs. Hernandez smiles as I take my seat. She's acting a little too sympathetic, as if she knows something I don't know. I wish it were Friday. I badly need a weekend.

Carly is a no show, again.

Steve slides into his desk as the tardy bell rings. He wags his eyebrows at me, as if everything were normal. When Mrs. Hernandez starts chalking a problem on the board, I use the opportunity to lean back and whisper, "I think Coach Ward threatened me."

I expect Steve to be shocked and say something like, *Whaaaat?* But he matter-of-factly says, "Yeah, he's steamed."

"Wait. You know he's mad? How do you know this?"

"He told us."

"What? Told who?"

"The team."

"The boys basketball team?"

"Yeah."

"When?"

"On Tuesday, after our last game."

Mrs. Hernandez is facing us again, explaining some nuance of polynomials. She lets slide my chat with Steve, which she clearly witnessed, in another show of leniency that only makes me more nervous. Like I'm so far gone, rules no longer apply. Helen raises her hand to answer whatever question Mrs. Hernandez has asked. She gets the answer wrong and Mrs. Hernandez turns back to the chalkboard as she goes into a more lengthy explanation, writing out a string of symbols and numbers.

I swing around and ask Steve, "What did he say?"

"He said you're trying to sabotage the boys sports programs."

I feel as if someone just pounded my back, knocking the air out of my lungs.

"You know that's insane, right?" I ask him.

He wags his eyebrows again, this time in a kind of mock prurience. "He told us you were a lez."

I turn back around to face forward, every part of me flaming hot. I don't even know how to assimilate this new information bomb. Coach Ward told the whole boys basketball team I'm gay. Because I asked for equal rights. Like, no straight girl would ever want equal rights. Clearly he figures being a lesbian is the most damaging thing you could call a girl. It probably is. Obviously his intention is that the guys will spread the word.

In Nathaniel Hawthorne's novel, *The Scarlet Letter*, which we read in English last year, the townspeople made Hester Prynne wear a big red A for Adulteress pinned onto her clothes. Coach Ward might as well have pinned a big red L on me.

I glance around, wondering if anyone else heard Steve's and my whispered conversation. Mort, sitting in his usual place in the very back row, camera as always around his neck, catches my eye. He has a copy of this week's *Statesman* on his desk, which he holds up and flicks a finger at the first photo, the one of me being overrun on the court. Then he points to his own mouth, at mine, and back at his, sign language for let's talk. He's requesting, again, an interview. I shake my head and look away.

"Ah!" Mrs. Hernandez says. "I believe Louisa just volunteered."

I guess my period of clemency is over. I can tell by the look on her face that she thinks I've taken advantage of her kindness. She holds the chalk out toward me, and I rise from my desk and take it from her. I walk to the chalkboard and face the algebra problem. I'm good at algebra. I like the way letters stand for numbers and how it's a whole language with a perfect logic. But right now I just feel blank and shaky. Worse than shaky. My legs are about to collapse under me. I stand there, chalk in hand, while the numbers and letters in front of me are a dull blur. I try to bring them into focus, but I can't think.

I whirl around to face the class. I feel completely exposed. Who has heard Coach Ward's proclamation? There are twelve boys on the basketball team. They each have a few good friends, and each of them has a few more good friends. This thing is a wildfire.

And it all started with the front page story of this week's *Statesman,* written by Mort. I can't wait to get out of here, out of this school, out of this town, off the entire west coast. I want to be as far away from here as possible. Williams College is all the way on the other side of the country, in Massachusetts. I'm hoping the kids there will be more mature, not to mention the teachers and coaches.

I'm standing here, the piece of chalk in my hand, gaping at thirty kids. They're all staring back, wondering what's wrong with me. My mouth is probably hanging open. I'm thinking about my whole life, how to save it, and not about the algebra problem at my back. I can't even turn around to face the chalkboard.

This is Mort's fault. He's sitting back there in his corner looking smug with his newspaper and camera. He put all of this in motion. If he hadn't followed me around, taking pictures, taking notes, recording everything I say and do, Coach Ward would never have known what happened at the school board meeting. He would never have shoved me against the wall under the bleachers. No one would have called me a liar. The boys basketball team would not be spreading a hot rumor about me being queer. All of this is because of Mort's photographs and story in the *Statesman*. If it hadn't been for him, this whole situation would have faded quietly into oblivion.

My anger concentrates in my fist and I hurl the piece of chalk right at Mort.

He looks surprised and a bit hurt, but catches the chalk, rises slowly from his desk, and walks toward the chalkboard. I bump into him roughly as I charge back to my own desk.

"Are you okay, Louisa?" Mrs. Hernandez asks.

She'd asked me the same thing yesterday morning. If the adults in this school were doing their job, they'd know I'm not okay. They'd do something about it.

But I don't answer her and I don't look at her. I slam into my desk and glare at the chalkboard, as if I'm fully engaged in learning algebra. I can see Mrs. Hernandez in my peripheral vision watching me, everything about her softening sympathetically, but I don't want her sympathy. I want—

What? What do I want?

Fairness? To play basketball? For adults to tell the truth? Yeah, all of that.

Mort meticulously works the algebra problem, and then I get mad about that, too. I could have done that problem. I'm good at algebra. Instead, I turned it over to a boy. What is *wrong* with me?

While he's still at the chalkboard, I lunge back to Mort's desk and grab the newspaper. Returning to my own desk, I look closely at the two pictures. In the first one, I look defeated and a bit feral. In the second one, I look brazen and also a bit feral.

Later that day, as the swim team coach passes me in the hall, he points at me with his forefinger and cocks his thumb. Could mean hello, or could mean *pow*. Since I don't know him, not even a little bit, have never had a class with him, I'd say the gesture does not mean hello. Besides, as he does that with his hand, he shakes his head from side to side, as in a great big general *no*. No to my entire existence.

Then, right before lunch, the young track coach with the muttonchop sideburns and tight polyester pants stops by my locker as I'm dumping off my American history text. He can't make eye contact and seems embarrassed, as if he's following a script against his will.

He says, "Hey. Um. Cool it. Okay?"

Barb is in the stream of kids flowing down the hall and she waves at me, calls out, "Chica! Laugh! Love!" Right on her heels, Judith Langstrom also goes by, the words *Hell No* scrawled on her leather book bag. The tension in my head and stomach loosens. It loosens a lot.

I turn to squarely face the track coach and say, "Really?"

"You know," he says, obviously uncomfortable. "Like with the statements."

"Statements," I say, as if what I don't understand is the meaning of that word rather than his request that I not make any.

"The false ones," he says. "Uh. The false statements."

"You're the third coach to warn me. I don't get what the problem is. I only—"

But he doesn't stay around to hear what I think. I blink and he's gone.

The way Barb walks, how she fully inhabits her body, is a statement. The war protest penned across Judith's leather bag is a statement. Mort's article is a long statement of facts. I wish that I'd found the words to tell the track coach about the First Amendment, which protects my right to make *statements* about my personal opinions and experiences any time I want.

Meanwhile, here comes yet another one, this time the baseball coach, a trio of bats hanging from the grip of his hand. He stops a few feet away from me but, like the swim team coach, can't bring himself to actually say anything. Even so, his presence is menacing.

I finally realize that the fight, which I'd thought was won after the school board meeting, has only begun.

22

SPRING COMES TO PORTLAND AS A pink and yellow glimmer. Even though I'm upset by the attacks from all the coaches, the cool, sparse rays of sunshine calm me as I walk up the highway. A chorus of birdsong, my private cheering section, greets me when I step into the woods. At least I talked back to the track coach!

The path is still muddy, so I'm watching my feet going down the hill, trying to keep from falling on my butt. I don't see the person sitting on a log on the other side of the clearing until I reach the bottom.

When I finally look up, I think, Steve!

He does unpredictable things like this, skitter away when I'm trying to connect and then show up somewhere else unexpected.

But no, it's Mort.

"What are you doing here?" I ask him, not disguising my annoyance.

"Stalking you?"

"That's not funny."

"I gather you're mad at me. The evidence being the look on your face right now. Plus you throwing the chalk at me in algebra. Clinched by the fact that you didn't show up for the scheduled interview."

"I didn't agree to that. Your article—" I look up into the trees as the sun goes behind a cloud and everything gets gloomy again.

"Uh huh," Mort says. "I'd like to hear you finish that sentence. Got you into trouble? No doubt. I told you it would. But you should be thanking, not blaming, me."

"It just made them madder."

"Of course it did. You told the truth. And exposed their discriminatory, never mind unlawful, behaviors."

"Yeah. Well." The sun bursts back out from behind the clouds and beams down through the forest canopy. He's right. I told the truth. Next thing I know, I'm quoting Gloria Steinem. "The truth will set you free. But first it'll piss you off."

Mort grins. "I like that!"

"I didn't make it up. Someone said it to me. I have to get home. I haven't started my Steinbeck paper. And by the way, don't stalk me."

"Getting your attention is difficult."

I take three big steps to the side, intending to move on, but Mort steps in my path.

"Stop it."

"I just need you to—"

"I just need *you* to leave me alone."

Then I feel bad. Mort looks genuinely hurt.

I put a hand on his shoulder, and maybe that's a mistake, because there's a buzz there between my hand and his body, coming right through the green army jacket. "Look. I appreciate you trying to help me."

"It's not personal," he's quick to say. "It's about the Constitution, which guarantees every citizen equal rights under the law."

"Debatable."

"You're right," he says. "It sort of *is* personal."

"No. I meant the part about guarantees in the Constitution. The Senate just passed the Equal Rights Amendment—" I only know this from hanging out with Mrs. Armstrong and her friends, who had a giant celebration when it passed, but I'm inordinately pleased to be so informed right now. For some reason I want Mort to know I'm smart. "—but it needs to be ratified by 38 states to get into the Constitution."

He's grinning again. "You're right. The Constitution's guarantees are debatable. I'd like to have that debate with you."

"Look—"

"Nevertheless, I'd argue," he carries on, "that equal protection under the law is *already* covered in the Constitution, but because of asshats like most politicians, teachers, administrators, etcetera, we need the ERA to bolster what should be women's God-given rights."

I know he's on my side, and that he's trying to make me feel better about everything that's happening, but he doesn't know the half of it. He doesn't know a *tenth* of it. Maybe for him it's about a law. But for me it's about my life, my whole life. Right now all I want is to get home. Doing homework, getting a start on my Steinbeck paper, is far preferable to thinking about Carly's absence and Coach Ward's character assassination.

"Actually," Mort says, "it's definitely personal."

"What?"

"I said it wasn't personal. Which I meant. It's not. Or, I mean, it's not exclusively personal. But it's *also* personal."

"Okay." Because what else am I supposed to say?

"Have you ever noticed," Mort says, "that the kids who were cool in grade school aren't so cool in high school?"

"Yeah. I guess."

"No, it's a fact. It follows, then, doesn't it, that the kids who are cool in high school aren't going to be the ones who are cool in college."

"Okay?" I say with a question mark, as in, why are you telling me this?

"I'm suggesting you take the long view," Mort continues. "Beneath this nerdy veneer is a cool guy."

For a second, in that tender yellow spring sunshine, spiked by the fresh tang of evergreen needles, I wonder what it'd be like. With Mort. Probably both sweet and ferocious. He'd be clumsy. Understatement. Mort is like a mental volcano.

"Okay," I say. Then realize that maybe that sounded like agreement when I only meant to say I heard what he said.

Now he's just staring at me. I take a step back because I swear he's about to kiss me. Like talking about the Constitution is an aphrodisiac. For him it probably is.

"I have to get home and study," I say, trying to interrupt the energy between us. With Steve the word *study* was a buzz kill. But for Mort it might be as exciting as the word *Constitution*.

"Can we do the interview this weekend?"

"No," I say.

"Did I talk too much?" he asks. "Just now? Like stupidly explaining things you already know?"

I shake my head and start walking backwards.

Mort nods, says, "Got it. Fine. But I'm not letting go of the interview. You're the hottest story at school." He smiles and licks his chapped lips, then pauses and says, "You are."

23

THE NEXT FEW WEEKS ARE HELL. Carly doesn't come back to school, and her mom won't even let her talk on the phone. Steve is friendly enough in class, but we have no more "dates" and he stops meeting me in the English Resource Center on our free period. Mort asks me several more times for the interview, and each request just reminds me of the mess I've made of my life. I've managed to lose Steve and Carly, infuriate the entire coaching staff, and get labeled a pariah.

The basketball season is over, and I miss my team so much. I see Helen in class, but she's one hundred percent focused on acing every paper and test between now and the end of the year. If she was studious earlier this year, she's now practically a walking library. I don't have any classes with the other girls. Barb smiles at me in the hall when we pass, but compared to talking in the locker room and making plays together on the court, that's a pittance.

I can't wait for this year to end.

On a day in mid-May, I'm on my way to Mr. Murray's English class when Coach Ward ambushes me in the hall. He must have looked at my schedule to find out where I'd be. I look around for an escape, but there is none, short of just running, which I do consider. He doesn't touch me this time but I still feel his hand clamped on my arm, still smell his nasty coffee breath, still feel like a bull's eye target in his blurry vision. He doesn't even speak, just hands me a stapled sheath of papers and walks away.

I start reading the published minutes from the school board meeting with a wash of relief. This report is in print. It's gone out to the entire city. My testimony will be seen by everyone. I will be vindicated. For a moment, I even have a tiny kind thought about Coach Ward, that he can admit when he is wrong.

Then I start to actually digest what the report says. And I can barely breathe.

I shoot out the nearest school exit. A couple of stoner kids, including the girl who responded to my survey, sit under a stairwell smoking. I drop down to sit with them, my back against the brick wall. The girl offers me a cigarette. I say no thank you, and she shrugs but smiles. She pulls a joint out of her jeans' pocket and holds that up.

"You look like you need a toke of this."

"Oh, no thank you," I say again.

"I do," the boy sitting on the other side of her says, reaching for the joint and lighting it.

I wrap my arms around my knees and pull them tight against my chest, squeeze my eyes closed, and wait for the school day to be over.

"You sure?" the girl asks, taking the lit joint back from the boy and holding it out to me.

I shake my head.

"It's cool what you're doing," she says, after taking a long drag herself.

I swing around and look at her. I'm surprised that she even knows. Or that she cares.

She laughs and says, "They can all go screw themselves."

I laugh too. Maybe I'm not as alone as I thought.

I get up and head back inside, going directly to the admin offices and charging through the reception area. Mrs. Hodge's door is open, and she looks up from her desk as I shoot by. I consider stopping to talk to her, since she's the one who started all of this, but I need to go all the way to the top.

Dr. Merble's office door is shut and so I knock.

"You're not allowed back here," scolds the secretary who's been chasing behind me. "You need an appointment."

I flap the sheath of papers in my hand, as if that'll explain everything to her, which it would if she read them, and again knock on Dr. Merble's office.

The principal opens the door, looking as if he's just woken up from a nap. Besides appearing permanently drowsy, he's tall with pasty white skin, and black hair brill-creamed over his bald spot.

"I'm so sorry, Dr. Merble," the secretary says from behind me. "I couldn't stop her."

"Louisa Carmichael!" He pronounces my name too heartily, as if forcing himself to sound available. He says to the secretary, "It's okay," and then to me, "Come on in, Louisa."

"Thank you. I need to talk to you."

The secretary makes an exasperated sound before huffing away.

"I always have time for fine students like you, Louisa," Dr. Merble says, exuding a bland benevolence as he holds an arm out toward a chair. I swear, his manner is so mild he sometimes seems drugged. "How are your brothers? They were such outstanding student athletes."

"Fine."

"And your parents, Louisa?"

"They're great. This report from the school board—" I shake the papers in my hand and then place them on his desk. "It's totally inaccurate."

"I'm glad you've come to talk, Louisa. This is a good opportunity for learning the importance of adhering to strict facts."

"Yes. Exactly. This guy, this Mr. Voigt, the 'communication specialist' for the school board, misquoted me right and left. For one thing, he's attributed comments from people in the audience to me. He's made other things up and said I said them. But what really gets me is that for all the comments he attributes to me, he uses the verbs 'alleged' and 'complained.' Everyone else 'said' their comments."

"Mm," he says, as if that's an answer to anything ever.

"He totally botched his job."

"Now, now. Have you ever taken notes for a meeting? It's a challenging task, getting every word down exactly as it was spoken. I'm sure he's captured the gist of what was said at the meeting."

"That's my point. He *hasn't*. He's made up a whole different gist."

"The problem is, Louisa, these things take time."

Did the principal learn from some "communication specialist" to use a person's name in every single sentence?

"What things, Dr. Merble?" I pick up the school board report and brandish it above my head. I probably look like one of those people who stand on a box in Pioneer Square downtown and preach to the air, but I'm so frustrated. "Coach Ward wrote a letter to the school board saying that the statement I made at the meeting was, and I quote, 'totally and unequivocally preposterous and unfounded.' He wasn't even there."

"Well, from *his* point of view—"

"This isn't about point of view. It's about facts. I said there is no girls basketball program. Is that not a fact?"

"Well, now, Louisa . . ." He can't even finish his sentence.

"Plus," I rant on, "the school board attached a copy of Coach Ward's letter to the meeting report, but *not* a copy of my statement. So anyone reading this only hears his words, but not mine."

Dr. Merble holds his flattened hands out over his desk and pats the air in a "calm down" gesture. He pauses a long, instructive time before speaking. I wait him out. I really do want to hear what he has to say.

"Hewing closely to the truth of the matter will aid your cause."

"I didn't say anything untrue. It's a fact that the boys get to have a basketball team, a coach, and prime gym time. While the girls do not. Is that not one hundred percent true?"

"Listen. Louisa. I understand. And goodness knows, if we could have sports programs for girls, we would have them. But there's not enough money to cover even our boys programs. Never mind gym time."

"It's the law. Equal opportunity."

This finally gets a genuine response. A visual one, anyway. Dr. Merble draws back and blinks. He almost flinches. As if I'd used the f-word or something.

He regains his composure fast, though, and says, "All in good time. Patience, young lady. What's needed here is patience."

The word zaps me with the opposite, *im*patience. I shoot over to the window where I can see the beautifully groomed baseball field, complete with plump white bases, tidy caged dugouts, and a meticulously raked infield. A groundskeeper is mowing the outfield grass in advance of today's baseball game. All of this is for the boys team. There is no girls softball program.

"I have a suggestion for you, Louisa."

"Okay." I'm still holding out hope that the principal is here to help, wishy-washy as he is. It's his job to be an advocate for students. To implement the law as it applies to education. I'm ready for his suggestion.

"It would be much more productive for your cause if you directed your energies toward getting more girls involved in athletics. If we see some interest, then there will be more impetus for expanding the programs."

Yes, he really does say this. There is no polite way to point out the absurdity of his "suggestion." I try to keep my voice calm as I ask, "How can I get more girls to play on teams that don't exist?"

Dr. Merble stands up and smiles sadly. At what? How pathetic he thinks I am? How hopeless he thinks my "cause" is?

"Your family has been an outstanding part of the Wilson High School community. I've asked the school board to not refute you publicly."

"Refute me? Publicly? They already have."

"Don't forget you have a whole year to complete before graduation. And, by the way, I hear you're applying early decision to Williams." He walks to the door and holds it open. "I trust you're keeping your grades up and staying out of trouble. Early decision is highly competitive. You wouldn't want any blemishes on your record."

He's still wearing that fake smile and now he punches the air in a gosh darn gesture. "I'm glad we had this talk, Louisa."

Then, as if things couldn't get worse, they do. I'm leaving the admin offices, trying to figure out how I'll explain my tardiness to Mr. Murray, and here in the empty hallway, plodding slowly my way, comes Mr. Stanton, aka *Coach* Stanton, head of the football team, his eyes pinned on me.

I'm completely alone. With him.

I glance around for an escape route, but see nothing but the long rows of metal lockers on either side of me. Their gray verticality morphs, for a second, into prison bars, making me think of the suffragettes, how they were thrown in jail for wanting the simple right to vote. How they were manacled to the prison bars and some were even beaten.

I'm only seventeen years old! I want to scream. *Leave me alone!*

As Coach Stanton draws closer I look straight ahead, as if by not looking at him, I might be able to ward off the attack. When we are side by side, him going in one direction and me in the other, I think maybe I'll get off free. Just keep walking, I tell myself. Just keep breathing. If I can find any oxygen at all in this rank hallway. What's even left for Coach Stanton to say or do? Mr. Voigt and Coach Ward have already taken care of the problem of me. I'm toast. A lying dyke.

But no, Coach Stanton makes a U-turn, slings an arm across my shoulders, and walks wordlessly with me down the hall. Physically, I'm about to collapse under his big arm. Mentally, his total silence wrecks me.

I want to scream, *You won! Okay? Get off of me!*

After about thirty yards of this side-by-side promenade, with me aiming for the exit to the outside, where with any luck I'll be able to breathe and walk freely, he says, "Did you say hi to your brothers for me?"

"Uh." I remember he'd asked me to do that a long time ago, on the day this all began.

"Hm?" he presses.

"Yes. I mean, I haven't talked to them in a while. But I will." Weak. But at least honest.

"Good. I hope they're doing well."

I nod. Then squeak out, "They are."

"Glad to hear it. Summer plans?"

"Me or my brothers?"

"You."

"I have a job with the county parks."

"Excellent."

We pace another five yards, and then he gives me a squeeze with the arm that's still around my shoulders.

I could swear it's a friendly rather than hostile squeeze.

When I look at him, his watery blue eyes are kind. He steps back and says, "I'm with you all the way, girl."

24

ON THE LAST DAY OF MY junior year, I find Barb in the cafeteria on my free period. I know she'll be there because the English Resource Center is right outside the cafeteria and I often see her sitting at a table with her friends.

I get a peanut butter brownie and a carton of milk and take a seat at her table.

"Hey," she says, and I notice she doesn't call me *chica* in front of her friends.

"Hey."

The other kids at the table look at us curiously, but then they jump back into their fiery argument about the school counselor Mrs. Evans, who some are defending and others are calling a sell-out.

"You know what?" Barb says to me, turning her back on the others. "I need a basketball nickname."

"You do?" So maybe she misses basketball, too.

"Yeah. I mean, Spider is perfect for Helen. What about me?"

She waits, and it just pops into my head. "Lucky!"

"Lucky? That's totally corny. Also bland."

"It's not bland. For one, it's an L word."

We both glance at the other kids at the table who have moved on to heatedly evaluating Mr. Hoppenburger, the boys counselor.

One kid calls him a fag, and another tells him to shut up. Then that kid is called a fag for defending one.

Barb turns back to me and I'm afraid I've said something too forward. Or too suggestive. But she rolls her eyes at the kids at her back, then gives me a big grin and says, "Lucky, huh?"

"Plus," I tell her, "there's nothing bland about luck. We're going to need it."

"We?"

I flush. "I mean, next year, our team."

"We're playing in the rec league again?" she asks.

"Aren't we?"

"Sure. Yeah. I guess. If we can."

"We'll need to be lucky," I say. "To pull a team together. To win games. For everything."

"*You* need Lucky," she says. Then adds, "I mean if you want to win."

"I do," I say and flush again. "What are you doing this summer?"

"I'm counseling at church camp."

"Oh. Is Church Girl X a counselor too?"

Barb looks away. I've overstepped something. Again.

"I just mean—" I don't know how to clean this up, and besides, I really want to know. "The girl you did the pushup contest with."

"You keep bringing her up."

"I do?"

"Would it make you happy if I told you that you can do more pushups than her?"

How am I supposed to answer that? Luckily Helen, aka Spider, joins us with a plastic bag of apple slices she's brought from home. She's wearing a far-out pants suit of patched denim with a hot pink blouse.

"What's up, team?"

I say, "I'm thinking we should get a pickup game together over the summer."

Helen makes a face. "You know I won't be leaving the house this summer."

"But a *basketball* game?" I ask.

"Yeah, that ought to be innocent enough."

"Except that I'll be there," Barb boasts, as if she's trouble. She bats her knee against mine.

Helen smiles that gracious smile of hers and eats an apple slice. She doesn't take Barb as seriously as I do. Which seems like a mistake to me. Barb is deep behind all that goofing around. I can see it in the way she observes everything so accurately, even in the precise way she plays basketball.

"What study plan did your dad come up with?" I ask Helen.

"Actually," she says, "I managed to finesse that one a bit. He was all about African history, like from hundreds of years ago. Kings and queens, all that. It was going to be a total bummer. I countered with a reading list that Mrs. Jones—a teacher who goes to our church—helped me put together. I'm stoked."

"Yeah? Let me see."

"For real? You're interested?"

I nod and so she digs a piece of paper out of her backpack, announcing, "Twentieth century Black women writers."

"That's cool," Barb says.

I look over Helen's summer reading list. I haven't heard of a single one of the authors.

> *The Bluest Eye*, by Toni Morrison
>
> *The Third Life of Grange Copeland*, by Alice Walker
>
> *I Know Why the Caged Bird Sings*, by Maya Angelou
>
> *A Raisin in the Sun*, by Lorraine Hansberry
>
> *Their Eyes Were Watching God*, by Zora Neale Hurston

"Read them with me," Helen says to Barb.

"Nah." Barb backs down fast. "My summer is full."

Helen smirks at Barb, as in, *yeah, right, you lightweight.*

I want to defend Barb. She's not a lightweight. She has a unique kind of insight and savvy. "I will," I say. "I'll read them with you."

Now Helen smirks at *me.* Maybe she doesn't believe I'd be interested. Or follow through.

I take out my English notebook and write down the titles.

"All the books we read in school are by men," I say, realizing it for the first time.

"All the books we read in school are by white people," Helen adds.

I tuck my new summer bibliography into my backpack.

"I have to write a report on each book," Helen says. "You going to do that too?"

"That'd be going a little far," I say.

Barb cracks up and knee-bats me again.

"Hey," I tell Helen. "We have a new nickname for Barb. Next year she's going to be Lucky."

Helen nods without smiling. "We're going to need to be lucky. All of us."

I want to ask, *for what?* But I'm afraid she'll scoff at me for not already knowing. Anyway, I sort of do know what she means. Life is full of so many obstacles. More, and bigger ones, every day. Everyone needs a little luck, maybe a lot of luck, to get through.

"What about that summer basketball game?" I ask.

We promise to call each other. But somehow I know we won't.

Later that day, when the final bell rings, kids burst out of classrooms, throwing notebooks and pens in the air, hooting like freed animals.

Someone shouts, "Let the summer begin!"

And I think, *Let the* lonely *summer begin.*

We've already turned in our textbooks, so cleaning out my locker is easy. I just have to decide which of my junior year memorabilia to keep and which to toss. I save notes from Carly, slipping them into my English notebook. I wad up old homework assignments and drop them in a discard pile on the floor in front of my locker. Broken pencils and eraser stubs go on the same pile. I definitely keep the funny drawing of me that Barb did way back in February, tucking it into my English notebook with Carly's notes and Helen's reading list.

Resting on the top shelf of my locker is the typed statement I made at the school board meeting at the end of March, along with Coach Ward's more recent angry rebuttal in the meeting minutes. I might as well throw all that in the trash.

"Excellent photograph."

It's Mort, standing right at my side. For a skinny kid, he has a deep voice, even if it does crack in the middle of every sentence. And he's bragging once again about his picture of me, published in his beloved *Statesman.* I ignore him. Even though he's standing close enough that I can detect his laundry soap smell.

"Did you watch the match last year?" he asks.

That's when I realize that he's not talking about his own photography. He's talking about the picture of Billie Jean King taped on the inside of my locker door. My whole family—pretty much the whole country—watched her match with Bobby Riggs, the jerk who said no woman could ever beat a man in tennis, and challenged the number one female player in the world. Billie Jean King beat him easily in straight sets.

"Of course I did."

"That was hilarious," Mort says. "Watching her destroy that idiot."

"Yeah."

"So the school year is over."

"Yep." I raise my elbows abruptly, the way you do to block out an opposing player for a rebound, aiming to make more space around me. Mort takes a step back. But he doesn't go away.

"This is my last chance," he says.

He wants me to say, *last chance for what?* but I don't. I continue packing my backpack.

"You've blown off all my interview requests. I've made four of them, two in person and two delivered in formal notes."

I sling on my backpack and face Mort. "Look—"

"I know. You said leave you alone. Which I have. Mostly. I mean, I've left you alone on a personal basis. Pursuing you for the interview is strictly business. I'm risking triggering your wrath this one last time because it just seems like, given the outrageous set of lies in the school board's report that came out last week, you'd *want* to talk to me, to clear the record."

"My wrath?"

"Point taken. That was too strong a word. It would do you good to show some wrath, actually. How about that interview? We could let them have it."

"Hello? School's out for the summer. As of ten minutes ago. There are no more issues of the *Statesman*."

"The interview would run next year. Obviously. Although, and I realize this is ambitious, I could try to place it in the *Oregonian*."

"I lost. We aren't getting a basketball team. There's nothing more to say."

"So you're giving up?"

"Maybe you didn't hear me. *I lost.* It's over."

"I'd still like an interview. We could start with an easy question. What are you doing this summer?"

All around us kids are celebrating, shouting jokes and shooting rubber bands, freely using language not allowed at school, because what can anyone do now, school is over. For three glorious months.

Or three months that *would* be glorious if I had any friends. I look past Mort—way past Mort—down to the end of the hall where Steve's locker is. I don't see him.

But I do see Carly.

I shove the trash on the floor back into my locker, kick the metal door shut for the last time this year, and brush past Mort. I run all the way to Carly's locker.

"Where have you been?!" She's deep in her own locker, shoveling stuff into a big brown paper bag. "Every time I call, your mom acts like you just have the sniffles or something, but it's been *weeks*."

"Bad flu," Carly says, straightening up to face me. "I just came by now to clean out my locker."

She looks terrible. Her long black hair hangs limp and ragged at the ends. Her skin is sallow and saggy, and she has dark circles under her eyes, the opposite of her old vivacious self. She sees my shock at her appearance.

"Bad flu," she repeats.

"You missed finals and everything." My voice comes out in a worried hush.

"I know. It's a drag. Now I have to do summer school to catch up."

"Summer school?" Like I don't know what that is. But I feel as if I'm only getting about one percent of the story.

"Gotta run. Mom's waiting in the car. I'm also grounded."

"For having the flu?"

"You know how strict they are."

"But I miss you."

Carly tries to wrest her face into her former invincible smile. Instead she just looks like she's grimacing. She clearly doesn't want to talk. She kisses her fingertips and blows me a kiss. "Miss you too!" she calls over her shoulder as she totes her bag of stuff down the hall and out the door.

25

I LOVE SUMMER. BUT IT'S DEADLY without your best friend.

Carly's mom can't keep the flu story going forever, and so when I call a few days after school lets out, she finally lets me talk to her. Briefly. Long enough to find out that she's going to summer school in the mornings and working at her dad's insurance agency in the afternoons. Her parents will barely let her out of their sight, but after lunch she gets to walk from home to her dad's downtown office. We agree to meet on Terwilliger Avenue the next day.

It's a gloriously hot June afternoon, and I'm wearing cutoffs and the halter top I made by sewing a few red bandanas together, basking in the heat as I wait for Carly on a bench looking out over the city and Mount Hood. My job starts on Monday and I so wish she and I could just have some fun in the meantime. She shows up wearing office clothes, a drab beige blouse and a black skirt, as if she's already passed into adulthood. She's wearing sneakers but says she has pumps in her handbag and she'll change when she gets to the office.

I can't help it. I scowl at her, all of her, and shake my head disapprovingly. Carly looks worse than she did on the last day of school, as if she's both physically sick and depressed.

"I don't understand why you're grounded," I say as we start walking toward downtown. I feel like I have ten seconds to get the story before one of her parents sweeps in to take her away.

"I got incompletes in two classes."

"But that wasn't your fault. You had the flu." I pause. "Or something."

"They've grounded me for less."

"But why won't they let you see *me*? I didn't cause you to get those incompletes."

Carly looks over her shoulder, as if she's doing something illicit by walking along a woodsy street with her best friend. We both know that if anyone is a bad influence on anyone, it's her on me.

"It's not anything about you specifically. I'm grounded from any social life at all this summer. You know my parents. They think they're still living in a village in the old country."

I sigh with incomprehension. Carly thinks I should understand, but I don't. "It's going to be such a boring summer without you."

So many times last summer we'd walked along this exact same route on our way downtown to splash in the Forecourt Fountain. Or buy slurpees at the 7-Eleven. Or try on sunglasses at Nordstrom's. The whole time talking about the start of our lives, the real start, which would happen as soon as we graduated from high school. How did everything get so complicated in a few short months?

"You have Mrs. Armstrong," Carly says. "And all that."

"That's over."

"What do you mean?"

I'm relieved to finally hear a bit of fire in her voice. So I tell her the whole story: the aftermath of the school board meeting, the principal and Coach Ward's censorship of Mort's article in the *Statesman,* the confrontations by all the coaches, as well as the communication specialist's report and Coach Ward's letter of rebuttal.

"So?" she says, surprising me with the anger in her voice. She can be arch and saucy, but never angry. I can't quite tell who the anger is directed at now.

"Well," I say. "I mean . . ."

"Well," she mimics me. "You mean *what?*"

Tears actually surge up into my eyes. Now even Carly is attacking me?

She grabs my arm and spins me around. "You're not going to let them stop you, are you?"

"No. Yes. I mean, what choice do I have? We lost. Everyone thinks I made shit up. That I lied. Even Dr. Merble thinks I lied."

Carly finally laughs, and I'm happy to hear her series of snorts, even if it's at my expense. "You lying," she says. "That's hilarious. You're like Heidi. Or Maria von Trapp." Carly twirls with her arms out and sings, "The hills are alive . . ."

She makes me sound like a goody two-shoes. Or even priggish. Telling the truth isn't necessarily all that innocent or easy, as it turns out. She's missed everything that's happened the past two months and while maybe I've caught her up on the basic events, I don't know how to tell her about the emotional fallout.

"Coach Ward told the boys basketball team that I'm a lesbian."

"Worse things could happen."

"You're kidding, right?"

Carly shrugs.

She has no idea. What it's like to be labeled like that.

I want to tell her about that pamphlet the two women with the *Lavender Menace* T-shirts gave me after the Gloria Steinem event. "What is a lesbian?" the pamphlet asked and then answered.

"A lesbian is the rage of all women condensed to the point of explosion. She is the woman who, often beginning at an early age, acts in accordance with her inner compulsion to be a more complete and freer human being . . . than society cares to allow her to." Which is a different definition from the one I thought I knew.

"I'm not a lesbian," I say too loudly, too emphatically. "But I get all the exile vibes anyway."

She sighs. "At least you wouldn't get pregnant."

This drops like a comprehension bomb in my mind. First there's the hiss of a burning fuse as understanding makes its hot sizzling way to my brain. Then the explosion of a million thoughts at once.

"Wait," I manage to say.

We've arrived at Pioneer Square in the center of downtown Portland. Two long-haired hippies play hacky sack, kicking a small bean bag back and forth through the air. Another hippie couple sit facing one another, legs entwined, making out. A handful of protesters carrying signs—"Make love, not war" and "Bombing for peace is like having intercourse for virginity"— walk in a solemn circle.

I grab Carly by the arm and swing her around to face me.

"I have to go," she says. "Dad expects me by one-thirty."

"What you just said."

"It's so damn hot today," she babbles on as if she doesn't know what she just revealed. "I can't believe I'm going to spend the afternoon filing insurance claims."

"Why didn't you tell me? Why didn't you let me come with you?"

"You're like nonstop busy. Anyway, it's done. Taken care of. Gotta go. Dad's waiting."

Carly tries to walk away and I run along beside her.

"Wait. Carly. I need you. I need you to . . . You're so forthright and unapologetic and there's nothing wrong with love and . . . You can't do this."

Her face contorts back to the edge of anger. "Do what?"

I gesture at her whole body, sweeping my hand from her head down to her feet.

"Leave yourself behind." I don't mean for my voice to drop to a whisper, but it does. "Leave *me* behind."

Carly shrugs and stares into the distance. She's willfully deadening her eyes. I know that's not who she really is, someone who doesn't care. She says, "There was no love."

"What?"

"You just said, 'There's nothing wrong with love.' But this wasn't even love."

"Well. So?" Sometimes I feel like Carly is light years ahead of me in experience. "So what? I mean . . ."

Carly laughs, but without joy. "See? You're speechless. But actually, the no love is the best part. If my parents had their way, I'd be married now."

I gasp. "No way."

"I had to convince them to not talk to his parents."

"How'd you do that?"

"By making sure they understood that he'd deny everything."

"I would have backed you. I'm a witness."

"Louisa, sweetie, think what you're saying. You'd have helped Mom and Dad make me marry Doug."

"Oh! Ugh. Sorry."

"Which would have been a far worse fate than working in my dad's insurance agency, believe me."

"I do believe you."

"I gotta go."

"Does Doug know?"

"You're kidding, right?"

"But that's not fair. He's half responsible."

Carly looks at me like I'm missing nine-tenths of all the information in the world. Mort called me naïve. I guess I am.

The couple in the center of Pioneer Square are pretty much dry humping by now. I can't look and I can't not look.

"I'm late," Carly says.

"I need you."

"Summer school in the mornings, Dad's office in the afternoons, homework in the evenings. My life is so over."

"No!" I cry out with too much emotion. "I mean, mine hasn't even started!"

Carly stops, turns, walks back to me. She puts her hands on my cheeks, gently. She looks me in the eye and says, "Well, then start it."

She walks away, and I watch her pull open the ground floor door to the building that houses her dad's insurance firm and disappear inside. Her last words echo between my ears.

26

CARLY CHALLENGED ME TO START MY life already. She's right.

I run all the way to Steve's house, and I'm in luck. He's out in the driveway, shooting buckets. I like how loose his jump shot is. I like the way his head tips to the side as he releases the ball. I like how light on his feet he is as he rebounds his own shots. I stand, at the top of his driveway, watching him for a couple of minutes.

Enough meetings with Mrs. Armstrong and her friends. Enough speaking in airless rooms to panels of adults who can't listen. Enough weathering the hurricane-force blowback from simply telling the truth. I need to put my real life together. I want the biggest L word, Love.

"Hey!" I call out as I step down the driveway.

Steve drops a thirty-footer and says, "If it's not Gloria Steinem's right hand woman."

"Yeah. Right. Good one. That's over."

"Moving on to more ladylike pursuits?"

"Want to go to a movie tonight?" I just blurt it.

He sinks another shot with graceful confidence. As the ball falls through the net, he says, "It's Friday night date night."

"Yeah!" My voice nearly screeches and I clear my throat.

"And I got me a hot one," he says.

He's so corny, making fun of the way some of the jocks talk. It's not really even funny. But I don't care. I'm psyched. He said yes.

I say, "I could probably get the car."

Steve drives for a layup, misses, gets his own rebound, and tosses the ball to me. I'm not expecting the pass and it hits me in the stomach, hard. I emit an unpleasant grunt.

"Damn," Steve says. "Sorry about that."

"Do you have today's *Oregonian*?" I ask, recovering from the bullet pass, trying to act cool, trying to start my life already. "We could see what's playing."

"As it turns out, Judith and I are catching the zoo concert tonight."

I hear the words but for a long time they're scrambled. They have no meaning. I'm just plain confused.

Several seconds tick by. My brain refuses to comprehend. It doesn't want to. But I can't keep the truth at bay for long. He said he's going to the zoo concert. Tonight. With Judith. Not to a movie with me.

"Judith Langstrom?" I try to make my voice light, unfazed.

"The one and only."

On cue, Judith emerges from Steve's house with two pale green, iced drinks sloshing in tall glasses. Of course she wouldn't drink something as banal as soda pop.

"Speak of the devil," Steve says.

"The *she*-devil," Judith corrects. She lets fly with a devilish laugh, low and seductive.

Barefoot, and wearing much shorter cutoffs than mine with an avocado green tube top, she looks like summer. One of her peacock feather earrings is stuck in her hair and she swings her head a couple of times to free it. The motion causes some of what I guess is an herbal concoction to slosh from both glasses.

"Louisa," she drawls in that moody cool voice of hers. "How're you doing?"

It's all I can do to remain standing. A hot flush of feverish embarrassment is jellying my legs. I just asked a guy out and thought he'd said yes. When he hadn't. When in fact, *as it turns out*, to use his words, he has a date with another girl who is right here. Thank God she didn't hear me ask him out.

"You know," Judith carries on, "it's awesome what you did this year. I dig your activism."

Is it possible to feel glad that the amazingly smart and ravishing Judith Langstrom says she digs what I did? While simultaneously feel crushed that she and Steve are, apparently, together?

I have to find a way to talk, to say something, to act as if nothing both mortifying and devastating has just happened.

I start with an accusation. "You said you didn't believe in sports."

"True." Judith hands Steve one of the iced drinks and then uses her free hand to ruffle his hair. "But I believe in political action. And justice. For real, you were right on."

I notice the past tense, as in *were* right on.

Steve takes the other drink out of Judith's hand and sets both on the side of the court. He gives her the ball, gently, takes a defensive stance, and challenges her to get around him. She dribbles—more like a cross between slaps and fumbles because she has zero ball-handling skills—and he lets her go past him. When her shot misses, he jumps and tips it in for her. The way they are playing one-on-one looks more like sex than basketball.

While I stand and watch.

Talk about being benched.

"Okay," I say quietly. It's pretty clear I'm talking to myself. "I gotta go."

But Judith does hear me. "Call me!" she says. "Let's hang out this summer."

How I would have loved this invitation. Up until about five minutes ago. Judith Langstrom wanting to hang out with me.

"Cool!" I enthuse way too loudly, almost hysterically. "I will."

Neither of them stop me as I walk the length of the driveway and head back up the street toward home.

27

I LEAVE FOR WORK AT SIX o'clock, four days a week, and swing heavy tools all day. At least it's good for strength-building. I like most of the other kids on the trail crew, and best of all, they are not from my high school and know nothing about my notoriety. I like the woodsy air and the chance to sweat out my junior year . . . my junior year *what*? Let's just call them difficulties. Although on some days I'd go all the way to calling them torments.

In the afternoons, I sit at Grandpa's bedside until dinnertime. He has a low fever and keeps throwing up. He's taking strong antibiotics for an abdominal infection. I overhear Mom and Dad using the words "hospice care," and really, that's just more than I can bear.

Grandpa's always been a big talker and so I figure I'm going to chat him back to health. Every afternoon I ask him to tell me about his 1945 championship game, the Cougars versus the Wildcats. I listen to every word and ask lots of questions, even though his answers are just a repetition of the same couple of sentences, spoken in a barely audible mumble. He thinks I'm Grandma, his wife now dead some twenty years, and I let him think that.

When I've exhausted his need to talk about his championship game, I talk about what's on my mind. I tell him a lot of things I never would have told him in the past, but he doesn't comprehend much, and I know he just likes the sound of my voice. I tell him that the principal and coaches at my high school, working in concert with my city's school board, made a fool of me. That I'm afraid to go back to school in the fall because I'll have to see Coach Ward again. That Steve is going out with Judith Langstrom. And how sad I am that even Carly is mostly off-limits this summer. On Fridays, which I have off from my job, I can meet her on Terwilliger Boulevard in the middle of the day for a twenty-minute visit while we walk downtown, but she looks like some nineteenth century girl who's taken the vapors, pale and vacant. She walks like she has lead in her feet. She told me that she'd found three notes in her locker, shoved through the vent slats, calling her a slut. One said she was going to hell. When I asked her if she thought Doug Carter had written them, she said no but that he'd probably talked to Chris McMahon, another boy on the football team. I only needed to glance at her, and she only needed to nod, for me to realize she'd slept with him, too. Another wildfire.

To top it all off, by now Dr. Merble has probably written to Williams College, telling them I'm a lying lesbian. After high school I'll end up flipping burgers at some fast food joint and living at home.

The main thing keeping me from total full-on depression is Helen's reading list. I read at Grandpa's bedside, I read under the covers at night, I read while eating my breakfast at dawn in the mornings. Through these stories, I'm walking into whole new worlds, meeting extraordinary people, and getting introduced to so many ideas. Toni Morrison shows me what it means to be the little girl named Pecola at the heart of her story. Zora

Neale Hurston bursts open my understanding of love through her character Janie. The revelations in their stories, the fullness of the characters' beauty and pain, give me hope.

Something else gives me hope, too. Grandpa somehow—through his fever and dementia and with a bad systemic infection—remembers our ritual. Every evening when Mom shouts for me to come to the dinner table, I rub the top of his bald head. He always winks. Every single time he remembers.

One night at the end of June, sitting there in the dark beside Grandpa, I decide I'm sick and tired of wallowing. Feeling sorry for myself. It makes no sense. None at all. For one thing, there are all the people in Morrison, Walker, Hurston, Angelou, and Hansberry's stories, loving and working and fighting their way through their days, weeks, years. Telling truths, telling lies, succeeding and failing. But *living*. And here's Grandpa almost at the end of his journey, still in love with his wife, even if she's dead, and still excited about winning a championship which happened decades ago. If he can find the will and love to get to the next day, then so can I.

In fact, I make a bargain with Grandpa.

"You get well," I tell him, "and I'll quit wallowing."

"Good stuff," he says.

"Help me make a plan?"

I no sooner say the words out loud than ideas start bursting to life in my head.

You won't shut up, though, right? Helen had insisted in her clear, bell-like voice. *You've just gotten started.*

So you're giving up? Mort had asked.

You're not going to let them stop you, are you? Carly had said.

Helen is right. Mort is right. Carly is right. I've let them stop me. I've just given up. I've allowed the communication specialist for the school board, otherwise known as Mr. Voigt, or the *mis*communication specialist, to retool the story. *My* story. I've let Coach Ward fling false accusations at me. And I just slunk away.

I run up to my room and sit down at my desk. I write out the whole true story: what the Title IX law says, what I'm asking for, and how the adults who are supposed to be supporting students, not to mention following the law, tried to stop me by misconstruing my words and actions. It's a long letter, but I decide I need every word. I use Mom's typewriter to make a neat copy, fold the sheets of paper in thirds, and slip them into an envelope. I find an eight cent letter stamp, lick the back, and stick it on the upper right corner of the envelope. I walk the letter out to our mailbox and raise the little red flag, the signal to our mailman that there is an outgoing letter.

I feel so much lighter. The next day I drive to the record store and buy Stevie Wonder's *Talking Book* album that has "You Are the Sunshine of My Life," so I can listen to the song whenever I want, and when I do, I think of Barb pointing at me and saying, "Our song." If we have a song, you'd think I could call her. But I don't.

A week later, the *Oregonian*—a newspaper read by everyone in the state—publishes my letter. They didn't change a word, either. I'm completely blown away.

Even better, that very day Grandpa's fever breaks. He sits up and eats a bowl of chicken noodle soup and then asks for ice cream, which I sneak him later that night. The next day he swings his legs out of bed and walks on his own to the bathroom. No one can quite believe it. He gets dressed and roams around the house as if he hadn't been on his deathbed for a couple of weeks.

Grandpa is honoring his end of our deal.

Meanwhile, my story explodes. Dozens of other people write letters to the editor in response to mine. Some castigate me.

They call me a women's libber and argue that I'm just trying to destroy the school sports programs for boys. But many more people applaud my speaking out for fairness. Reporters call and interview me. Our state representative, Mary Rieke, writes a strong letter of support for me personally as well as for equal opportunity for girls in education. The *Oregonian* publishes her letter, too. By midsummer, nothing can be more clear: the State of Oregon is not in compliance with the Title IX law. And a lot of people care.

PART THREE

28

ON THE VERY FIRST DAY OF my senior year, Dr. Merble calls me into his office.

"Welcome back," he says. "You've had a busy summer." He looks like he's sucking on a lemon.

Between my job hacking trails through the Oregon forests, spending as much time with Grandpa as possible, and reading some out-of-sight novels and one awesome play, yes I have. But he's not talking about any of that. He's talking about my letter to the *Oregonian*. And the brouhaha that followed.

I say, "I had a job."

"Ah, good. Very good. Waitressing?"

"I was on a youth trail crew for the county parks."

"Good heavens," he says, as if I'd admitted to having worked in a strip joint.

He recovers from the shocking news of my having had what he considers a boy's job and continues. "Very good. Very good. I trust you're planning on having a constructive senior year?"

Nodding, I shift my weight from one foot to the other, impatient to find out where this is going.

"I have news for you. The Portland Public Schools will be having a girls basketball league this year."

I'm floored. This *is* news.

"Your complaints found some sympathetic ears," he says in a tone that makes me feel chastised.

But I let it go. I'm just trying to take in the idea that my voice, my words, helped change an entire city.

"What do you say to that?" He's smiling, but his question sounds accusatory.

"For real? Are you serious?"

"You didn't leave us much choice, did you?"

I want to say that it's the *law* that doesn't leave anyone much choice, not me. But again I keep quiet.

"Of course there are a number of obstacles, including gym time and money for uniforms and referees, that need to be overcome." He levels me a look that says this is my fault. "I'm asking for your patience."

I almost laugh out loud. He's acting as though I'm the one holding the cards here, as if I have any say in the matter. A seventeen-year-old student.

But . . . I guess . . . maybe I do. I already have.

"You'll only get in your own way if you run back to the school board with complaints."

"I didn't—"

"You have no idea how much we've had to scramble. The cuts we've had to make to the boys programs. But after much arm-twisting, we've finally found you a coach. Mrs. Wiggins has agreed to do it."

"The French teacher? She's the most unathletic person on the faculty."

"You're lucky to have her."

"We need a real coach."

Dr. Merble stands up, signaling the end of the meeting. "No one else wanted to do it. She believes in your cause."

"It's not a cause. It's a basketball team. We want to play basketball."

I'm *still* struck by the simplicity of the request, even after all that's come down. I just want to play basketball.

"I don't think you understand how much you've disrupted the sports programs in this city. You're very lucky to have—" He makes finger quotes around the next word "—won. But let's be clear: all the letters you and the other gals wrote to lawmakers and newspapers over the summer, they do a disservice to your reputation. Now your brothers were fine students, and fine members of the Trojan football squad, and I respect your parents. For those reasons, we're going to just go forward from here, but I want you to know—"

I turn and leave his office in the middle of his sentence.

I head straight for Mrs. Wiggins's classroom. Looking through the little window in the door, I can see the French teacher gesturing and laughing and talking in front of her class. She's a cool person, but the most unlikely basketball coach in the entire building. She has Cher-like hair, dark and straight, hanging all the way down to her waist, dozens of bangles on each arm, and long red fingernails. She's wearing a flowing red, orange, and yellow top and billowy pants to match.

I turn and press my back against the door, knowing I need to just let it go, take the crumbs Dr. Merble has offered. Instead, I whirl around, pull open the door, and burst into the middle of her class. Startled, Mrs. Wiggins breaks off her rapid-fire French monologue and gives me a look of amused inquiry. I can tell she knows who I am, the girl who got her a job as a basketball coach.

"*A quoi ai-je l'honneur de cette interruption?*" she says to me.

I have no idea what she's just said, although I do recognize the word *interruption*. "May I talk to you please?"

"Can you wait until class is over?" Thankfully she's switched to English.

"No." I realize that five minutes after Dr. Merble asked me to be patient I'm acting supremely impatient.

Mrs. Wiggins actually gives me a sympathetic look before resuming her French lesson. I step outside the classroom and wait for the bell to ring. When it does, Steve and Judith are the first students to emerge, as if they just can't wait to get out in the hall where they can make out. Which they do, right there in the middle of everything, Judith dropping her copy of *Madame Bovary*, in French of course, on the floor so she can use both hands. Neither even notices me standing there.

I push past the last students coming out of the classroom, a salmon swimming upstream, and find Mrs. Wiggins at her desk.

"Dr. Merble told me that you volunteered to coach the girls basketball team."

"That's true."

"But—"

"No one else would do it, honey. I'm all you got."

"Do you even want to coach?"

"Of course not. But if it's the only way you can play, isn't it better than nothing?"

"What do you know about basketball?"

"Zip. Nada. Rien. But practice doesn't start for another couple of weeks. I'll read some books."

I stand there staring at her in disbelief. Dr. Merble told me a few minutes ago that I had "won," with finger quotes. But this doesn't feel like winning. It feels like getting outfoxed. You want a girls basketball team? No problem, we'll give you a girls basketball team—and make sure it fails.

29

IT'S A GOLDEN LATE AUTUMN DAY, maybe our last sight of the sun for months to come, and everyone is eating lunch on the quad, the big grassy lawn outside the cafeteria. The row of maples lining the sidewalk in front of the parking area are brilliant red, and the sun feels honey warm. I'm sitting with Helen, and she's telling me about her book reports this summer. She's surprised I really did the full reading list. I'm shy talking to her about the books, as if I'd been peeping in on other peoples' lives, but I want her to know how meaningful the stories were to me, how they helped me get through a hard summer. How they're still helping me as I try to navigate the beginning of senior year.

Steve and Judith walk up and plunk down in the grass with us. It still stings, seeing them together, but I'm getting used to it. I like that she's not afraid to tell him off. There's a lot he doesn't get, and sometimes I'm glad it's her and not me having to set him straight all the time.

Carly joins us, too, which makes me happy because even though she's back in school this year, she hardly ever hangs out. She spends most of her free period in the library, more often sleeping than studying. Sometimes I think the notes someone shoved into her locker last year upset her more than the pregnancy. I don't know how to talk to her about it. When I try, she tells me to lay off.

"What colleges are you applying to?" Helen asks her now, not knowing it's a fraught issue. I try to ward Helen off with my eyes, but she's looking at Carly, not me.

Carly shrugs, like it doesn't matter. Like nothing at all matters. I want to scream, *You're going somewhere with a strong literature program and then moving to Paris to be an expat writer!*

I take out my notebook and write down exactly how each of my friends look, trying to capture their body language, too—Steve's cocky head tilt, Judith's sweeping glances, Carly's soft collapse, and Helen's clear-eyed focus. Maybe Carly's given up on being a writer, but I haven't.

"Look who's coming," Carly says, sitting up straighter. She elbows me.

"Who? Mort?" Judith says in a tone that means, *so what.*

I look over my shoulder. Yep, it's Mort heading our way. He stumbles, then stops and examines the grass, as if there's an obstacle there that tripped him. There isn't. He shrugs and forges on until he arrives at our circle.

Carly tells him hi, but he just stands there not speaking.

"Hey, Mort," Helen says. "I'll have that piece on the new art installation in the south hall for you by Friday."

"You joined the *Statesman*?" I ask her.

"Yes. I need to improve my writing skills."

"You already have the best writing skills on staff," Mort says.

"That's not true," Helen says. "I need to learn how to be more concise. Journalism will help me with that."

"I have my best shirt on," Steve says to Mort. "Take my picture for the paper." He spreads his legs wide and leans back on his straightened arms, hands planted in the grass.

Mort nods, lifts his camera, and takes a series of shots. But of me, not of Steve, not of anyone else at all. It's embarrassing.

Lowering his camera, he says, "Congratulations."

"Thanks."

"I daresay you've changed the world."

"Uh. We got a basketball league."

"Okay, I'll be more specific," he says. "You've changed the face of girls sports in Portland. Which is major."

"I just want to play."

"Own it, girl," Judith says. "Mort's right."

"It's not like I'm the one who passed Title IX."

"False modesty is unattractive," Steve says kicking my shoe with the toe of his sneaker.

"And yet you've still never given me a real interview." Mort is persistent if nothing else.

"Do it now," Carly says. I guess since she's backed out of her own life she's going to be more pushy about mine.

"There's nothing to say," I try.

"Steve is right," Judith says. "Enough already with the false modesty."

"I think there's plenty to say," Mort says. He takes his notepad and pen out of the front pocket of his short-sleeved plaid shirt.

"Do you want to sit down?" Carly asks him, her voice carrying a tiny hint of her old self.

Mort shakes his head. Then, totally out of the blue, he asks, "Do you have a date for Homecoming?"

Awkward! He's so not Carly's type.

She says, "Really, Mort? Right here in front of everyone?"

At that, everyone—Carly, Judith, Steve, and Helen—all look at *me*.

Mort stands there with his notepad in one hand, pen in the other one, poised for writing, as if he'd just asked an interview question. The moment is excruciatingly revealing. Because clearly Mort is asking me, not Carly, to Homecoming.

Judith snuggles up against the side of Steve, and he kisses her forehead. Carly is actually smiling for once, looking in fact downright lascivious. Leave it to her to return to her old self in my name rather than her own. I glance at Helen, who is always spot-on astute, hoping for a clue about what I'm supposed to say, but she's gazing away from all of us, out over the tops of the red maples. Her hair is even bigger this year.

Why, anyway, am I looking to my friends for their reactions? What do *I* want? Can't I figure out yes or no on my own?

Shyness creeps from my feet up to my head. It's a sweet shyness, a curious shyness, mingling with the late September sunshine. It surprises me. What the hell. It's my senior year. All bets are off. I say, "No."

"No, what?" Mort asks.

Maybe he *was* asking Carly. But he's staring at me.

Carly huffs impatiently. "Louisa! Speak."

"I meant no, I don't have a date for Homecoming!" I practically shout it.

Mort nods hard once and says, "I personally wouldn't be caught dead at Homecoming."

Okay, if I was mortified before, now I'm full-on disgraced.

"Mort!" Carly says with even more exasperation than she had for me. "Would you please explain where you're going with this?"

"For real," Judith puts in.

"Is this, like, a news story?" Carly uses her hands, gesturing above her head to indicate headlines: "Title IX Activist's Date— or lack thereof—for Homecoming."

Judith snorts and calls out, "Title IX Activist Home Alone— on Homecoming."

"Not a news story," Mort says, flustered.

"Why not?" Judith says, that wide mouth of hers open, showing her tongue. "Maybe the *New Yorker* would be interested in Louisa's plans for Homecoming. Try pitching them with the story."

"I was thinking the *Washington Post*," Mort says and everyone cracks up. Encouraged by our laughter, he adds, "Now that Nixon has resigned, I think I can get Louisa top of the fold."

I roll my eyes.

But Carly pats a patch of grass. "Sit, Mort. Seriously. Explain yourself."

"Thomas Pynchon is reading at The Rose that night," he says without sitting. "And the Laurel is showing *Harold and Maude*, which happens to be my favorite film. So it'd be possible to both catch Pynchon's reading and make it to the second showing of *Harold and Maude*."

We stare at Mort, the silence stretching taut.

"Mort?" Carly says. "Are you asking Louisa out?"

"Only if she wants to."

"Oh," I stutter. "I don't think—" After almost saying yes to going to Homecoming with him, I feel like I have to deploy a no now. To save face.

"You're damn cute, Mort," Carly interrupts. "And Louisa says yes."

Mort looks at me for confirmation. He's still hovering his pen over his notepad. Carly kicks me. Hard.

The best part is that the Mort situation has zapped a bit of life into Carly. A bunch of boys have asked her out this fall, and she's turned them all down, because their invitations are obviously based on her reputation. I guess she's enjoying this scenario today because it's about me, not her. I want to make Carly happy.

I nod. Okay. Why not?

"I read that as a yes," Mort says. "Can I get a confirmation?"

Everyone laughs, but in a friendly way. Mort laughs too.

"Yes," I say. "Okay, yes."

Mort writes YES in huge letters on his notepad, adds an exclamation point, and holds it up for us to see. He says, "Exclamation points should almost never be used. They're almost always superfluous. In this case, it's warranted."

With that, he walks away.

Steve says, "Wow."

Carly says, "Man, that's one diamond in the rough."

Judith adds, "Smart as shit, too."

"I like his smile," Carly says. "I'm a sucker for dimples."

"Great eyes," Judith says. "Deep."

"Pynchon? *Harold and Maude*? Kind of freaky, actually," Steve snarks, and I have to wonder if he's a tiny bit jealous.

Helen jumps to her feet, gathers her books, and lopes away. I guess she's above all this silliness and just wants to study. Or maybe her bad experience with the student body president of Jefferson High has put her off the entire topic of dating.

The rest of us are still watching Mort, who's doing a goofy skip step, like he's dancing across the quad.

"Kind of a dork," I say.

"And I repeat," Carly says. "The cutest dork on campus."

Judith snaps her fingers.

Steve says, "Whatever."

I lie back and look up at the blue sky, feeling at least for a few moments a little bit in love with everyone in the world.

30

"GOOD EVENING," MORT SAYS WHEN HE calls me shortly before he's supposed to pick me up. "I slipped and fell on a banana peel."

I laugh. He does have a sense of humor, if a quirky one.

"My brother can't break the habit of just throwing stuff he doesn't want on the floor."

I laugh again, but I'm nervous, so it comes out in a big awkward guffaw.

"No, actually I'm serious," he says. "I broke my arm. I'm in a cast."

"What is your brother's *problem?*" I bleat, trying to cover for laughing. "Younger siblings are such a pain in the butt."

"He's my *older* brother."

"And he just drops banana peels on the floor? What an idiot."

"Yeah, well, he's special."

"Sounds *real* special." I laugh yet again, and yet again too loudly.

"No, I mean that literally," Mort says. "My brother has Down's Syndrome."

I feel like the biggest jerk on the planet. "Oh! I'm really sorry. For laughing."

"No need to apologize. It *is* kind of funny. The banana peel gag is iconic."

"Are you okay?" Of course he's not. He just broke his arm. Just shut up, Louisa.

"You probably think I'm a total klutz. I should have been able to finesse the fall. Or at least I wish I'd been doing something heroic like chasing Danny, saving him from some kind of disaster. I did once catch him before he stepped into an open manhole in the middle of a street."

"Wow, that *is* heroic," I say, trying to cover up my insensitivity with an inane comment. I realize Mort is working up to canceling on me.

"Do you want to reschedule?" he asks. "I'm in a cast. I can't do much."

"Okay," I say, but I'm thinking, we're going to a coffeehouse and then to a movie, not playing one-on-one. Can't he do that in a cast?

"Also a little goofy on pain pills," he adds. "It just happened this afternoon."

"Okay," I say again.

"Okay what?"

"If you want to cancel."

"I don't want to cancel. I asked if *you* want to."

"I'm okay with our plans. If you feel all right."

"I feel stupid for falling."

"It was your brother's fault." I pause, again embarrassed for possible insensitivity, and add, "I mean, even if he can't help it."

"Good point. I'm going to go with that."

"I think we should still go."

He's quiet.

So I add, "To the coffeehouse and the movie. If you want to."

"Good. Do you mind if Helen comes too?"

"Helen?"

"She was here at my house when it happened. We were working on a story for the *Statesman*."

"She's still there? She went to the doctor with you?"

"No, but I'd already told her what you and I were doing tonight and she was so nice about the fall and everything that right before she left, as Mom's racing me out to the car to go to the doctor's, I asked if she wanted to come with us."

"And she said yes?"

"Not exactly. But I thought it'd be nice to call and ask her again. The moment was kind of chaotic."

"Sure. Okay." But I'm disappointed. It's my senior year, and Carly is right, I need to get on with my life. I've had some false starts with a few guys, and Mort may not be the love of my life, but a little practice can't hurt anything, can it? I've been trying to channel Carly and Judith's assessments: diamond in the rough, cutest dork on campus.

"Uh, do you mind driving?" Mort asks. "My cast and pain meds and all."

"I'll ask if I can have the car. Where do you live?"

When I pick him up a few minutes later, he tells me that Helen said she has too much homework. Who does homework on a Saturday night? I guess Helen would.

"That's too bad," I say and look to see if he thinks so too. He gives me a big grin, those X-ray eyes reading all my thoughts.

We get to The Rose a few minutes later, and the reading is just about to begin. A hippie with long frizzy blond hair is testing the mic. A bunch of mismatched rugs cover the cement floor. The tables, all different sizes and heights, look like they've been scavenged from Goodwill. A wide-bottomed chianti bottle, holding a lit candle, sits on every table. We find the last two open seats together, and Mort starts picking the hardened candle drips off our table's wine bottle. The frizzy-haired hippie comes to ask what we want to drink.

Mort orders something called an espresso, so I say I'll have that too. It comes in a tiny cup and tastes like a cross between mud and bleach. Luckily, Thomas Pynchon steps up to the mic and begins, so Mort doesn't notice that I only take one sip of the drink.

When Pynchon is done reading, Mort asks more questions than any other audience member. I'm tripping at how un-shy he is in front of all these smart people, which I tell him afterward, when we're back out on the sidewalk.

"Oh. Sorry. I do that sometimes. Get overly inquisitive. Did I embarrass you?"

"No." I liked seeing how much he cares about books, language, and complicated story ideas. How unafraid he is to show it.

"Good. I'm going to take you at your word."

"You should. I'm quite trustworthy."

I meant that to be funny, or light-hearted, maybe even flirtatious.

But he just says, "Good," in this dead-serious tone of voice. Then he takes off at what is practically a run down the sidewalk to where we've parked my car. The Laurel movie theater is across the river and we'll have to find parking again. He's mentioned twice already that he hates missing the openings of movies, even ones he's seen before.

"Pynchon was intense," I call ahead to him.

"Understatement," he calls back to me. "You should read *Gravity's Rainbow*."

"Okay."

"Do you mean that? You'll read it?"

"Sure."

"Excellent. Can you walk faster? We're going to be late."

"Yes, I can walk faster."

But I don't. In fact, I stop walking altogether and wait to see when Mort will notice. When he gets to the car and stands waiting by the passenger-side door, he looks around to see where I am. I'm about twenty yards back, leaning against a parking meter.

I expect him to tell me to hurry up. But he doesn't. He walks, now kind of slowly, back to me.

Judith is right about his eyes. They're deep. And expressive. It's easy to tell when he thinks something is funny or smart. Now he looks curious, like he's wondering why I've stopped, what I'm doing propped against this parking meter.

I'm channeling Carly, is what I'm doing. I'm following her instructions to get on with my life.

Mort says, "Uh, you look kind of wild right now."

That's something else I like about him. The way he comes out with pretty much whatever is on his mind. It's refreshing. You don't have to guess or wonder. So different from Steve who is always masking his feelings and making fun of anything earnest.

Mort says, "Looks like Thomas Pynchon had quite an effect on you."

"I guess so. Does that hurt?" I nod at his bright white cast.

"Yes."

"Do you want to go home?"

"No. Wait. Maybe? My parents are out tonight."

Yep, he pretty much blurts whatever's on his mind. That wasn't what *I* meant by going home. Not exactly, anyway. But . . . what would Carly do?

As we stand there just looking at each other, I'm thinking of my moment with Steve at Council Crest, when I looked away and broke the spell. So I force myself to not look away now.

"I can do that," Mort says, staring hard as if it's a game to see who will blink first. I laugh but still don't look away. He steps closer yet.

Next thing I know our noses bash together. I grunt with surprise and jump back. "Sorry!" I say.

"For what?" he says. "I'm the one who's a klutz."

"It's a habit. I say sorry too much."

"Better than people who don't know how to say sorry ever."

True. It's a sweet, thoughtful comment.

"Take two," he says. "Ready?"

This time he turns his head to the side, rather than coming straight forward, and kisses me. I can feel his teeth through his lips, but he keeps his tongue to himself, which I appreciate for a first kiss. When Mort steps back, he asks, "Was that okay?"

I nod. Then he takes my hand and we walk to the car. On the drive we chat about Thomas Pynchon and act as if we haven't just kissed. But at his house we go straight to his bedroom which feels a little direct to me. Shouldn't we sit and talk somewhere more neutral for a while? Maybe have a snack and a drink?

"Is your brother with your parents?" I ask.

"Yeah. They're all over at my aunt and uncle's. They'll be back pretty soon."

"Oh."

"Yeah. So."

I guess that "so" means we should hurry. My feelings are completely tangled. On one hand, I'm glad we're just moving along here. At the same time, I wish it felt a little more romantic. Or maybe a lot more romantic.

I sit on his bed and look around. Stacks of books with brainy titles. Photographs—I guess ones he took—stuck on the walls. An array of pens and pencils scattered on his desk. He tosses his army jacket on top of a couple of barbells in the corner, as if he wants to hide them. The weights, and the thought of Mort working out, melt me a little.

He takes his wallet out of his back pocket and starts to set it on his desk. But then he pulls it back and opens it up. "This is Danny. He's eighteen." He hands me a photograph. Danny has a flattish nose, upward slanting eyes, and thick brushy hair. He has a big goofy smile on his face. He's adorable. My heart goes all gooey at the idea of Mort carrying around a picture of his brother in his wallet.

"He looks really sweet," I say.

"He is. He's the best part of our family. Even if he's a huge pain in the butt. Or, in the case of today, a pain in the arm." Mort holds up his cast. "Hey, you can be the first to sign it."

He finds a felt-tip marker on his desk and sits on the bed next to me. I take the marker and draw a big heart on the cast, and then I write my name in the middle of it. In an immediate wash of regret, I realize that everyone at school will see this. The red marker ink is permanent.

Mort sits staring at the heart holding my name, as if he's decoding a message. His hands are trembling a bit. I take one and hold it.

"So I should tell you," he says. "I'm a virgin."

Oh. That was abrupt. I say nothing because I can't think of a single thing to say.

"Are you?" he asks.

"Um, I guess, yes, technically. I mean, define virgin." Oh boy, way too much information. I try to clean it up by summarizing, "I've messed around with boys before." Is he going to ask me which "base" next? This is definitely not feeling very special.

He nods. "The other thing?"

I wait for the other thing.

He holds up his cast.

"Oh! Sorry! You're probably in a lot of pain. I should go."

"No. It's just . . . the other thing is embarrassing."

I wait some more.

"I'm *really* left-handed."

"Um."

Again he holds up his left hand which is encased in the rigid cast.

Honestly, I guess I should be happy he's talking a lot. Most boys just lunge and grab. But this just isn't going how I've fantasized having sex should be. In fact, never once yet with a boy has it been how I've fantasized it being.

But maybe I'm overthinking everything. I always do.

It's my senior year. Mort is a diamond in the rough.

I lean over and kiss him. He puts his arms around me, the cast clunking me lightly on the head as he does, but we don't stop. Sitting side by side, we make out for a long time, without his teeth getting in the way. Up close, he smells like pencil shavings, and though he's pretty clumsy, he's not oafish. This is definitely better than it was with Jason who used to sort of disappear, his eyes going flat and lifeless, and I felt like I was just a hand, any hand. Mort is definitely breathless, but he pulls back often to look at me, to see where I am, and I mean, those eyes.

Eventually, holding his bad arm in the air, he pulls me down onto the bed and lies next to me. He looks like he's trying to ask a question, but then just rolls away from me to pull open the bedside table drawer, reaching in and pulling out a small foil packet. "I told you the truth," he says, his voice cracking big-time. "I'm a virgin. That doesn't mean I'm not prepared."

I want to say, *maybe let's not this time.*

He tears open the condom package and pulls out the flat ring of rubber. He sets this beside the pillow and then shifts onto his left side, holding his casted left wrist in the air over his head. "I can try with my right hand," he says. "But like I told you, I'm very left-handed." He unbuttons my jeans.

I say, "It's just, I don't really know you."

"That's not exactly right," he counters. "We've known each other for over three years now. We've had six classes together, if you count the two we have together this year—three freshman year, none sophomore year, two last year, and one this year."

His right hand slides under the waistband of my undies. I want him to move it lower and I don't want him to. I squeeze my eyes shut.

"But wait," Mort says. "I didn't mean to argue. If you're not ready, that's cool."

It's not that I'm not ready. I am so ready. But the question is, for what?

No, maybe the question is, for who?

"It's okay," I whisper.

"Yes?" he asks.

"Yes," I say.

31

ON THE FIRST DAY OF TRYOUTS I hustle to the gym and find the locker room empty. Val, Barb, Diane, Helen, and Marcia all said they were coming, but only Helen and Marcia were enthusiastic. Val groused that the city rec league would be better than being coached by the spectacularly unathletic French teacher.

I keep hearing Dr. Merble's "suggestion" to me at the end of last year, that I get more girls involved in sports. If no one, or only a handful, show up, then he'll have proof that this is a big waste of time and money and resources.

I did all I could to spread the word about tryouts, but the only official announcement, the only one coming from the school administration, was a small, hand-scrawled sign, placed in an inconspicuous spot in the locker room next to the showers. The ink ran and the paper crinkled from the shower steam. When last week I asked Dr. Merble about this, he said that it'd only be the girls who took P. E. classes who'd be interested and they were sure to see the sign. At least Mort, who's been promoted this year to editor-in-chief of the *Statesman*, prominently placed an article in the newspaper announcing tryouts. Though he was forced to also print an opinion piece by another student writer on what The Powers That Be call "the other side of the story."

I carry my basketball out to the court and start warming up. A team of one.

Admittedly, I'm a little eager, and therefore a little early.

Five minutes later, Diane comes in to the gym. She's by herself. Every time I've run into Diane this year she's been with her new boyfriend, a leggy guy from the north hall gang, the boys who live to take apart and rebuild muscle cars. It's like Diane has had a lobotomy: besides still being skinny, she now wears lots of makeup, short skirts instead of slacks, and platform shoes so high they make her hobble. I was actually surprised when she agreed to show up today.

"Hey!" I shout, forcing cheerfulness. "Get changed! This is going to be a blast!"

Diane stops, looks at me, and then smiles tentatively. At least she's here.

A few other girls trickle out of the locker room, including Barb, Helen, and Marcia. We barely look at each other, as if this is all a mirage that will disappear with a direct stare, as we start warming up our shots.

Mrs. Wiggins arrives and stands helplessly on the sidelines. She's wearing a brand new—the price tag still dangles from the back of the pants—purple tracksuit. A shiny silver whistle, which looks more like jewelry than sports gear, hangs on a chain around her neck. Maybe she read some books about basketball, but just the expression on her face makes it quite obvious that she doesn't have a clue.

More girls emerge from the locker room. By three-thirty, the official start of tryouts, I'm amazed to count over forty girls on the court. Wow.

The bad news, besides Mrs. Wiggins, is that most of these girls are completely lacking in skills. They shoot air balls. They carry the ball without dribbling—and without even knowing that this is called traveling in basketball and disallowed. Perfectly executed passes fly right by them. They laugh at their mistakes, as if we're all just actresses in a sitcom. As if this is a hilarious way to spend a couple of hours.

What did I expect? I know I'm lucky. I have athletic older brothers who've spent hours coaching me, teaching me skills that, so far as any of us knew, I'd never get a chance to use in any real situation.

Then again, looking more carefully at the mayhem on the court this first day of tryouts, I see that I'm not the only girl who has brothers or fathers who've spent hours teaching her. I'm not the only girl who's learned, on her own, to love basketball. I'm not the only girl who's practiced every shot, every aspect of her game, on home courts. The gym full of girls trying out for the team looks, at first glance, like a disaster. But here and there, among the novices, are some girls who've been waiting their whole lives for this chance.

I'm keeping an eye out for Val. We can't win games without her. She's our power forward. I gather Helen, Barb, and Marcia and ask if they've seen her.

"We have algebra together," Marcia says. "When I asked if she was coming to tryouts, she said 'Maybe.'"

"I think it's about Diane," Barb says.

None of us know what to say to this. We've never spoken about them being a couple, if that's what they were, so it's hard to speak about their apparent breakup.

Meanwhile, our "coach" claps her hands and shouts, "Defense! Defense!"

I pull away from the meeting with my teammates to tell her, "Mrs. Wiggins, there's no defense when you're just warming up."

She's clearly an intelligent woman. And she obviously wants to be supportive. But we really don't need a babysitter and she knows it.

"Oh," she says. "Gosh."

"Also, the price tag on your tracksuit pants is showing."

"Oh, boy." She reaches around and yanks it off. "I'm sorry, Louisa. I wish I knew more."

"Do you want me to just—?" I point at the mess of girls on the court.

"Could you? Maybe just for the first couple of practices?"

"This isn't a practice. It's tryouts."

She nods helplessly.

I step back onto the court. I clap my hands and ask for everyone's attention. I quickly explain what a fast break drill is and have the girls form three lines. I guess I haven't explained it very well because a lot of them just stand there, arms hanging loosely at their sides, mouths open, acting like I'm the librarian shushing them and ruining their fun. One girl, completely out of the blue, decides to demonstrate a dance move, and a bunch of the others join her, laughing uproariously.

I sigh. Put my hands on my hips. Throw back my head in exasperation.

That's when I notice Val sitting on the highest bleacher, in her street clothes, watching. Maybe Diane isn't the deterrent, or not the *only* deterrent. Maybe her fear about changing clothes in front of other people, or the embarrassment of changing in a toilet stall, is why she isn't doing tryouts. I run up the bleachers and sit next to her.

"Why aren't you on the floor?"

She shrugs, won't look at me. Her face is all broken out. She nods at the court. "This isn't real basketball. It's definitely worse than the rec league."

"Still. We need you. It'd be *more* like real basketball with you on the court. We'd have the six of us, anyway."

She scoffs, looking angry. That line from the *Woman-Identified*

Woman pamphlet pops into my head: *the rage of all women con-densed to the point of explosion.*

We both look down at the court where chaos is reigning. My hope sinks hard and fast. Nice move, Dr. Merble. Make us look like clowns.

I slowly clunk back down the bleachers.

"I'm sorry, Louisa," Mrs. Wiggins says. "I don't know—"

"You tried. Thank you."

"I wish you'd advocated for a feminist book club. Or even, I don't know, a bonfire to burn bras. I could be so much more help if—"

"No one burns bras," I tell her. "That's like a metaphor."

"Yes. Okay. I know. I'm really sorry."

I plunk my basketball on the court and sit on it, gazing at the exit on the far side of the gym. Just beyond that is another exit, the one to the outdoors. All I want now is to get home and see how Grandpa is doing. Maybe shoot a few on my driveway, in peace.

I'm still staring at the exit when the rotund figure of Coach Stanton fills the opening. He's wearing gray sweats, the kind that gather at the ankles and have a drawstring at the waist, or in his case, under his huge round belly. I figure he's having a look at the spectacle of a girls basketball team, the joke of it all, before heading out to the football field for his team's practice.

No, probably the word *joke* doesn't apply. I'm guessing he doesn't find it one bit funny to witness the sloppy waste of prime gym time and school money.

When he raises a whistle—a big sturdy one very different from Mrs. Wiggins's warbling ornament—to his lips and blasts a loud, piercing blow, I literally fall off my basketball and onto my side on the floor. He strides in the door, his sausage arms swinging, his crew cut at attention. I scramble to my feet, trying to gather my wits and figure out what to do about this new interruption. It was one thing when the boys were messing around on the court we'd reserved in the early morning hours. It was another thing when Coach Ward—and the swim coach, and the track coach, and the baseball coach—accosted me. But walking right into the middle of our practice, our official school-sanctioned basketball practice, is outrageous. How dare he.

I stand tall, searching for a response. The boys have had *years* of sports teams, from early grade school on, both at school and in the wider community, like Little League for baseball and Pop Warner for football, to develop their skills. We have to start somewhere, even if we have to start this late in our lives, even if we have little to no skills at all. The Title IX law says—

Coach Stanton blows his industrial-strength whistle again. He's now standing on the center court line. He gruffs, "Line up on the end line, ladies. Suicides."

No one moves. The other girls are looking around, dismayed.

"Wait," someone says. "He just told us to commit suicide?"

"That's what I heard," says another novice player.

"Louisa," Coach Stanton growls. "Demonstrate."

Wait. What?

Then I remember that afternoon, at the end of last year, when he walked down the hall with me, that one-armed hug. His body language had surprised me by being friendly, not threatening, and his eyes had been kind. What had he said to me? "I'm with you all the way, girl."

"You do know what a suicide is, don't you?" he says looking right at me now.

I feel as if I've been awakened by a big splash of cold water. I sprint to the end line where I wait for his whistle. When I hear the harsh blast, I take off, running the suicide alone, giving it one hundred percent, no, one hundred and ten percent. I sprint to the quarter-court line, tap the floor, back to the end line, tap the floor, and without a pause, I'm off again to the half court line, tap, end court line, tap, three-quarter court line, tap, end court line again, tap, and then the full length of the court and back. I run the fastest suicide I've ever run in my life and finish heaving so hard I might throw up.

Coach Stanton blows his whistle and shouts, "Everyone!"

Barb, Helen, Marcia, and Diane are the first ones on the end line, but they're soon joined by a bunch of other girls. We run five suicides, some girls with more enthusiasm than others, and one girl tripping and falling on her face. After the sprinting, Coach Stanton orders us to the bleachers.

As we take seats, all of us gasping for oxygen, Mrs. Wiggins drops down near me and breathes, "Oh, thank God."

"Let's get a few things straight from the get go, shall we?" Coach Stanton says.

I nod, endorphins from the killer workout lighting my heart and mind into athletic bliss. I glance up at Val who's still sitting on the top bleacher. I beckon her down but she stays where she is, elbows on her knees, chin in her hands.

"I have my own convictions about how to play this game and they might not match yours," Coach Stanton says. "But if you're on my team, you're playing my game. Are we clear?"

"Yes!" I answer.

"First," Coach Stanton says and lets a long dramatic pause fill the gym, "games are won and lost with free throws. You'll shoot one hundred every single day after practice. If you ever want off the bench, you'll find a way to shoot another couple hundred over the weekends. Understood?"

Some of the girls look doubtful, but I'm beaming.

"I believe in the underhanded free throw. You have fifty percent better accuracy with that style, and it unnerves the opponents."

He lumbers to the free throw line and demonstrates.

"That looks really dumb," Diane mumbles.

"I can shoot a regular set shot from the free throw line," Val says, as she slides into the place on the bleacher next to me.

Coach walks over and bends down in front of her. His nose is almost touching hers, and yet he seems more grandfatherly than intimidating.

He says, "Anyone wanting to follow his own whims is welcome to leave the gymnasium right now. There's the locker room."

I almost speak up. Val is by far our best forward. We need her. It'd be better if Coach Stanton doesn't get into a war of wills with her. Val can be super stubborn.

"Her," says one of the novice players. "*Her* own whims."

Val's knees start to straighten as she makes to get up off the bench. I put my sneaker on top of hers and press down hard.

"Ouch," she says and scowls at me.

Coach Stanton has wisely paced to the other side of the seated team, giving Val a chance to think about her decision. I keep my foot on top of hers and she lets me. I know she wants to play serious basketball as badly as I do. And that's what this is going to be with Coach Stanton. He's not going to fool around. That much is already obvious.

"Our first game is in three weeks," he says. "Suffice it to say, we have a lot of work to do. We'll be practicing after school every other week and in the mornings before school on the alternate weeks. You'll be on the court, already warmed up, by the start of practice. Anyone thirty seconds late will sit out that practice. Anyone late twice will be benched the next game."

He stops talking and looks squarely into each player's face. Several girls get up right then and slouch to the locker room. He watches them go, nodding his head, a look of satisfaction on his face, as if to say, we don't need quitters or wimps. Then he blows his whistle and says, "Another suicide."

Three more girls quit. The rest of us line up on the end line. Mrs. Wiggins rises from her spot on the bleacher bench and presses her hands together in front of her chest, fingers pointing up. She bows to Coach Stanton. *Thank you*, she mouths. Then, smiling, she exits the gym.

Two hours later, I'm soaked with sweat and happy to have just run the hardest practice of my life. Actually, it's the *first* practice, real one anyway, of my life, period. All the girls trying out for the team are shooting underhanded free throws at the baskets around the perimeter of the gym. I finish mine and run over to talk to Coach Stanton.

"Are you going coach us all season?"

"Yes. Objections?"

"No! No objections. It's just, I mean, what about the football team?"

"My assistants are perfectly capable of handling those coaching duties."

"You gave up football to coach us?"

"You have a problem with that?"

"No!"

"One hundred free throws."

"But I've already done mine."

He raises an eyebrow and I hightail it over to an available basket and shoot an additional hundred, all underhanded.

32

I'M LIVING FOR THE MUSIC OF hoops: hands slapping onto the ball, the echoing bonk of dribbling, hard breathing and grunts of effort, sneakers squeaking on the varnished wood floor, the ka-clunk of a rim shot, and the nearly silent swish of a net-only goal, all punctuated by the repeated blasts of Coach Stanton's whistle.

Keeping Val on the team isn't going to be easy. She arrives at tryouts already dressed, so I figure she's changing in a toilet stall in a hall bathroom. She leaves the gym in her sweaty practice clothes. But worst of all is the rift between her and Diane. They aren't even speaking to each other. Val wears her sadness like a skin.

At the end of the third day of tryouts, as everyone heads for the locker room, I call last year's teammates over, throwing an arm around Val's neck to keep her from escaping.

"It's up to us," I tell them, "to hold this team together, whoever else Coach chooses to join us."

Coach Stanton has already winnowed the team down to eighteen girls. Everyone who is left desperately wants to be on the final squad of twelve, and the competitive energy on the court is seriously jacked up.

"We're the core," Barb agrees.

"We have the most experience," Helen says. "But we gotta be welcoming to the new girls."

"Sure. Yeah. Of course," I say. "But that doesn't mean we don't have our own history together."

Diane says, "Yeah. A history of flat tires and public buses." Her beige foundation has blotched and some sweaty eyeliner runs down her cheek. "We don't even know if we'll make the team."

"You're joking, right?" Barb says. "He cuts any of us, and I'm walking."

"Stealth here," I say, my arm still around Val's neck as I get to the main point of my calling this impromptu meeting, "is going to be crucial to us winning any games."

"Stealth!" Barb, aka Lucky, shouts. "I like that!"

"Good one," Helen, aka Spider, says. "You definitely don't see Val, I mean, Stealth, coming. Her skills are understated. She has the ball, and you think, so what, and then, pop, she's just put one up in your face."

It's true. She slips inside the key before you even know she has the ball. If she doesn't have a shot, she pitches out to Barb so smoothly you don't even see the pass. Stealth is the perfect nickname for Val.

I feel her shoulders soften under my arm and when I look at her, Val is even smiling, a weak little cockeyed smile set in her acne-inflamed face, but it's there, I see it.

"We're the power core six," Barb shouts. "Lucky, Spider, Stealth, and . . ." She looks at me, Marcia, and Diane, who are all without nicknames.

But I want to keep this special for just Val right now, so I say, "Stealth. You're our secret weapon. See you all tomorrow."

Coach Stanton teaches us a two-one-two zone defense, fast break strategy, blocking-out positioning, and a couple of different ways to set a pick. I can tell he's watching to see who learns quickly. When a girl does something right, he twirls his hand in the air above his head, meaning do it again. Then again. And again. He's all about repetition, honing our basic skills. At the end of each day, we shoot a hundred underhanded free throws. I do another hundred every night in the driveway, in the rain.

On Friday, we scrimmage. Coach wants to see who has good synergy with whom, who can execute and think while they play. Good shooting is an obvious needed skill, but making the assist—seeing and passing successfully to an open teammate—is just as important. I'm thrilled to have a coach who understands the game, the deep game, of basketball, who asks us to be better than any of us ever thought we could be.

Even so, even with just the best players remaining on the court, we have some rough interludes. Once I throw a long pass to Barb who's sprinting for the far basket, and I miss her by about five yards.

It is just after this moment that I see Coach Ward standing in the gym doorway, arms folded and legs spread in a stance of contempt, watching. He slowly shakes his head, outrage emanating from behind those thick-lensed glasses. I guess he doesn't much like having to practice in the early mornings, every other week, and for what, so a bunch of girls can blunder their way up and down the court?

All weekend long, that look on his face, the anger in his stance, keep me off balance. I know I shouldn't worry, or even think, about Coach Ward. But it's hard not to be intimidated by a teacher, a coach, who is so hostile. I spend most of both Saturday and Sunday on the driveway, practicing my shooting and dribbling. It's the only way to counter his bad vibe.

On Monday Coach Stanton posts his squad of twelve players. I make the team.

33

Mort is rhapsodizing in Mr. Murray's philosophy class about René Descartes' assertion, *I think, therefore I am.*

"It's an absurd claim," Mort says.

Mr. Murray's eyes get all twinkly as Mort lays out his argument against the famous philosopher. He loves when we take contrary points of view, as long as we support them with reasonable arguments.

Mort's cast is now covered with multi-colored inscriptions, but everyone has left space around my name inside the heart. In other words, no one has missed that statement on Mort's cast. We're pretty much considered going together at this point, even though we've only had two actual dates.

Carly thinks it's funny we went to the Oregon Museum of Science and Industry on our second date. She also thinks everything between me and Mort is strictly theoretical, in spite of what I wrote on his cast. It sort of annoys me that she assumes neither of us is capable of getting past handholding. But the truth is, I haven't really wanted to tell Carly about the sex. She's been so depressed and out of it, and I haven't wanted her to think I'm moving on, even though it's been her example spurring me. She's supposed to be the wild, experimental one and I'm supposed to be the cautious, tame one. I'm afraid of breaking our pattern, leaving her behind, losing her completely.

Also, in truth, I feel a little ashamed about my ambivalence, and I wouldn't know how to tell Carly about that. At the science museum, they have this giant human heart made of plastic, and you can walk inside it and see all the arteries and other blood vessels. The best parts are the way it glows deep pink, with the rivers of red veining through all the walls, and the way it thumps really loudly while you're inside. I felt like I was standing inside my own heart—strangely booming and outsized and too bright, and well, just plain weird. Mort and I hung out inside the plastic beating heart for a long time and held hands, but our hands were so sweaty it was kind of gross. I pretended I wanted to go see the incubating chicks in another part of the museum as a way to let go of his hand. After the museum, we took a hike in Forest Park and ended up making out in a small grove of Douglas firs. But he didn't pull out a condom again. I think he's a little embarrassed about how it went in his bedroom. He blamed it on his cast, and that's fair. Still, I guess we're both trying to figure out how to make it amazing, the way sex is supposed to be. When Carly asked about what happened on Homecoming night, I just rolled my eyes and said, "His broken arm."

As Mort carries on about René Descartes in Mr. Murray's class, Judith passes me a note that reads, "Diamond in the rough."

She's never passed me a note before and I want to pass one back. But it has to be clever, funny, impressive in some way. Some big way. Big enough to equal Judith who today has her hair pulled up on top of her head and held with a scrunchie, so that most of it looks like a fountain, with a few loose strands dangling down her neck. The fabrics of her clothes—a deep purple satin blouse with wide cuffs and long, pointed collar tips and pants in black velvet, flared at the ankles—make you want to pet them. I pass her a one-word note: "Hot."

She passes me another one that says, "He's 100% Louisa material."

I know she means it as a compliment, but I'm not sure it feels like one to me.

Meanwhile, Mort's getting even more worked up in making his case against Descartes, big words flying, arguing that just because we think we have consciousness does not mean we exist. We could be figments of some other being's imagination, for example. We could all be a dream. René Descartes may only *think* he thinks. Someone else altogether might be doing the thinking. Mort reads a lot of science fiction.

Doug Carter raises his hand. When Mr. Murray calls on him, he says, "Our thoughts are given to us by God. Period." A full sentence! Impressive. I'm crafting a note in my head to Judith, making fun of Doug's Neanderthal voice, and he's looking around smugly, thinking he's nailed this discussion, when the classroom door flies open. A cheerleader frolics in. She searches the room, finds Steve, and pins a construction paper cut-out of a planet on the front of his shirt: *Send the Vikings to Mars!*

We both have our first games of the season today, the girls here at home and the boys away. Judith, who's sitting next to Steve, rips the Mars bar off the tag, peels back the wrapping, and takes a big bite. I guess she's still protesting against sports.

When I face forward again, Mr. Murray is standing in front of my desk. He hands me a lined index card onto which he's scotch-taped a green lifesaver. A straight pin is threaded through the top part of the index card so I can attach it to my blouse. Below the candy, he's written, in blue ballpoint pen ink, "Win, Miss Carmichael."

His eyes are even more twinkly than they were when Mort was taking on Descartes. He's so cool, a teacher who gets it. He's making fun of the cheerleader ritual, but at the same time, acknowledging that I also have a game today. I pin the paper and candy onto my blouse and smile at my favorite teacher.

Over my right shoulder, I hear Judith say, "Far out!"

34

THE GYM BLEACHERS ARE NEARLY EMPTY. A couple of moms show up, but mine says she's too busy making dinner and watching Grandpa, and Dad is at work. I'd been hoping, okay, outright fantasizing about the Wilson High School student body coming to root for us, but apparently they have better ways to spend their afternoon. Or maybe they all got on the booster buses to go to the boys game.

Mort is here, taking pictures for the *Statesman*. But that's about it.

At the start of the fourth quarter, the game is tied. I drive to the basket for a layup, miss, but get fouled. As I stand at the free throw line, lowering the ball held in both hands between my bent knees for the underhanded shot, several girls on the opposing team's bench jeer.

"What dorks," one shouts.

"Check it out! They *all* shoot that way!"

"I'm surprised they don't still think they have to keep the offensive and defensive players on separate sides of the court."

"Or have six players out there."

I glance over at our opponents' bench and see the girls cracking up.

"Focus," Val growls under her breath. She's standing in the first spot under the basket, waiting for the rebound if I miss. I don't. I sink both underhanded shots.

But the other team immediately executes a fast break to tie the score again.

We take possession, and I'm about to inbound the ball, when I see Grandpa shuffle in the gym door. I get a dropping elevator car feeling of shock as I watch him make his way to a seat in the front row of the bleachers.

The referee blows the whistle. I've failed to inbound the ball within the required five seconds. The ball is turned over to the other team. Their point guard takes it down court and pulls up for an easy jumper.

Coach Stanton calls a timeout.

His face is as red as a slice of baloney as he growls at me. "What is *wrong* with you? Wake up, Carmichael."

He actually waits for an answer, but I don't have one.

"Helen. Go in for Louisa."

Rather than sitting down on the bench next to my teammates, I run around the end of the gym, nearly knocking over Mort with his camera. I can hear Coach Stanton shouting at me. "Carmichael!"

I squat down in front of Grandpa as the game goes on behind me.

"Grandpa, is Mom here?"

"I wouldn't miss your game for all the world."

"But how'd you get here?"

"Where?"

I frantically look around for help. I beckon Mort over.

"This is my grandpa. He has dementia. I think he walked here. Please, will you stay with him until the end of the game?"

"I'm on it. Consider the mission accepted."

Before returning to the Trojan bench, I rub the top of Grandpa's bald head. Without missing a beat, he winks at me. When the play surges down to the other end of the court, I sprint around the end line and take my seat, as far from Coach Stanton as possible, next to my teammates. At the next timeout, I expect him to yell at me, but he's completely focused on strategy and motivation. To call his huddle commentary a pep talk doesn't begin to capture the passion of his competitiveness. Coach Stanton's will to win is steely.

When the end-of-game buzzer sounds, we Trojan girls leap off the bench. We've won our first game—by one point. Coach Stanton is shaking his head, unhappy with our play, saying we should have won by forty points. But he can't curb our elation, and I'm mid-air in a victory leap when I see Mom rushing into the gym, breathless and frantic. She nearly collapses when she spots Grandpa, who is clapping vigorously from his seat on the bottom bench of the bleachers. I break away from my celebrating team and run over to them.

"Are you out of your mind?" Mom yells at me. "You know he can't—"

"I didn't bring him."

"I leave the house for thirty minutes to go to the grocery store and when I get home he's gone. Gone! I've been driving all over town. I finally figured out that you must have—"

"I didn't bring him! He walked."

"He can't find his own bedroom. How'd he even know you had a game?"

"I told him I had a game. I told him I wished he could be here. But I never thought he'd actually try to come."

While I'm arguing with Mom, Mort is talking with Grandpa. He has his notepad and pencil out and is taking notes, listening carefully, as if he's conducting an interview.

"Yep, the 1945 champs," I hear Grandpa saying. "We were playing the Wildcats, and we were the Cougars, so it was a feline thing . . ."

Mort nods respectfully and scribbles on his notepad.

"You were there when we were talking about the game at breakfast," I say to Mom.

"He has no idea what we're talking about at breakfast. Or at any other time."

"Apparently he does."

"How could he possibly get here on his own?" Mom looks at me accusingly, as if I have some secret information, and I look over at Grandpa talking excitedly to Mort, clearly pleased to be interviewed by the press.

"He came to all of the boys games. For years. He must remember the way."

"That's impossible."

"Apparently not."

Mom huffs with exasperation and turns to confront Grandpa.

"Dad," Mom interrupts, "did you walk here?"

Her anger frightens him and he folds his hands in front of his stomach and stares blankly, losing track of where he is in his story. I hook my arm through his, and he relaxes.

"He's like your dog," Mom says, still upset. "He'd follow you anywhere."

"Mom?" She's acting a little over the top.

"Dad," she practically shouts at Grandpa. "You can't just walk out the door." She pauses and repeats more slowly and loudly, as if that will make him understand. "You can't just leave the house, Dad."

"Mom, we won," I say, trying to change the subject.

"I'm taking him home."

"We won because Grandpa came."

"That's ridiculous."

"It's not." I rub Grandpa's bald head and he winks at me, briefly appearing perfectly lucid.

"Are you coming with us?" Mom asks me.

I look beyond her, to the other side of the gym, at my teammates who are still whooping and dancing.

"I have to shower. I'll walk. But promise you'll bring him to the rest of my games."

Mom doesn't answer. She takes Grandpa's arm and shepherds him out of the gym. I run to join my teammates, and only later realize that I never thanked Mort for taking care of Grandpa during the game.

35

Mort calls me on Saturday morning and says, "I think we should talk."

"Okay." I wouldn't blame him if he's mad at me for being sort of rude to him at the game. I didn't treat him like a girl is supposed to treat a boyfriend. But hey, I had a game. And he had a job as a reporter. Plus, my family had an emergency. Under those circumstances, I can be excused from being a perfect girlfriend, can't I?

"How about now?" he says.

Why do we have to talk immediately? I want to finish my calculus homework and then jump rope to improve my footwork. But I say, "Okay."

He's at my door twenty minutes later.

"You got your cast off!"

"Yesterday after school." His left arm is extra pale and skinny.

That time in Forest Park when we tried fooling around after the Oregon Museum of Science and Industry, he'd been apologetic about being unable to do much because of his cast. A third time, when he walked me home, we made out in the woods by my house and we went pretty far, but it was awkward, at best. Maybe that's the cause of this morning's big rush? He's now free to use his much more dexterous left hand? I'm sorry, but that feels kind of businesslike rather than romantic.

I try to make small talk on the drive to Forest Park, but he seems overly nervous and unusually quiet. He parks in the dirt lot, and we start down the trail. There's a nice glen with a grove of firs for cover about a half-mile in. When we get there, he sits in the forest duff and I sit beside him. If we're going to have cast-free sex, I'd rather do it somewhere a little more private.

"So I'm not sure if we're dating or not," he says massaging his skinny left arm.

"What do you mean?"

He shrugs. "I've been sort of obsessed with you since last year. Getting your attention at all took months. And now that we've, you know, kind of hung out some—"

Obsessed with is different from *in love with*. I can't help noticing that. Plus, I'd say we've gone a little further than *kind of hung out some*. Where is he going with this?

He says, "It just sort of seems like you're not that into it. I mean, you've only said yes three out of seven times I've asked you to do something in the last five weeks. If we're talking about actual dates, there've only been two."

I'm silent for a long time. The way he counts everything is off-putting. It also makes me feel guilty. I say, "I really like you."

"Sure. I get that. And I know I'm not exactly Don Juan in bed."

So it *is* going to be about more sex. I like that Mort isn't pushy. But sometimes thinking too much gets in the way. I lie back and look up into the Douglas fir branches, deep green and sturdy, with bits of pale blue sky showing through. I guess my lying back is an invitation. I expect Mort to lie back beside me. I do want to have more sex. I think about it all the time. But in my fantasies the kisses are sweeter. Our hands are not just exploratory, they're tender, more caring. Maybe I want too much.

Mort says, "Because something has happened. I mean, come up. A change."

"What?" I ask.

"This is really awkward because, well, I don't really know our status. Like I said, I've been chasing you for months. Since last year. You've rebuffed me over and over again."

"But recently—" I realize I don't actually have a second part to that sentence. I feebly finish with, "We've, you know . . ."

"I've fallen in love," Mort says. "Kind of spectacularly in love."

Oh. I'm not sure what to do with that. I know I just said I want too much. Maybe not *this* much? I like Mort. But it's not spectacularly anything.

He says, "With someone else."

The soil against my back. The trees looming above. The cold November air in my lungs. For what feels like an eternity, that's all I can comprehend: soil, trees, air.

He says, "I mean, frankly, I didn't even know if you'd care."

"When?" is the question I ask. Not who or why.

"Recently. I mean, it's been developing for weeks, I guess, but I resisted the feelings because I've put so much energy into getting your attention that I felt like I should, you know, stay the course. But the dam broke and a tsunami of feeling broadsided me. Like an epiphany! Like a supernova! She's brilliant! And gorgeous! And it just hit me. I fell madly in love."

Probably a lot more detail than I need. Definitely a surplus of exclamation points.

"I know it's really sudden. I mean, it's so awkward because I haven't known what we're doing. You and me. But the truth is, you really don't seem that into me."

I'm still lying on my back, knees bent, with silent tears spilling from the corners of my eyes and sogging up the hair at my temples. I wipe them fast, not wanting Mort to see, and he doesn't. He's massaging his left wrist and thinking about what to say next.

"We've been working together on the *Statesman*," he says. "Since the start of this year."

I mentally scroll through the girls who work on the paper. Barbie Quade? Sue Nakadate? Ann Cox? I can't picture Mort with any of them.

"You know her," he says.

No way. It couldn't be.

Then, wanting to taste her name, as if he just can't help himself from talking about her gorgeousness and brilliance, he offers, "Helen."

I sit up. It's the stupidest thing I could say, but the words just come out. "She's not allowed to date a white boy."

"I know."

"So this is one-sided?"

"It's not one-sided."

Mort and Helen. Of course. It makes perfect sense. Two smart nerds.

Just like Steve and Judith make perfect sense. Two ironic luminaries.

Then there's Louisa. One weirdo. By herself. I guess that makes perfect sense too.

"Okay," I say.

"Are you upset?"

"It's not exactly fun to get dumped."

"I thought of not saying anything at all," he says defensively. "It's not like you and I have an agreement. The fact of the matter is, I haven't been able to tell how you feel about me. It's not something that should be unclear or murky or ambivalent."

He sounds argumentative, almost truculent.

Of course he's right. I wanted a boyfriend. I'm not in love with Mort.

"Sorry," I say. When he doesn't answer, I add, "For being murky and ambivalent."

Mort turns to look at me. Hopefully it's too dark under the evergreens for him to see traces of tears. He sounds a little angry when he says, "Whatever."

He gets to his feet.

"I'll walk home," I say.

"That's ridiculous. Come on."

"No. I want to. I'll run. It'll be my workout today."

I'm still on the ground and Mort stands over me, hands on his hips, probably dying to get home so he can call Helen and they can have cast-free sex, him using his much more dexterous left hand. I wonder how many books her father will make her read when he finds out about Mort.

"I hope we can still be friends," Mort says, his voice softening with what sounds like regret. Maybe he'll miss me. Murky, ambivalent me. But I doubt it.

"Sure," I say, my voice spiking to cover for the tears in my throat. "Why not?"

Mort doesn't say any more. He strides out of the Douglas fir grove and up the trail toward the parking lot. I imagine him gunning the engine, madly in love and free to pursue his passion.

I don't run home. I walk. Slowly. It takes me two and a half hours, and when I arrive I'm so thirsty I put my whole head in the kitchen sink and drink straight from the faucet.

36

A MONTH LATER, AS I BOARD the bus that's taking the team to a game at Roosevelt High School, I avert my eyes while passing Helen, who is sitting in the front row, as if the bus were a classroom. We still aren't talking to each other.

She tried. Right away, first thing on the Monday morning after Mort dumped me, she glided up to my locker and said, "I'm sorry."

"It's fine," I lied.

"I didn't mean to step into your territory."

"I don't think of boys as territory."

"We just . . . he and I . . . it happened so fast. I *really* like him."

"It's fine," I repeated.

"Mort said you weren't really that into him, anyway."

I made a show of getting my calculus book settled in the crook of my arm and banged my locker shut way too hard. In my peripheral vision, I saw several kids glance our way.

"He said you basically avoided him as much as possible."

This is all true, technically. But he was my boyfriend. So officially, she's betrayed me. The words sound hollow even in my own mind, and yet I still feel capsized.

"What about your Howard man?" I said.

It was a cheap shot, and her apologetic look turned into a glare.

I didn't shut up. Instead I continued with, "So I guess you should hide your journal better."

Helen shook her head and looked like she was considering cutting me some slack.

"Actually," she said, "I leave it in plain sight. With no incriminating information in it. My journal is basically a decoy at this point. I wouldn't ever write a word about Mort anywhere. My dad would kill me if he found out."

"That's censorship," I carried on, as if we were discussing an article of the Constitution in Mr. Larson's class. "You should be able to write what you want in the privacy of your journal."

She shook her head again, but this time as if I were a lost cause, as if she were a teacher looking at a hopeless student. "You don't understand. My parents met during the Montgomery bus boycott. My family is one hundred percent committed. . . . Never mind. You wouldn't understand."

That's when she burst into tears and ran away.

All I could think then was, why is *she* crying?

But she's right: there is so much I don't understand. About her. About me. I don't even quite understand why I'm mad at her.

Here's what I do know: Helen looks tragically in love. Her expression that morning, talking about Mort, matched the one on *his* face when he told me about her brilliance and gorgeousness. I'm jealous. I'm gut-wrenchingly jealous. But not because I want Mort. I'm jealous because I want to feel that way about someone. I want someone to feel that way about me.

In the meantime, for our away games, I sit by myself in the very back of the bus to avoid the awkwardness. Of Helen. Of being the weird girl who has no one special.

As I settle into my seat for our ride to the Roosevelt game, I watch the rest of my team board the bus, everyone happy and connected. Val and Diane sit together. Marcia opens a bus window and stretches her entire top half out to kiss her boyfriend. Helen scratches away in a spiral notebook, undoubtedly drafting something for the *Statesman*, some story for her secret Romeo.

"Hot damn, our own bus," Barb, the last to climb on, shouts. She says this every single game, and I know what she means. It's kind of miraculous. I should be happier.

I watch her make her way down the aisle and wonder where she's going to sit. Or, more to the point, who she's going to sit *with*. She pauses next to Alicia, cracks a couple of jokes, and looks pleased to have made Alicia laugh.

Then Barb keeps walking. All the way down the aisle to my dark hideout.

"I'm sitting here," Barb says, plopping down in the seat next to me.

For a second I think she means for me to get up and move, like she wants the whole seat, but she says, "Phew, it's quiet back here. Peaceful. Those girls up front are all—" She twirls her finger in the air around her ear.

I laugh.

"They're cool," she says. "Most of them, anyway. But they're exhausting."

I love that she thinks I'm *not* exhausting. Or nuts.

"What's so exhausting about them?" I ask, wanting more.

"Stealth and Diane? I mean, together, not together, together."

I laugh again. "Mostly together now, though, right?"

"The funky boyfriend is kaput," Barb says, "from what I can tell. Haven't seen him in ages."

It's true. Val and Diane seem to be inseparable again. Diane hasn't exactly gained the weight back but there's a renewed heft in her body, as if her spirit and personality have returned. Val's skin has cleared up and she's playing killer basketball. Diane's game is less reliable, but she's our best post player. They both still look afraid, as if the world is their enemy, but at least they're taking it on together again.

"Okay, Marcia," Barb says. "She's a hoot. I like her. But 'boy crazy' is an understatement. She's on, like, her tenth boyfriend this month." Barb makes kissy noises in my direction.

"Then there's Spider," Barb says. "She's so damn serious all the time. Look. She's studying now. On the bus. On the way to a game. There's not time for that later?"

I want to tell Barb about my standoff with Helen. It's so stupid. And pointless. I'm trying to figure out how to explain it to her when the bus doors hush open and Coach Stanton comes aboard.

"Listen up, girls." He wears a weary, weight-of-the-world expression on his face, as if a girls basketball team is the height of responsibility. I love him for it. He's deadly serious about our team. About winning.

Coach Stanton talks for five minutes. He tells us that we need to win this game if we want to even think about the city title. That's exactly what I mean—I *haven't* thought about the city title. It hasn't occurred to me that we could dream of that. Coach Stanton says he expects it. Then he tells us that Roosevelt, our opponent tonight, has a really tall post player who's dynamic inside the key. Diane, our tallest player, the one who plays the center of our two-one-two zone defense, will be responsible for keeping her from scoring.

"It's up to you, Diane," Coach says. "You have to stop her."

That's way too much pressure for cringing, half-terrified Diane. All that weight loss. The mask of makeup. The shield of an inappropriate boyfriend. She's taken steps away from all that camouflage, but still, I don't want Coach sending her running from herself again.

I'm wrong, though. No sooner does he give her the job of defending their tallest player, in front of the whole team, than Diane blats out, "I got this, Coach!"

At first I'm amazed. Then I get it. Coach Stanton isn't faking anything. He's not reciting coach-like words. He does believe in us. Every single one of us.

"It's do or die," he tells Diane, piling on the pressure. "You have to stop her if we're to win this game."

Barb shouts out, "Do or Diane!"

The whole team starts chanting, "Do or Diane!"

And you know what? Diane is basking in the attention.

The bus driver turns the key in the ignition and the big engine rumbles to life. Coach Stanton, still wearing an expression as serious as a funeral, lowers himself into a seat. The bus rolls out of the parking lot and up the dark highway.

We play a hard game against Roosevelt, battling for every single possession, but we win, with Diane keeping that tall post player to just five points. By the end of the game, everyone is calling Diane, *Do Or Di*. I'm the only one of the original five who still doesn't have a nickname. It's stupid, but I feel kind of left out.

As I get back on the bus, Helen is already sitting in her front row seat. I look straight ahead and keep walking, but she reaches out and grabs my wrist.

"Hey," she says.

I stop and face her. "I'm sorry," I say, because even though she took my boyfriend, I know that's not really how everything came down.

She laughs. "I thought you were working on saying 'sorry' less."

I shrug, wishing I had Helen's grace.

Smiling, she says, "Love means never having to say you're sorry."

We both crack up at that line from the novel *Love Story*. We'd agreed, earlier this year when we were talking about it in the locker room, that it was the stupidest line ever written. She gives my wrist a little shake and lets go of me.

"We cool?" she asks.

"Yes," I say. "Totally."

Feeling ten pounds lighter, I make my way back to my spot in the rear of the bus and find Barb already in the seat. I start to ask if I can sit there too, but then remember she's in *my* spot, and so I just slide in. She's looking out the window, and doesn't even turn around, but I know she's sitting with me on purpose. The rest of the team gathers in the first rows, so we have half of the bus to ourselves. The darkness is comfortable, like a cozy shelter.

When the bus starts rolling, I ask her, "Do you ever feel lonely?"

"Nah," she says.

I look past her, out at the shadowed streets.

"You have the boyfriend," she says, finally turning to face me.

Barb is way too observant to have not noticed that Mort and Helen are now together. It's like she's prodding to see what I'll say.

"We broke up."

"Really? Why?"

"I like him a lot."

"But you weren't feeling it."

"Something like that." My voice is too soft, revealing. I clear my throat to compensate. "Didn't you know that he and Helen are together now?"

When she doesn't answer I know that she did in fact know this and had in fact been digging for more information. Not about Mort, though, and not about Helen. About me.

"I want to show you something." Barb digs a notebook out of her backpack. It's not a regular spiral-bound notebook. It's one of those with a stitched binding like a novel, but with blank pages and nice thick paper. She opens it and flips through what look like a bunch of drawings. I can't see them very well because it's dark in the bus, but I catch glimpses as we pass under streetlights. When she finds the drawing she wants to show me, she holds the open notebook next to the window.

In the passing light I see a detailed black ink drawing that fills the entire page. Two huge and verdant evergreens frame the picture. Nestled in the one on the right is a treehouse with four walls, roof, big window, and a walkway leading to a platform, like a deck, surrounding the trunk of the tree on the left.

"You drew that?"

"Yeah. I'm going to be an architect. I want to design out-of-the-ordinary living spaces. Whole houses in forest canopies. Homes that float freely on the sea. I have one in another notebook, a house that's attached to a bicycle. It's tiny, obviously. But the person who lives there can pedal the house anywhere. I know it sounds impossible. But it's not. The materials for that one have to be incredibly light."

I look at Barb's face as she talks. And then back at the treehouse.

She taps the drawing. "It's my refuge."

"Like in your mind?"

"Not just in my mind. It's real. I'm going to finish building it this summer. I've salvaged a bunch of the lumber from a couple of construction sites near our house. I didn't steal the wood," she says, pausing to scowl briefly at me, as if I'd accused her of stealing, as if I'd think she would do that. "It was all scrap. The contractor said I could have it. I've already built the platform and floor. It's a full twenty-five feet off the ground—that's the part my dad doesn't like—and big enough to sleep in."

I love Barb's picture. The way she's imagined a haven for herself, and the way she isn't just fantasizing and wishing, but has drawn plans, scavenged materials, and is actually building the place. I feel as if Barb has shown me her heart. And as if she's just admitted that, yeah, she's sometimes lonely too.

37

BY THE END OF FEBRUARY, WE'RE undefeated. I love being part of a team: the jokes, the coach lectures, the satisfaction of perfectly executed plays, and even the analysis of badly executed plays. I love Coach Stanton's sky-high expectations. I love winning.

But I miss Carly.

On the eve of the city championship game, where we're going to play Lincoln High School, a team that has two players over six feet tall, I finish my homework and brush my teeth. Coach Stanton insists we get eight hours of sleep before a game, and I'm all for that rule. I want more than anything to take the city trophy.

Yet something about this momentous game, how far I've come from just a year ago, makes me feel extra sad about Carly's absence. In so many ways, her feisty example is what got me here. But she's been pretty listless all year, only rarely showing her old fun-loving, take-charge spirit. Plus, I've been so busy with my team that I haven't had time for hanging out. I didn't mean to leave her behind.

I sneak out the backdoor and walk to Carly's house. It's already after nine o'clock, so I pad around to the backyard. I grab the drain pipe and give it a shake. Securely attached to the side of the house, the thick cast iron tube doesn't budge. If it can hold Doug Carter's weight, I guess it can hold mine, too. Gripping the pipe and bracing my feet on the house siding, I work hand over hand, inching up toward Carly's window. With all the pushups and other strength training Coach Stanton's been making us do, the climb is not that hard. When I get to Carly's window, I tap quietly.

She doesn't have the curtains drawn, and I can see her sitting at her desk, face down on an open book. Is she crying? Sleeping?

She doesn't hear me, so I have to knock harder on the window.

Carly bolts upright and swings around in her chair. What's the look on her face? Maybe a mix of surprise, anger, and hope. As if she wants, more than anything in the world, for her former carefree joy to be sneaking into her bedroom to visit.

I realize that she's in a lit room and I'm out in the dark, so she can't see me nearly as well as I can see her. She must wonder who this is. It couldn't be Doug Carter, could it? He's practically engaged to Marylou Fitzpatrick. Yet who else knows this route? Me, of course.

Realization dawns on her face. Carly rushes over and shoves open the window.

Just in time, too. Sure, I'm stronger than I used to be, but the bottoms of my sneakers are slipping on the house siding and I don't know how much longer my arms can hold onto this drain pipe.

"I can't believe you," she whispers. "What are you doing?"

"Sorry. I mean if you thought I was some hot guy or something."

Carly grabs me like she would a toddler, a hand under each armpit, and tugs. I push off with my feet and dive headfirst into her bedroom, landing on the floor with a much too loud thud.

She sits down on the tangled sheets of her bed and runs a hand through her messy hair. She's wearing an old ratty T-shirt, sweatpants, and socks with holes in the toes. I stay seated on her powder blue shag rug, quietly celebrating having not fallen off the side of the house and broken my neck.

"Why didn't you just knock on the front door?" she asks.

"It's after nine o'clock."

"Oh. Wow. I had no idea. I must have—"

"Fallen asleep." I finish the sentence for her and as I do, I realize I mean in a much bigger sense than just this evening. I add, "That's because you're totally checked out."

"Okay. Fine," she says, becoming annoyed. "What do you want? Why are you here?"

"I want my best friend back. My *gutsy* best friend. I want you to stop hating yourself. I want you to know you're, like, my role model. I want to be you when I grow up. Or, I guess, I want to be the you you used to be."

She's quiet for a long time. Then she says, "You have the team."

"My teammates are cool. I like them. Most of them, anyway. But you're my best friend. You used to tell me things like . . . like sex is the best thing in the world. And you'd just say it, like it was a fact. Remember that night we ate a whole pan of cold lasagna with our fingers? That was the first time you told me you were going to live in Paris after college. And write novels."

Carly rolls her eyes and runs her fingers though her hair again, as if world weary, as if that's all such old news. But I can tell she's listening.

"This whole basketball thing, I wouldn't have been able to do it without you. Remember that time last year when I was watching the boys basketball practice after school and you thought I was looking at Steve? I *was* looking at Steve. But even more, I was wanting his fully-supported basketball practice. You told me to do something about it. I knew you were talking about Steve, not basketball, but I listened to you. Later, that first time we met on Terwilliger over the summer, you said, 'you're not going to let them stop you, are you?' You said it so hotly, so defiantly, like I would disappoint you royally if I did let them stop me. Like you wouldn't get well yourself if I failed. Your words spurred me on. You helped me find a way forward." I'm speaking so fast I've forgotten to breathe, and now I stop and gulp air.

She's just staring at me. With maybe a tiny smile twitching her mouth.

"We're playing for the city championship tomorrow night."

"I know."

"You do?" This surprises me. We haven't talked much all winter, at least not about anything consequential, and I didn't think she cared about what I was doing anymore.

"You should be home sleeping," she says.

"Come to the game."

"Oh. I don't know."

"Why not? I want you there."

Carly rubs her bare arms, as if she's feeling her own skin for the first time in a long while. Quietly she says, "I'll ask."

"It's a school event. Surely they'll—"

"No," she says. "Their answer to everything is no. I have four more years, at least, here at home before I'm free. *If* I get into Portland State. If I don't, I'll work in Dad's firm and live at home for the rest of my life."

"You have good grades. You could get in anywhere."

"Did have. But it's not about my grades. They're terrified I'll mess up again if they don't keep an eye on me every second." She sighs and shifts her eyes to the door because we both hear footsteps climbing the stairs.

"Carly? Who are you talking to?"

I hit the floor and roll under Carly's bed. From my hiding place, I can see the bottom of the bedroom door swing open. I could have just stayed where I was—it's not like I'm a naked boy in Carly's bed—but explaining to Mrs. Mazza why I climbed in the house via the drain pipe and came in the window, why I'm here at all, would be awkward at best.

Carly says to her mom, "I'm reading my government book out loud to myself. It helps me remember what I've read."

A long silence tells me that Mrs. Mazza doesn't quite believe this. After all, Carly is sitting on her bed, not at her desk. She used to have a phone in her room, powder blue to match the rug, but her parents pulled it out after last year's debacle, as if she'd use it to arrange secret dates. So she can't now say she was talking to a friend on the phone. I watch Mrs. Mazza's feet cross the room to the open window. She pulls it shut. Her feet step back to stand in front of Carly. Mrs. Mazza's fuzzy pink house slippers are about ten inches from my face.

"You'll catch your death with the window open like that." Mrs. Mazza's voice quavers with emotion, maybe at how much she loves Carly and also maybe at how afraid she is for her.

The word death makes me emotional, too, and I pull up my knees and fold my arms against my chest, making my body into a ball, hugging myself silently. One afternoon this past summer, while I was writing letters and stuffing envelopes with Mrs. Armstrong and her friends, the older women forgot I was there as they talked about the most personal details of their lives, including sex. All of them said how relieved they were when twelve years ago, in 1962, the pill was made legal and now they had access to safe birth control. Before then, two of the women had had abortions—illegal ones. One got an infection from the procedure, and when she went to a legitimate doctor to get anti-biotics, he turned her into the authorities. Another can no longer have children as a result of the operation. A third told in a teary voice how her sister had died of a botched abortion.

Carly is lucky. Just two years ago, the Supreme Court decision *Roe v. Wade* made abortion legal everywhere in the country. This means that the simple procedure can be done safely by real doctors, and that women no longer lose their lives.

Looking at Mrs. Mazza's bare ankles and slippers, I think that Carly is double lucky. She was able to tell her parents about her pregnancy. And they loved her enough to protect her, to help her make a safe choice. But no wonder Mrs. Mazza is afraid. So many women in her generation died—"caught their death"—as a result of backroom hack jobs.

Mrs. Mazza sits down on the bed next to her daughter. All these intense thoughts are making me feel like I need extra oxygen and it's hard to not breathe audibly. I should have just knocked on the front door.

"Sweetie," Mrs. Mazza says. I imagine her hugging Carly and then pulling back to look into her face. "Get some sleep. It's late."

"I will, Mom."

Mrs. Mazza gets up slowly with a grunt and leaves the room. She shuts the door quietly behind her and I almost think she knows I'm under the bed.

I roll out and get to my knees. I take Carly's hands as I whisper, "You're smart. And beautiful. And you used to be so intrepid. I need you showing me the way."

"Intrepid." She clears her throat. "Me. You're joking."

"I'm not. You're the one who told me that kissing is like melted chocolate, only better. I'm still waiting for that kind of kiss."

A sly smile sneaks up on her face, as if at long last she's remembering what kissing feels like.

"Listen," I say. "Last year I did that thing at the Civic Auditorium with Gloria Steinem and—"

"Duh. I was there."

"You *were?* But I saw you on the fountain with Doug. I figured—"

"That I skipped your big event to hang out with that jerk?" She blows a raspberry.

I smile. "Okay, do you remember when she said, 'Any woman who chooses to behave like a full human being should be warned that the armies of the status quo will treat her as something of a dirty joke?'"

Carly nods.

"Do you remember how it ends?"

She nods again, smiling.

Together we quote, "'She will need her sisterhood.'"

Carly's whole face crinkles up in her old grin.

I say, "I need my sisterhood."

"Carly?" her mom calls from downstairs.

I move quickly to the window and hoist it open, turning to grin at Carly before climbing out. As I start to slide down the drain pipe, she shuts the window behind me. I try—unsuccessfully—to brake with my feet. The ride is fast and I don't have time to think about how treacherous, and stupid, this is. If I break an ankle, then I can't play in tomorrow's city championship game.

When I reach the bottom of the pipe, I let go, tuck into a ball, and roll onto the grass. Once I come to a stop, I stay in my pill bug position for another few seconds, mentally checking my parts. Luckily the thick muddy grass softened the impact on my hip. It hurts, but not a lot. I stand up and brush myself off. I'm about to duck into the shrubbery, so I can sneak up to the street undetected, when I see a figure standing at the corner of the house, backlit by the porch light.

Mrs. Mazza waits in her bathrobe and slippers, hands on her hips. I could run. But a lot of good that would do.

So I walk up to Carly's mom and simply say, "She's a really good girl."

"I know it."

"Everyone makes mistakes."

I expect her to scold me for sneaking around, for hiding in Carly's room, but instead tears fill her eyes. I know they're tears of love. And of fear. I also know that Carly has a big beautiful life ahead of her.

The words come out my mouth without forethought. I just say them, and I say them forcefully. "Let her go."

38

THERE ARE THIRTY-SEVEN SECONDS LEFT TO go in the last quarter of the city championship game and we're up by ten points. The Lincoln High coach calls a timeout, but they don't have a prayer. I can't believe it's about to happen. We're about to become the city champs.

No one at all came to most of our regular season games, no fellow students, and only a handful of family members. But tonight, for the city championship, the gym is packed with parents, teachers, and even Portlanders who don't have a connection to Wilson High School. I've spotted Vice Principal Hodge, in her cat-eye glasses and lumpy hairdo, shouting encouragement. Mrs. Wiggins the French teacher, wearing a cobalt blue and lime green dashiki and all her bangles, is on her feet, hollering for our team. Mrs. Armstrong has brought an army of old feminists, all of whom are chanting along with the cheerleading squad, who has also shown up for our game. During the timeout, the cheerleaders do a choreographed cheer: "Look to the left! Look to the right! The Trojan girls will fight, fight, fight!"

Coach Stanton tells us which play to run. He's as deadly serious as he'd be if we were down by one point rather than up by ten. He never, not for one second, lets us take a game for granted. He demands total effort on the floor right up to the final buzzer.

We inbound the ball. Barb and Helen fire it back and forth around the top of the key, looking for a way inside. I'm cutting under the basket. So is Val. Finally Barb gets a bounce pass to Val who lays it in one second before the buzzer. We've won the city championship by a solid twelve points.

The fans erupt into cheering as my teammates and I charge onto center court. Family members flood off the bleachers to join us. I'm looking for Dad and my little sister—Mom stayed home with Grandpa—when Mort steps right in front of me, holding his pen and notepad prominently in front of his chest. Despite his saying he wants to remain friends, and me agreeing, we've barely spoken since we broke up in Forest Park. He and Helen hang out together as much as possible at school since she's not supposed to be dating him in the first place and they don't get to spend time outside of school. I once spied them in a dark corner of the north hall making out, and I figured they'd done much more. Maybe in Forest Park. Maybe in our glen. I guess I was Mort's practice girlfriend.

"Would you like to comment on your win?" he says. "For example, are you feeling exonerated perhaps?"

I'm distracted by Carly, who is standing just behind Mort, theatrically pointing at him and then at me and then back at him. I'm so happy she's here, that she came to my game. But the thing is, I never told her that Mort and I are not happening anymore. Worse, I can tell that she thinks he and I are still in development, like in the early stages of something, like I need her encouragement to make it happen. At least half of the gap in our friendship is *my* fault. There is so much I haven't told her this year.

Mort looks exasperated. He's asking me in this significant moment to help him just this once with a quote and he thinks

I'm stonewalling him, again. He scowls and says, "Like one sentence, Louisa. Could you do that much?"

Carly, misreading *everything*, says to Mort, "She doesn't seem shy, what with all her Title IX chatter, but she is."

I jump in, needing to move this all along. Maybe move *her* along before she says something even more awkward. "I don't know about *exonerated*," I say, wanting him to know that I do know what the word means. "But I'm happy."

"She's *really* happy," Carly says, throwing an arm around my shoulders.

"So, like, are you ready for the state championship?" Mort asks.

"We have to practice."

"But she's a natural," Carly says. "With a little practice, she'll be a . . . a champ."

"What kind of defense will you use?"

"You'll have to ask Coach Stanton, but we've been using the zone all season and obviously it works well for us."

"Obviously," Mort agrees.

Carly stands there grinning, swinging her head back and forth as Mort and I talk, like there's something to see here. I don't want to draw any more attention to her antics by giving her pointed looks, so I try to tune her out. But then she says, "The question is more like: what kind of offense should she plan on using?"

"Okay," I say, shoving her away from me. "You are so embarrassing."

But I laugh. Because it appears that Carly, the real Carly, is back. It's like she's had an infusion of zeal. Mort looks just plain confused.

"So I don't see your Grandpa," he says, his pen poised over his notepad, refusing to be distracted from his interview. "He's been at all the other games. And you rub his head and he winks."

"You've noticed that?"

"Hard to miss. You do it right before every game."

"He's sick," I tell Mort.

"I'm sorry to hear that. Will he be at the state tournament?"

"For sure. Definitely."

"Good. Well, okay, that's it. You should celebrate with your team." He glances at Carly who is now watching me with what I can only call suspicion.

When Mort leaves, I say, "Thanks for coming to my game."

"What's going on with you and Mort?"

"There's a lot I have to catch you up on."

"Did I just make a fool of myself?"

"Pretty much."

We both watch Mort who is now interviewing the gorgeous, brilliant Helen, the girl with whom he is spectacularly in love. He's practically slurping his enthusiasm for her, and while, yeah, they're perfectly suited intellectually, I have to say I'm a little surprised Helen is okay with his, let's just call it ardor. While we watch, he steps back and takes a few pictures of Helen. I imagine him printing them in giant format and papering his bedroom walls with the photos.

Carly looks at me. I nod. "Yeah, Mort and I didn't work out."

"Bummer."

"No. It's okay. I should have told you."

"Well, yeah. You should have. I mean, every single detail."

"There are some really good ones, too."

Her eyes glitter with anticipation. I can't wait either because I know we're going to laugh hard. I mean, the toothy first kiss, the sex with cast, his pretty much useless right hand, the walk-in thumping heart, the abrupt breakup. It's all kind of hilariously heartbreaking.

For now I just say, "I'm so glad you came to my game."

"Are you kidding? I wouldn't have missed it. You're my role model. I want to be you when I grow up. The you you are *now*."

We smile at each other. I'm so relieved to have the comfort of my best friend back. Someone who knows me through and through. No currents of confusing energy. Just plain goodwill and honest talk and shared sense of humor.

Carly lifts her chin, pointing it at Mort and Helen, still engaged in their "interview." She says, "Do you think they're . . . ?"

"Oh, yeah. Yes. Definitely."

"Whoa," she says. "I never would have seen that one coming."

"Which one?" I ask. And we both laugh so hard we have to bend at the waist.

Before I recover, my teammates swoop in and physically lift me off the ground. Two of them brace their shoulders under mine and two others each take a leg. They carry me over to a ladder positioned beneath the home team winning basket and set me on the bottom rung.

"Up you go," Coach Stanton says, a huge smile on his face. After I climb halfway up the ladder, I stop and look down at the top of his head where sweat glistens on his pink scalp under the short crew cut. Then I look out at the gym full of fans, all of them watching me, waiting for the winning ritual. I feel dizzy, not just from the height of the ladder but from how fast and far I've come in just a few months.

Surrounded by my teammates, friends, family, students, teachers, and people from the community, I have this huge, full-throated feeling. I've gained a basketball team, but now I know, from listening to Mrs. Armstrong and her friends' stories, from everything Gloria Steinem said, from my own personal experience this past year, that this is just the beginning. Speaking up, telling the truth even when people don't want to hear it, demanding a fair shot, all that is part of this moment, too. We won this game, and winning is fun, but it's only a start, one step in a long journey.

The best part? I'm ready for that journey. I have my sisterhood. I have my team. I have my voice. I have a new feeling in my arms and legs, a new feeling at my very core. Playing basketball, strengthening muscles, tuning physical precision, makes me know myself on a skeletal level. A cellular level. It's the best feeling in the world: knowing I'm here and strong in this body.

When I get to the top of the ladder, a beaming Coach Stanton hands me a pair of scissors. I cut the white net off the orange rim, and then swirl it in the air over my head. I know I look totally goofy: my mouth wide open, eyes bright with happiness, arms flung wide, the net dancing in the air.

Mort captures this picture of me. He publishes it in the *Statesman* under the headline, *Hoop Girls Take City, On to State.*

39

Coach Stanton calls a special practice for the Saturday before the final state championship game. All season long I've been all in for the team, down with any of Coach's requests, large and small. Making a commitment to the other girls, to hard work, to being the very best teammate and player I can be. I've wanted this my whole life. No one dreamed our team would get this far.

But this morning I don't want to go to the practice.

Grandpa has been unconscious for three days, his breathing raspy and irregular. All week I've run home right after school and practice to sit with him. He no longer talks about the 1945 championship. Or thinks I'm Grandma. Occasionally he mumbles incoherently. Once I heard him say my mom's name. She was standing in the doorway to his bedroom and when I turned to look at her, tears were streaming down her face.

Mom and I sat up with him through all of last night. Neither of us ever went to bed. Grandpa's lips moved a bit now and then, but no more words came out. A couple of times his breathing stopped altogether and we thought that was it, but then in a great gasp, his lungs sucked in air again. His hands twitched and he breathed. Mom wiped his head with a cool damp cloth. I asked him questions about basketball strategy and pretended that he answered.

As the sun rises, I'm holding his hand and nodding off in the chair next to his bed. Mom takes my other hand and I jerk awake. She tells me to gather my gear for the special practice. I shake my head. I'm not leaving Grandpa.

"Go," she says.

I shake my head again.

"You made me bring him to every one of your games that he was well enough to attend," she says. "It was the last great pleasure of his life. He would want, more than anything, for you to be prepared for the state championship game. That means joining your team for this practice."

I try to think of an argument but know she's right.

Dad takes me because he doesn't want me driving in my condition of sleeplessness. When I step into the gym, I'm glad I've come. The cold malodorous air, simultaneously foul and energizing. The hollow sounds of voices and basketballs in that big space. My scattered teammates loosening their muscles. All of this needs to be harnessed into one coherent, sure-fire game plan for the state championship on Tuesday. Coach Stanton will do that. He'll find a way to motivate even sleepless, sad me. Barb tosses me a ball and I start warming up.

"Nice shot, Karma," Barb says as I drop one from twenty feet out.

"Carmichael," I say, hurt that after all this time she gets my last name wrong.

"Excuse me," Barb says passing me another ball. "I know what your last name is. Karma is your team name. As in good karma. Goes with good luck. Or good Lucky."

Barb rebounds someone else's shot and doesn't look at me again for the rest of the warm-up, but the other the girls heard

Barb give me my nickname and they're all calling me that, laughing. I can tell it's going to stick.

Just before practice officially begins, Spider, Stealth, Do Or Di, Lucky, and I—now aka Karma—have our own quick huddle. Barb's arm is around my waist and I love her for giving me the nickname. It soothes my sadness about Grandpa. I tell my teammates, the original five, "You're all my champions, no matter what happens on Tuesday."

"What are you talking about?" Lucky chides. "Only one thing is going to happen on Tuesday. That's not an open question. Get in the game, Karma."

"I'm in the game," I tell her. "I'm definitely in the game."

"We need good karma," she says and gives me a squeeze.

"We need good luck," I reply and squeeze her back.

Barb moves her arm up to hook it around my neck and pulls me toward her. She bumps her forehead on mine. Then she swaggers away as if that was a normal thing to do. It isn't. No one has ever bumped foreheads with me. But it feels exactly perfectly right.

At eight o'clock, Coach Stanton blows his whistle and tells us to take a seat on the bleachers. I sit down with the other girls, a little woozy from sleep deprivation, but ready. Ready for everything.

Coach Stanton paces in front of us, a frown on his face, looking as though he's choosing his words carefully. I love his dead seriousness. His exacting demands. I look forward to hearing how he plans for us to win this game. He stops and rubs his jaw.

That's when Coach Ward comes out of the boys locker room. He stands off to the side, legs spread wide and arms crossed. Why is he even here?

Coach Stanton finally begins speaking. "I couldn't be more

proud of you girls. Each and every one of you. You've worked hard and played your hearts out."

He starts pacing again, as if he doesn't want to look at us while he talks. Usually he makes use of direct eye contact, like he's extracting every ounce of will and commitment from us. Today his pale blue eyes are a little glazed and he's looking over our heads. I begin to wonder what's wrong. There's no money left in the budget to get us to the game? We've broken some league rule and been disqualified? *What?*

"We play Grants Pass on Tuesday for the Oregon championship," he says. He does like to state the obvious. It's his way of honing our focus. "It's going to take everything we have to win. They're a first-rate team. Undefeated like us. Tall, too."

"We got this, Coach," Barb calls out. "Don't worry."

He gives her a doleful smile.

"We need to win this game," Coach Stanton says. That statement is a little too bald even for him.

He flings an arm in the direction of the boys coach, who has been sidling closer. "You all know Coach Ward." He waits for a few of us to nod. "He's head coach for the Wilson High School basketball program."

Where is this going?

I clarify, "The *boys* coach."

"Actually," Coach Stanton says. "He's head coach. Over both of the school's basketball teams." He pauses to let this information sink in. "So he'll be joining us this morning to help out."

Coach Stanton steps back and Coach Ward comes forward.

I loathe him. I've never told the other girls on the team the whole story about his pushing me against the wall under the bleachers, his threats, but I feel his hands and words all over again now. I start shaking and can't stop. It's as if everything we've won is being yanked away.

"As Coach Stanton pointed out," Coach Ward announces, "I'm head coach of the basketball program here at Wilson High School. That makes me head coach of this team, too. I'm sorry I haven't been able to help out sooner, but a state championship is too important to leave it to—"

This is wrong, dead wrong.

My voice is firm, clear, and loud. "Coach Stanton is our coach."

Coach Ward bares a bitter smile. "He's done a fine job. Certainly no one expected you girls to win city and advance to the finals in state. But here we are. I'm happy to help out."

I jump to my feet. Coach Stanton, standing behind Coach Ward, shakes his head at me. As I start to speak anyway, he shakes his head more vigorously. Reluctantly, I sit back down.

"For starters," Coach Ward continues, "know that the Grants Pass girls are tough cookies, if you catch my meaning."

My teammates and I exchange looks, clearly *not* catching his meaning. It sounds vaguely derogatory. They're excellent basketball players, is what they are.

"They'll destroy a zone defense," Coach Ward says. "It's time you all learned a real defense: today I'm going to teach you a man-to-man. Believe me, the Grants Pass gals can play a man-to-man. Stanton, get me five players on the floor."

Coach Stanton points at Val, Diane, Marcia, Barb, and me. We set up on the court in our usual two-one-two zone defense.

"In a man-to-man, one player is responsible for guarding a single player, not an area—or zone—on the court," Coach Ward explains.

"We know that," Val says. "But we play a zone."

"Your name is?" Coach Ward asks. A warning is buried in his question, even though he smiles as he asks it.

"Val Smith. Starting forward."

"I haven't named the starters yet."

Val's nostrils flare and she looks to Coach Stanton. He keeps his face neutral.

"Val Smith," Coach Ward says, "are you left- or right-handed?"

Val's face, her entire body, hardens against this man and she doesn't speak. I close my eyes briefly, wondering how to interrupt this disaster. Val is impetuous. She'll walk off the court if she feels disrespected. We need Val if we're going to win this game.

"She's right-handed," I call out.

Val looks over at me, her face impassive as she makes her decision about what to do. I try to smile encouragingly.

"In that case, as I guard her, I'm going to stay to her right side," Coach Ward says. "Never, never ever, let a player drive in the direction he wants to drive in. Go ahead, Val. Try to get past me."

He puts the ball in her hands. She dribbles a couple of times, looks up at the basket, and lackadaisically moves to her right, into his blocking body. Coach Ward remains in a defensive position, arms up and legs spread, as he calls over his shoulder to the watching team. "See? She can't get past me. Deny the offensive player a lane to the basket. Always deny access."

This is beginner stuff.

Coach Ward positions himself to guard Val again and nods at her. As she starts dribbling, she looks over at Coach Stanton and then at us, her teammates, on the bench. Coach Ward gets an *ah ha* look on his face, excited about what he thinks is a teaching moment. He lunges, swatting at the ball, thinking he can steal it as she's looked away. Think again. Val steps back, switches dribbling hands, and keeps possession.

Then, in one quick move, Val bounces the ball behind her back, swapping her dribbling hand again, and drives to the left, easily losing Coach Ward and making the layup.

"That's what I'm talking about," Barb says quietly, elbowing me.

Coach Ward forces out a fake laugh. "See? That's exactly what happens when you let down your guard."

"You didn't let down your guard," Val says. "I got by you."

"Uh huh," Barb says, this time more loudly.

"Good work, Smith. Take a seat." He's pretending it didn't piss him off.

After going through a lengthy explanation and demonstration of the basics of a player-to-player defense, which we all already know, he sets out to change our free throw protocol.

"I know you're capable of making a respectable free throw," he says.

"We're 72% at the free throw line," Coach Stanton says. "The underhanded shot has worked very well."

"We'll be laughed off the court," Coach Ward scoffs. "We'll shoot our free throws the right way in the championship game."

The entire practice is hell. For one thing, we hardly play. We listen. To Coach Ward lecture on his ideas about the game. He not only completely changes our defense, from a two-one-two zone to what he calls a man-to-man, he tosses out our best offensive plays and teaches us two new ones. By the time he stops talking, drawing lines and arrows on the chalkboard, we only have time to run the new plays a couple of times.

Dad wanted to pick me up after the practice, but I told him to stay with Mom. So I run home now, feeling sour from Coach Ward's hijacking of our team, and anxious about Grandpa. Emerging from the woods and onto our street, I see an extralong, shiny black car parked in our driveway. I get to the front door as two men in dark suits carry out a zipped body bag on a stretcher. Mom follows them, her face so blanched she looks like a ghost. Dad tries to put his arm around her, but she shakes him off. The men slide the stretcher into the back of the vehicle.

I don't believe it's Grandpa. I know that's crazy. But my mind just bounces off the truth, refuses to accept that he's in that bag, on that stretcher, and now in that big scary car, even though I know he's been dying for weeks. As if that body could be someone else's, I run into the house and check Grandpa's bedroom. A part of me truly expects to see him lying there, sheet and blanket pulled up to his chin. He's not. The bed is empty.

"I wasn't here," I cry. "I wasn't with him when he went."

The idea of not being with Grandpa when he died is unbearable.

Dad has come into the room behind me. He gives me a hug. "Mom says he died shortly after we left the house. That happens all the time. People want to stay with their loved ones as long as possible. They wait for their favorite person to leave the premises before they let go. He would have wanted you to be playing basketball when he went, moving toward your championship."

Maybe Grandpa died at the exact moment that Barb christened me Karma. Or maybe he died at the moment Coach Ward announced he was commandeering our team. I don't know how to process this amount of gladness and sadness, anticipation and anger, all mixed up together. So I just drop down onto Grandpa's bed and cry.

40

I BARELY LISTEN TO WHAT COACH Ward tells us in the locker room at halftime of the state championship game. We're behind by a staggering seventeen points. Just three days ago, he changed our entire game—our defense, our free throw style, and key parts of our offense. We're confused and sloppy on the court.

As Coach Ward rants about our performance, his rangy legs lurching back and forth across the locker room, his gangling arms waving, I watch Coach Stanton. He's standing off to the side, neck rigid, hands folded in front of his large belly. I meet eyes with him for a second and try to ask a question, but it's a silent one, and he just shakes his head and looks away.

At the end of the halftime break, we walk out to the court, already defeated, while the Grants Pass Cavemen trot triumphantly into their positions. Coach Ward has only played me a few minutes of the game, and I take my place on the bench. As the referee tosses the ball to start play, I search the audience for Grandpa. For a quick moment, I've forgotten he's gone. It hits me all over again, and I lean forward, almost nauseous with sadness. So much has gone so wrong, so fast. I don't know how I can come to terms with losing this game. Losing Coach Stanton's leadership. Losing Grandpa.

I watch helplessly as my team battles on. Val drives for a layup and makes the shot. Grants Pass inbounds the ball and answers with a pick—easy to execute against our flimsy player-to-player defense—and a successful jumper. Barb takes the ball down court and, in her frustration, guns the shot rather than patiently waiting for a good opportunity. Grants Pass gets the rebound.

My groan is loud and almost teary.

Coach Stanton is sitting on the far end of the bench and he reaches across a couple of girls to tap me on the knee. I know what he means: sit up and look sharp. I do.

Then, inexplicably, he winks at me.

Or maybe not inexplicably. Maybe he's seen Grandpa's and my ritual.

The wink rockets resolve into my whole body. The resolve is a kind of knowledge. I'm buzzing with it, and now I just need to interpret what it means.

Only a couple of weeks ago I was flush with the triumphant joy of victory. I remember the feeling of being on that ladder after the city championship game. How my euphoria was as much, if not more, about having spoken up for what is right than for having won the game. I still have my voice. And I know what's right.

Diane fouls the shooter.

"Louisa," Coach Ward shouts. "Go in for Diane."

I leap off the bench, check in, and jump onto the court.

After the Grants Pass player makes her free throws, Helen inbounds the ball to me. It's now or never. Speak or don't speak. I tuck the ball under my arm and raise my hand, flat and vertical. I slap my other hand horizontally on top. I shout, "Timeout!"

The ref whistles the timeout and both teams run off the court to their respective benches. A hushed bewilderment falls on our huddle. The silence is so intense it's almost painful. I want to be the one who breaks it, but I'm not.

Coach Ward glares at me. "Are you injured?"

He knows the answer to that question. I'm fit and healthy.

I can practically see the steam coming out of his ears. He says, "I call the timeouts. Not you."

Now or never.

I beckon Coach Stanton, who's standing on the outside of our huddle. My teammates look at him, at me, and back at him, and then step aside to make room. He hesitates, but Val takes his arm and pulls him forward.

"*You're* our coach," I tell him. "We need *you* in charge."

"Sit down, Carmichael," Coach Ward seethes. "You're benched for the duration."

I remain standing. "Your approach obviously isn't working," I say to him. "We want to return to the game we've been playing all season with Coach Stanton."

I use the word "we," but I don't actually know, as I'm speaking, if my teammates will support me. Then—

"Yep," Val gruffs.

"Yeah," Diane agrees.

"We need Coach Stanton," Barb says.

There's another silence, and then Helen speaks in her "going to be a lawyer" voice. "Coach Stanton is our coach. Period."

A chorus of voices, loud and urgent, all the girls now talking at once, back me up. We're a team.

Coach Stanton meets eyes with a glowering Coach Ward. For a moment I think Coach Stanton is going to defer to his supposed boss. His pale blue eyes are watery and sad, but I know there's a steeliness, hard as dry ice, backing them up. He wants this win every bit as badly as we do. Still holding the other man's gaze, Coach Stanton quietly says, "Here's the plan," and he lays out our strategy. We listen with complete attention as he reminds us how to draw fouls, block out for rebounds, and find the open players in our two most effective offensive plays, the ones we won games with all season, not the new ones Coach Ward taught us a few days ago. As the referee blows his whistle for the game to resume, the last thing Coach Stanton says is for me to go back in the game.

By this time in the season we have so much trust in Coach Stanton that his voice alone instills confidence in us. We run back out onto the court. After Val banks in a shot from top of the key, we set up our zone defense and work so relentlessly that the Cavemen can't get the ball inside. Their point guard is forced to put up an off-kilter shot, and Diane leaps to block it with a loud smacking sound.

Our fans go out of their minds.

We make ten straight points, reducing our deficit to nine points. Grants Pass calls a timeout.

As we run back to our bench, there's a short period of confusion as Coach Ward still stands in the head coach's position, hands on his hips, looking as if he remains in charge of the team, as if he's responsible for our remarkable scoring streak. Coach Stanton takes a more humble stance. It's up to us girls to choose. We're like bees looking for their hive, but we quickly find it, gathering around Coach Stanton. He wants zero turnovers, flawless defense, and smart passing. Take open shots. His coaching is straightforward, fierce and locked in. He believes in us. Which is saying a lot, given how far we still have to go to win this game.

We drive to the basket, over and over again, drawing fouls, and then dropping our underhanded shots. We refuse them their offense. Our zone defense, tried and true all year, denies them access to the hoop. All those suicides we've run this season hold us in good stead because we're in great shape and Grants Pass is getting tired. Barb snags two crucial steals in the last three minutes of the game and converts them to scores. Helen even makes an unlikely hook shot that drives the fans to their feet.

With five seconds left to go in the game, we're down by two points. Barb puts up a twenty-five-foot jumper, and the ball swishes through the net. Better yet, Grants Pass fouls her. She makes the free throw. We're up by one point and Grants Pass has possession with three seconds to go. They inbound the ball and have no choice but to heave it from midcourt. It hits the backboard, bounces down onto the rim where it teeters, and then rolls out.

We're the 1975 Oregon state champions.

41

My teammates and I throw ourselves on top of each other until we're a big ecstatic pile of girls in the middle of the gym floor. The school band plays the Trojan song at full volume. Fans storm off the bleachers and onto the court. Our friends and family members pull us to our feet, and everyone is hugging and hooting.

A crew from the local TV station circles me and my teammates, one guy holding a microphone and another hoisting a big black camera on his shoulder, recording and filming our celebration. Val is so shy that when they try to get a word from her, she literally puts her hands over her face. Barb hams it up for the reporters, practically acting out her two late-in-the-game steals, the cameraman filming her antics.

I'm about to go find my parents when I notice the TV crew moving over to our team bench where Coach Ward stands with a smile plastered on his face, as if this win has anything at all to do with him.

I don't want to feel angry, to have my celebration marred by bad feelings, but when the reporter holds the big fuzzy microphone up to Coach Ward's mouth and the other reporter steps in close with the TV camera, I know I need to do something. I glance over at Coach Stanton who is sitting on the far end of the bench, hands dangling between his knees, looking almost sick with the relief of our win, despite his goofy smile of happiness.

Mort gets there first. He's shoving his notepad and pen in his shirt pocket, a big scowl on his face, as he shouts—he has to because it's so noisy in the gym—in the TV cameraman's face. I can't hear what he's saying, but he's saying a lot and pointing at Coach Stanton. The TV reporters look confused. They glance back and forth between the two coaches as Mort keeps talking, keeps gesturing. I run over to provide backup.

"He's right," I tell the TV guys. "Coach Stanton is the brains and heart behind our win. He's our coach."

The two reporters still look unsure. I guess it's not what they've been told. Coach Ward is speaking loudly, trying to keep their attention with his long-winded verbal analysis of the game.

Mort and I are not the only ones who've noticed him trying to reap the glory.

My whole reveling team swarms over to Coach Stanton. I join them and we try to lift him up off of the bench. He's too heavy, though, and shaped like a giant basketball, so we only get him a couple of feet in the air. We lose control and drop him. He falls on his back and butt onto the bleachers, and for a moment he looks stunned, like maybe he's really hurt, but he starts laughing uncontrollably, a big, red-faced man completely silly with joy.

The TV crew catches the whole thing on film, and that's what airs that night on the local station: our giddy jubilation with Coach Stanton.

42

LATE THAT NIGHT I GO INTO Grandpa's room to tell him about the game. I'm no longer in denial. I know he's gone. Still, I stand before his made up bed, my eyes filling with tears.

"See it was 1975, and we were playing the state championship game. Trojans versus the Cavemen, so it was a . . . I don't have any idea what kind of thing it was. And anyway, there are no cavemen, anymore. For that matter, no real Trojans, either. Oh, Grandpa, I miss you so much."

43

I'VE JUST FINISHED MY LAST FINAL of the year. Actually, the last final of my entire high school career. The rest of the week is all about being with friends and saying goodbye. Carly and I are meeting on the quad for lunch. I don't need to say goodbye to *her.* We'll be friends for life. But there's still a bittersweet taste to every last second we have together on this campus. So much has happened in these four years.

I open my locker to put my books away before going to meet her, and a thick textured piece of paper flutters to the floor. I pick it up and hold it in two hands. It's Barb's treehouse drawing. She's eased it into my locker through one of the air vent slats, gently folding it without making a crease so the paper and picture didn't get bent. I stand there holding the drawing, looking at every amazing detail, as if it's a sacred text. Maybe a secret message. Since that night in the bus, I've wanted to ask to see the picture again. But somehow her showing it to me felt like a private and exposed moment, and I've been too shy to ask. Now here it is, in my locker, as if she's made a gift of the picture.

I want to see the inside of her refuge.

The gift, if that's what it is, is especially surprising since I've barely spoken to Barb since the end of basketball season in late

March. Our paths don't cross all that much at school, and the few times they have, we've glanced at each other and then away quickly. I haven't known how to break through. What does she mean by giving me this drawing on the last week of school?

Very carefully, so I don't bend or wrinkle or rip the paper, I slide it into a notebook. Rather than leave the notebook in my locker, I carry it out to the quad where I'm meeting Carly.

It's a beautiful spring day and all the kids are eating lunch outside. The rhododendrons and azaleas on either side of the quad bloom pink and yellow, the blossoms tinged with brown because it's already May. The sun feels warm and tender. I don't see Carly yet so I sit on the grass, right in the middle of everything, so she can easily find me. I take out Barb's drawing to look at it some more. I don't even hear Carly come up behind me.

"Cool," she says standing over me. "Who drew that?"

"Barb. On the team we call her Lucky. She's super, *super* talented. I mean, as a point guard, obviously. But also, she's going to be an architect and is actually building this treehouse." The words tumble out and I curb myself from saying more. She knows how to change a flat tire. She's adopted. She has white parents. She's the most observant person I know. She's funny. Her friend, Church Girl X, dumped her for Jesus. She bumped foreheads with me at our last practice. She calls me Karma.

Carly squats and takes a good long look at the drawing. Then she falls back on her butt and scoots up to sit beside me. She peels back the wax paper from her tuna sandwich, takes a big bite, chews, swallows, and then another bite.

I can't take my eyes off the magical treehouse.

"You going to see her this summer?"

"What?"

"Barb the super talented point guard architect."

"Oh. No. I mean, no."

Carly puts the uneaten half of her tuna sandwich on top of her backpack and leans back on her hands, squints at me, twists her mouth to one side.

"I'm just wondering," she says.

"Wondering what?"

"You. Basketball. Girls."

"What?" I say, though of course I heard her.

Zipping through my mind is, *Why are you always everywhere first? Why do you know me better than I know me?*

"Because," she says as if I'd spoken out loud. Had I? "I'm your best friend."

"I don't feel that way about *you!*" I practically scream.

Not until Carly grins do I realize that I've given myself away with the emphasis on *you.*

She says, "I know that. Not about *me.*"

"Wait," I say. This train is leaving the station way too fast. "It's not like that."

"What's it like then?"

"It's about basketball. I'm in love with basketball."

That's true. I mean it. I mean it with my whole heart.

Carly nods slowly, still looking as wicked as possible, enjoying every moment of what she sees as a revelation. She says, "It's a whole package then—girls *and* basketball."

Thankfully, Steve and Judith show up and throw themselves down on the grass next to us. I dig my transistor out of my backpack and click it on. As Barbra Streisand sings "The Way We Were," Carly keeps looking at me with that smirk on her face, like she's just discovered something amazing. She starts singing the dippy song along with Streisand, looking at me and starting to crack up, so I spin the little ridged dial to shut off the transistor.

Then, in a fully offensive move, I turn the conversation onto Carly's own secrets. I say to her, but am really speaking to the whole group, "Did you tell them?"

"Tell us what?" Steve says. "You're skipping college and moving directly to Paris?"

"Close," I say.

"I talked to the admissions people at U of O," Carly says. "They're letting me in."

"Hot damn," Steve says. "Congratulations."

"Mom and Dad are letting me live on campus, too."

"Well, I guess *so*," Steve says. "That'd be a two-hour commute from Portland."

"What changed their minds?" Judith asks.

Carly laughs and looks at me. "My mom is superstitious. She thinks she saw a ghost one night."

"Whaaaat?" Judith says. "No way."

"The ghost told her to let me go."

"Like a dream maybe," Judith says in her corrective voice, as if somehow Carly and I really do believe in ghosts and need to be brought in line with reality.

"Yeah. Maybe."

Carly and I smile at each other, enjoying the sunny drama.

"I still don't understand why you didn't just apply to colleges when everyone else did," Steve says.

"You don't need to understand that," Judith tells him.

"Okay, fine," Steve says. "It's a girl thing, apparently. Whatever."

"Not a girl thing," Judith says. "Just none of your business." Then to me, "*Thank* you for turning off that song."

I see Mort coming through the cafeteria doors, balancing a full tray. He glances at Helen sitting over by the parking lot with another group of friends, and then makes his dogged way to our circle. He sets down his tray and drops onto the grass. Without saying hello, or anything at all, he opens his carton of milk, drinks half of it in one gulp, and then saws off and eats five consecutive bites of his enchiladas.

"Earth to Mort," Carly says. "You have such cute dimples but lately you hardly ever smile."

"Rough year," he says, fingering his camera if it's a comforting teddy bear.

"The *whole* year?"

Mort shrugs. "Some of it was okay."

"Just okay?"

He glances at me. "A bit of a roller coaster."

"Welcome to life, Mortimer." Carly reaches out a leg and presses the sole of her ankle boot up against the sole of his sneaker. He jerks a bit, like she sent an electric current through him.

"You win some, you lose some," Carly says, as if she's the font of all wisdom.

"Apparently the breakup hasn't affected your appetite," Judith observes. "I'll know I've found the man of my dreams when I come before his next meal."

"Ouch," Steve says.

"I *didn't* eat for a couple of days," Mort says, defending himself.

In April, Helen went with her dad to a welcome weekend at Howard University. At the very first event on Friday night, she met her Howard man. Robert is six-one and drop-dead handsome. In fact, he's the most handsome man she's ever met in her entire life, she told me, as if she's already lived for a century. He's pre-law, like she plans to be, and he got a 4.0 in high school and crazy high SAT scores. "His lips . . ." she said about five times, waving her hand around in front of her own mouth, as if words couldn't capture the glory of his lips. She also told me that her dad was right, and that she's so glad she waited. All I could think was, *she waited?* She came right home from that weekend and broke up with Mort.

"I'm glad you're recovering," Carly says in a soothing voice, much more sympathetic than Judith's tone. "Have a bite of your chocolate chip cookie. Looks like it's right out of the oven. The chocolate is all melty."

Mort does as he's told.

"She's not the only fish in the sea," Carly says. "Good looking guy like you."

You can practically see the hook in Mort's mouth. Carly may as well put up her hands and reel. His newly prominent Adam's apple is bobbing up and down.

She glances at me as if to say, *You don't mind, do you?*

For a hot second, I do.

"I'm so glad you're going to U of O, too," Carly tells him. "Can we hang out?"

Wait, I think. No. Just no. Wait.

Then, when I see the look on his face—yeah, he's definitely recovering from Helen—I just crack up. I send Carly a telepathic, *go for it.*

While she and Mort continue their dance, Steve and Judith start kissing, so I lie back and look up at the blue sky, holding up my hand to block the May sun. In three months, my friends are scattering all over the country. Judith is going to Smith in Northampton, Massachusetts, which is pretty close to where I'll be in Williamstown, Massachusetts. Steve is going to Washington University in St Louis. Mort and Carly to the University of Oregon in Eugene. Helen to Howard University in Washington DC. And yeah, my best friend in the family, Grandpa, is dead. Yet somehow I feel the least lonely I've ever felt in my life. Something big has shifted and snapped into place. It's as simple as this: I have me.

44

I NEVER GET A CHANCE TO thank Barb for the drawing. I see her twice in the last two days of school, both times at a distance. The first time I try to catch up to her but she disappears into a classroom. The second time I get shy and let it go. I regret this.

But here's the thing: she wrote her address on the back of the drawing.

I spend the first two weeks of summer trying to figure out what that means. Possibly nothing at all. I want to ask Carly, who's working in her dad's insurance firm again this summer, but she'll exaggerate the meaning of the address, insist it means way more than it probably does. I know this without asking her. Besides, she has a way of making things explicit and right now I don't want explicit.

I just want to see the treehouse.

I'm working the trail crew again. I don't have Grandpa to sit with in the afternoons before dinner. Sometimes I meet Carly downtown. Her dad lets her leave work early and we walk to the 7-Eleven for slurpees. On other afternoons I climb the willow beside our driveway, where there is no treehouse, just branches, but still, I love reading up there, being sus-pended in the air, the long thin willow branches with the thin pale green leaves making their own kind of fort walls. Maybe I should have outgrown forts by now, but when I think about treehouses being training for a career in architecture, it elevates them to something much more sophisticated. Besides, it's my last summer as a kid. I get to sit high in the willow tree and read.

It's in the evenings at dusk when I wonder most about the address on the back of Barb's drawing. She didn't include a phone number. Sometimes I read that like a dare: all or nothing. Show up or never mind.

After dinner on a Thursday, I ask to borrow the car, say I'm going to Carly's, and drive to Barb's street. I park a couple of blocks away and walk to her house. I arrive at dusk.

The treehouse looks exactly like the one in her drawing, tucked high in a Douglas fir, with the bridge to the platform in the neighbor tree. She's made a lot of progress because that evening on the bus, she told me she'd only built the floor so far. Now there are four walls and a window, glowing with a pale golden light. Music, Phoebe Snow singing "Poetry Man," drifts down from the fort. I just stand there listening to the beautiful, lilting words. The music seems to float softly in the twilight. When the song ends, an ad comes on the radio and someone turns it off.

What isn't in the drawing is the basketball hoop affixed to the trunk of the big tree supporting the treehouse. A ball lies in the dirt under the basket. I walk over and pick it up. I sink my first shot, all net. The next one bonks against the backboard and ricochets into the neighbor's yard. I chase it down and when I return to the hoop, Barb is standing on the deck of her treehouse, twenty-five feet above me. It's nearly dark now, but I can tell it's her by the way she moves, her shape backlit by the treehouse's window.

I'm nearly paralyzed with shyness. What am I doing here? Had I been invited? No, I hadn't been. No one invited me.

I manage to squeak out a, "Hey."

"Karma?" Barb says.

"Yeah." The word comes out like I'm choking.

"Chica! Come on up."

I set the basketball down and rub my sweaty hands on my cut-offs. She waits on the deck of the treehouse while I climb the ladder. When my head and upper body pop up through the hole in the deck, she grabs one of my arms by the wrist. I wrap my fingers around her wrist, too, and she helps me onto the deck.

"I didn't think you'd come," Barb says.

"Oh. Well, I did."

Still holding my hand, Barb pulls me inside the treehouse and shuts the door. She slides the latch to lock it. I can't look at her, still overwhelmed with shyness, so I look at the interior of her refuge, lit by a camping lantern. Later I'll ask how she managed to get that big armchair, with a matching ottoman, up here. A small bookshelf holds a few books. A red and orange patterned rug covers most of the plywood floor. Pinned all over the walls are Barb's drawings of other dwellings. Her notebook rests on the floor, open with a pencil on top, and I guess she'd been drawing when I arrived. I walk to the window and look out into the dark, into the tree branches.

I can't believe I'm finally here.

THE END

Author's Note

WHILE PRETTY MUCH EVERYTHING IN THIS story happened,
I don't remember exact conversations, or even the particulars of
certain events, so I've fictionalized the dialogue and used my
imagination to fill in my memories. I've also folded one or two
friendships from the following couple of years in my life into the
year of this story. All the events with teachers, coaches, the school
board, and the older feminists happened exactly as I tell it. The
quote from the *Oregonian* is verbatim. I changed the names of
most of the people to protect their privacy, but there are three
big exceptions: Mr. Murray is the best English teacher I've ever
had; meeting Gloria Steinem in person changed my life in the
best possible ways; and a certain coach is a hero to me. So I
wanted to honor these three with their real names. I am pleased
that Portland's Woodrow Wilson High School changed its name
in 2021 to Ida B. Wells High School.

There are no thanks loud enough for Reiko Davis, Kat Georges,
and Peter Carlaftes. Big gratitude.

About the Author

LUCY JANE BLEDSOE IS THE AUTHOR of eight books of fiction for adults and six previous books of fiction for young people. *Lava Falls*, stories about kickass survivor girls who take on the religious right and uranium mining lobbyists, won the 2019 Devil's Kitchen Fiction Award. *Ms. Magazine* called her novel *The Evolution of Love*, about how those who develop the muscles of compassion and inclusion will win the evolutionary lottery (in the long run), "fabulous feminist fiction." *The New York Times* said her novel *A Thin Bright Line* "triumphs as an intimate and humane evocation of day-to-day life under inhumane circumstances." Bledsoe's fiction has won a California Arts Council Fellowship in Literature, an American Library Association Stonewall Award, the Arts & Letters Fiction Prize, two Pushcart nominations, a Yaddo Fellowship, and two National Science Foundation Artists & Writers in Antarctica Fellowships. Bledsoe loves basketball, mountains, cats, and books. As a social justice activist, she's currently working on voting rights. She lives in Berkeley.

RECENT AND FORTHCOMING BOOKS FROM THREE ROOMS PRESS

FICTION

Lucy Jane Bledsoe
No Stopping Us Now

Rishab Borah
The Door to Inferna

Meagan Brothers
Weird Girl and What's His Name

Christopher Chambers
Scavenger
Standalone

Ebele Chizea
Aquarian Dawn

Ron Dakron
Hello Devilfish!

Robert Duncan
Loudmouth

Michael T. Fournier
Hidden Wheel
Swing State

Aaron Hamburger
Nirvana Is Here

William Least Heat-Moon
Celestial Mechanics

Aimee Herman
Everything Grows

Kelly Ann Jacobson
Tink and Wendy

Jethro K. Lieberman
Everything Is Jake

Eamon Loingsigh
Light of the Diddicoy
Exile on Bridge Street

John Marshall
The Greenfather

Aram Saroyan
Still Night in L.A.

Robert Silverberg
The Face of the Waters

Stephen Spotte
Animal Wrongs

Richard Vetere
The Writers Afterlife
Champagne and Cocaine

Julia Watts
Quiver
Needlework

Gina Yates
Narcissus Nobody

MEMOIR & BIOGRAPHY

Nassrine Azimi and Michel Wasserman
Last Boat to Yokohama: The Life and Legacy of Beate Sirota Gordon

William S. Burroughs & Allen Ginsberg
Don't Hide the Madness:
William S. Burroughs in Conversation with Allen Ginsberg
edited by Steven Taylor

James Carr
BAD: The Autobiography of James Carr

Judy Gumbo
Yippie Girl: Exploits in Protest and Defeating the FBI

Judith Malina
Full Moon Stages:
Personal Notes from 50 Years of The Living Theatre

Phil Marcade
Punk Avenue: Inside the New York City Underground, 1972–1982

Jililian Marshall
Japanthem: Counter-Cultural Experiences; Cross-Cultural Remixes

Alvin Orloff
Disasterama! Adventures in the Queer Underground 1977–1997

Nicca Ray
Ray by Ray: A Daughter's Take on the Legend of Nicholas Ray

Stephen Spotte
My Watery Self:
Memoirs of a Marine Scientist

PHOTOGRAPHY-MEMOIR

Mike Watt
On & Off Bass

SHORT STORY ANTHOLOGIES

SINGLE AUTHOR

The Alien Archives: Stories
by Robert Silverberg

First-Person Singularities: Stories
by Robert Silverberg
with an introduction by John Scalzi

Tales from the Eternal Café: Stories
by Janet Hamill, with an introduction
by Patti Smith

Time and Time Again:
Sixteen Trips in Time
by Robert Silverberg

Voyagers:
Twelve Journeys in Space and Time
by Robert Silverberg

MULTI-AUTHOR

Crime + Music: Twenty Stories of Music-Themed Noir
edited by Jim Fusilli

Dark City Lights: New York Stories
edited by Lawrence Block

The Faking of the President: Twenty Stories of White House Noir
edited by Peter Carlaftes

Florida Happens:
Bouchercon 2018 Anthology
edited by Greg Herren

Have a NYC I, II & III:
New York Short Stories;
edited by Peter Carlaftes
& Kat Georges

Songs of My Selfie:
An Anthology of Millennial Stories
edited by Constance Renfrow

The Obama Inheritance:
15 Stories of Conspiracy Noir
edited by Gary Phillips

This Way to the End Times:
Classic and New Stories of the Apocalypse
edited by Robert Silverberg

MIXED MEDIA

John S. Paul
Sign Language: A Painter's Notebook
(photography, poetry and prose)

DADA

Maintenant: A Journal of Contemporary Dada Writing & Art
(Annual, since 2008)

HUMOR

Peter Carlaftes
A Year on Facebook

FILM & PLAYS

Israel Horovitz
My Old Lady: Complete Stage Play and Screenplay with an Essay on Adaptation

Peter Carlaftes
Triumph For Rent (3 Plays)
Teatrophy (3 More Plays)

Kat Georges
Three Somebodies: Plays about Notorious Dissidents

TRANSLATIONS

Thomas Bernhard
On Earth and in Hell
(poems of Thomas Bernhard
with English translations by
Peter Waugh)

Patrizia Gattaceca
Isula d'Anima / Soul Island
(poems by the author
in Corsican with English
translations)

César Vallejo | Gerard Malanga
Malanga Chasing Vallejo
(selected poems of César Vallejo
with English translations
and additional notes by
Gerard Malanga)

George Wallace
EOS: Abductor of Men
(selected poems in Greek & English)

ESSAYS

Richard Katrovas
Raising Girls in Bohemia:
Meditations of an American Father

Far Away From Close to Home
Vanessa Baden Kelly

Womentality: Thirteen Empowering Stories by Everyday Women Who Said Goodbye to the Workplace and Hello to Their Lives
edited by Erin Wildermuth

POETRY COLLECTIONS

Hala Alyan
Atrium

Peter Carlaftes
DrunkYard Dog
I Fold with the Hand I Was Dealt

Thomas Fucaloro
It Starts from the Belly and Blooms

Kat Georges
Our Lady of the Hunger

Robert Gibbons
Close to the Tree

Israel Horovitz
Heaven and Other Poems

David Lawton
Sharp Blue Stream

Jane LeCroy
Signature Play

Philip Meersman
This Is Belgian Chocolate

Jane Ormerod
Recreational Vehicles on Fire
Welcome to the Museum of Cattle

Lisa Panepinto
On This Borrowed Bike

George Wallace
Poppin' Johnny

 Three Rooms Press | New York, NY | Current Catalog: www.threeroomspress.com
Three Rooms Press books are distributed by Publishers Group West: www.pgw.com